The Man in Room 204
by Phil Brackett

A Bangor Springs Story

For permissions, contact:
philbrackett75@gmail.com

This book is dedicated to the people who have helped me to believe most in its possibility. My wife, Jennie, as my closest friend and greatest cheerleader; my dear friend Nate, encourager extraordinaire and faithful ally; my colleague Chris, who wouldn't let me settle; my faithful blog readers and uplifting supporters, whose words have boosted me to heights unimaginable. While this effort is my effort, the energy came from so many. Thanks to you all.

Cover art by Rob White
By His Hand, LLC

Preface

The mind of the man in Room 204 was a house of many, many rooms.

Some of the rooms were similar to those one would find in any regular, normal house -- furnished with accouterments of different kinds and types. Wall decorations, pieces of furniture, paint choices and area rugs -- all symbolic dressings in his mind for rooms built out of memories from a long life. Memories that he shared with his wife while they'd spent their lives together. Memories of his childhood, with his mother and father and sister. Memories of one particular event in a living room and some other event in a kitchen -- these were the stuff of which the rooms in the house of his mind were built.

Other rooms, however, were dark and hideous, somehow malevolent. They weren't rooms that you would choose to be in, and they threatened anyone who might try to enter them. But of course, the only one who would enter them, who had *ever* entered them, was the man in Room 204. And he wasn't getting around his own house much anymore, at least not the house of his mind.

These dark, bitter rooms hardly resembled, in their reality, rooms akin to those that most people have grown accustomed to seeing in their houses here and there and everywhere. These rooms were more like the rooms that you would see in the haunted houses in the movies. In the horror films. They looked like they did, and they felt like they did, to the only man to ever enter any of them, because they were built of the bad memories.

However, these rooms weren't even the worst rooms in the house of his mind.

The worst rooms of all in the mind of the man in Room 204 were the ***going*** rooms.

The rooms that were 'going' in the mind of that man were rooms that weren't entirely there, weren't entirely *whole*. Parts of them were missing, incomplete somehow. A corner missing from this room, an entire wall missing in that room. They weren't whole, and in their incompleteness, they seemed to be portals to somewhere else -- somewhere terrible. Somewhere dark. The man knew not to venture inside of them. When you go into rooms you shouldn't be in, bad things happen.

During the good days, the house was mostly there. On the bad days, the house was mostly gone. And as the bad days and weeks turned into bad months and years, the parts of the house that were available for the man to explore were fewer and fewer.

The man in Room 204 was slowly losing what he'd been building in that house over ninety-seven years, and to a certain extent, this was to be expected.

But, it also happened to be the case that the deterioration of the house wasn't completely natural.

* * *

Kathryn Santos could tell, based on the look in the man's eyes, if he was stuck in his house, so to speak. On those days, he was capable of anything -- behavior ranging from calm catatonia to enraged, violent screaming and thrashing. Kate knew when a day was going to be a bad day by the look in his eyes. On the good days, the man had a loving, peaceful demeanor that Kate found endearing.

Thus were the final days of the man in Room 204.

Bangor Springs, 1993

He'd been trying for five long years, trying to make things work. For the fifth time, it had all failed. Standing in the middle of the open field, its dust and dirt blowing up in the breezes going by, Bob Smithers took a moment to remember the last five years -- all of the wasted time and effort.

Initially, he hadn't thought that the fourteen acre lot was going to make that big of a difference in his bottom line -- not really, anyway. He farmed many hundreds of acres -- some he owned and some he rented-- at different locations, all over Bangor Springs, so picking up an extra, small piece of land wasn't that big of a deal. On the other hand, Bob knew that every single acre was important and, in the tough times, having extra land could be the difference between surviving and not.

Bob had also realized --back in 1988-- that land prices were on the rise. Bob wasn't about to end up paying a fortune for the property, years down the road, when he could buy it for cheap right away. He'd been contacted by the Knox County Board of Realtors, in the spring of '88, notifying him of a land auction involving several pieces of property all over the area surrounding Bangor Springs. The bigger farmers in Knox County got notices like these, from time to time, because farm property was only likely to be purchased by farmers -- it made sense to market the opportunities their way.

Some of the pieces of property up for auction had more appeal, some less; Bob was really only interestcd in two or three of the auctions on the docket. He'd spoken with his wife, Joyce, about going to the auction and bidding on certain properties, and they'd put their heads together to try to figure out what they could afford to spend in order to be able to add to their total acreage.

The thing about a land auction is that, depending on the competition that's present, the prices often ended up being only slightly less than what you would have spent if you'd just bought the land from a seller, that is, after the prices get driven up by whichever competitors happen to be at the auction. Bob had been to plenty of farmland auctions before, and he'd seen some crazy stuff happen -- one time, he saw two farmers, ganging up on a third, bidding up the price on a piece of property, just to make sure that the third farmer would pay a hefty sum if he meant to have it.

Bob Smithers had been leery about going to the auction that spring, knowing that the question was often more a matter of who *else* was interested in the properties that you were interested in.

The single piece of land that Bob Smithers was most interested in at that auction was Miller's Field, and Bob hadn't been expecting a lot of competition for that particular piece of property. In fact, Bob was probably the only person in Knox County that day who'd even been interested. Bob knew what people had to say about Miller's Field, he'd heard the stories that went around -- the gossip -- and he'd been sure that it was all just hogwash.

Plus, Bob had thought back then, if the stories and the gossip about the property kept others from bidding on it, then that was going to work out even better for him.

But, look how that had turned out.

Bob looked around himself at the field on which he'd been completely unsuccessful, for five growing seasons, to get anything to grow. Not a darn thing.

Seems like they'd all been right and he'd been a fool.

Miller's Field was a piece of property with about five hundred feet of frontage on Old Smith Road. More than twice as deep as it was wide, the property would have been a great little farmstead for some family a hundred years ago. But in 1988, the property was just a giant speed bump for Bob Smithers; he used to spend so much time each spring driving his way around it -- in order to be able to plant the fields that he owned on all sides, to the north and the east and the south. Buying that property had made sense just as a way to save him some time in having to circumvent it.

But, all for naught. He'd wasted his money on this piece of junk property. Bob kicked at a clump of infertile dirt on the ground in front of him, busting it up with the toe of his boot. He regretted the decision that he'd made five years ago to buy the property. He regretted the work that he'd put --each spring-- into trying to make a crop grow on the land. He regretted the money wasted on seed, the sleepless nights spent trying to figure out the problem. Bob Smithers regretted Miller's Field more than he'd ever regretted any other business decision of his life.

The best laid plans of mice and men.

* * *

John Stuckey looked around the Hilltop diner at the other patrons, sitting in twos and threes in the booths and at the tables, on all sides on the group of farmers that were huddled together around a couple of long tables that had been pulled together in the middle of the restaurant to make a conference table of sorts. It was like this every time the farmers gathered together for breakfast.

And there were certainly times when John Stuckey was one hundred percent sure that he had other things to do --better things to do-- than to sit in this diner at these 'meetings', listening to other farmers running their mouths. There were other times --less busy times-- when it wasn't a half-bad proposition, spending time with people with whom you shared a livelihood, especially if there wasn't much else to be doing. If nothing else, John liked people-watching, and he would spend the time watching other people watching him and his fellow farmers.

But, in the middle of April, John had been hoping for some very valuable information to legitimize why he would take some time away from the fields that needed to be planted. So far, he hadn't gotten any. Instead, what he got was an earful of Warren Hobbs.

"Well, I don't have a lot of sympathy for someone who should've known better, is all I'm sayin'."

"What do you mean, 'He should have known better'?" John Stuckey spoke up, daring to question the great Warren Hobbs.

"You know what I mean, John. Everybody in town knows. Miller's Field is cursed. Always has been. I'm just sayin' that Bob should've known better." Warren replied.

Hobbs waited for anyone else at the table in the Hilltop diner on that Saturday morning to respond to his bold statements, but nobody did. It wasn't that the farmers there feared Hobbs, unless you counted the fear that most of them had about what Hobbs might be able to do to them, making life difficult for any of them if he felt like it. Rather, each of these farmers was keeping their silence because -- deep down inside-- each of them agreed with Warren; in their minds, Bob Smithers *should* have known better.

"I wouldn't farm that land if you paid me to do it." Hobbs continued, "Not that you *could* farm it -- everyone knows that you can't grow a thing on Miller's Field. And, just to prove the point for all of us, Smithers has tried, and failed, for five whole seasons now. And now, with that Clinton fella in the White House, who knows how things are gonna turn out for us farmers."

"Now, wait just a minute." John retorted, putting his index finger down hard into the table next to his plate, to make his point. "There isn't a farmer at this table that wouldn't buy a piece of land to make his plowing and planting easier, a piece of land that's adjacent to what they've already got."

Warren Hobbs looked at each of the farmers seated around the table, each in turn, to see whether or not any of them might agree with John Stuckey. Instead, each of them just stared down at the dirty breakfast plates in front of them.

"Listen, John. We all know that you and Bob are friends. So, you defending him at this table is something that each of us understands you doin'." Warren paused, for dramatic effect, almost to the point where it seemed like that was all he was going to say, but then he continued.

"But, buying that field was the dumbest thing that Bob Smithers ever did."

A few of the farmers around the table snickered at the insulting language that Warren had chosen to use, and as much as it annoyed John, Warren was right.

Nothing had ever grown on Miller's Field, certainly not a single crop that Bob Smithers had tried to plant since he'd bought the place. Smithers might as well give up on the whole damn piece of property.

As the chortling giggles died down among the good ol' boys, whose sense of humor was no more developed than their sense of Greco-Roman statuary, John Stuckey thought about getting up to leave. He was, however, still yet to receive anything to legitimize him coming here in the first place. Rather than going, he beckoned the waitress over for a refill of his coffee mug.

Leaning back in his chair a bit, surveying the others in the group, John sipped his coffee and thought.

There were times --like this one-- when John Stuckey thought that farming was more of a competitive sport than an occupation. Come to think of it, he usually felt this way when he was here, sitting in the Hilltop diner in Bangor Springs on a Saturday morning.

What a coincidence.

The local farmers, the big ones, had been meeting together for breakfast at the Hilltop for at least the past couple of decades. The meetings were equal parts local gossip, strategic planning, and allegiance forging. While these might not, on the surface, seem like worthy endeavors for a farmer, they most certainly had their purposes.

Warren Hobbs, who had enough wind in him to run these meetings well into the twenty-first century, was one of the most successful farmers in the history of Knox County. Warren's brother-in-law ran the feed mill in town, and the two of them knew every seed and feed distributor in southern Michigan or northern Indiana. If it was going on in Knox County, and it had anything to do with farming, Warren had his fingers in it.

Unfortunately for everyone else at these meetings, Hobbs knew how successful he was and it inflated his ego to the extent that he was obnoxiously pompous. John couldn't really stand to be around Warren for very long at all (in fact, he wondered how all of the other farmers at these meetings seemed so calm and agreeable), but he kept coming to the meetings because of the value of the information that was traded back and forth.

A large part of the competitive nature of farming was simple land-grabbing, and that could sometimes be quite fierce. Information about who owned what piece of land where, whose land butted up against who else's land, and who was looking to get rid of what land where, these were the things that often ended up being discussed on Saturday mornings at the Hilltop. That information made it worthwhile to be at these meetings, despite the fact that Warren Hobbs was an arrogant ass.

* * *

"He was talking about you again this morning. And, of course, I stuck up for you."

Bob Smithers always enjoyed talking to John Stuckey on the phone, but he enjoyed it more when the topic of the conversation was a bit more positive.

"John, you know I don't give two flying poops what Warren Hobbs has to say about anything at all. He's a pest, and I wouldn't give him the time of day if he asked."

"I know, Bob. Part of me just feels duty-bound to let you know that he's still running his mouth."

"So, let him."

The two paused in the conversation long enough to let things settle. Then, Bob picked it back up.

"Do you think I'm stupid, for having tried to farm Miller's Field?"

"Bob, come on. You know that I don't. I would have tried the same thing, had I been in the same situation."

"Have I thought of everything? Am I missing something? Tell me, old friend, is the answer staring me in the face and I just can't see it?"

"Listen -- we've been over this. Every farmer knows that there are a lot of reasons why a crop might grow poorly on a certain piece of land. Soil chemistry, the available moisture, exposure to sun, lots of different reasons."

"Right," Bob replied, "and I've been thinking about those things all along."

"I know you have. And, let's be honest: there are smarter farmers in Knox County than Bob Smithers."

Bob chuckled; "Granted." he replied.

"But, here's the thing, Bob -- it's not like you're doing anything different on Miller's Field than what you're doing on any of your other fields. You're a successful farmer, Bob. That's why I'm convinced that it's not you. It's that field."

John and Bob had had this whole conversation a dozen times, more and more often over the last couple of years. John didn't mind giving his old friend the pep talk every once in a while, because he knew that Bob would do the same for him, had the roles been reversed.

"And tell me, John, have you ever heard of a field anywhere else that is completely incapable of growing any green things -- crops *or weeds*?"

"You know that I haven't, Bob."

"I can't even grow ragweed on Miller's Field, my friend. Not ragweed or lambsquarters or velvetleaf or marestail. I've got fields where I can't stop that stuff from growing, but not on Miller's Field."

"I know." John reassured his friend.

"How is it that I can grow anything I want on any of the surrounding fields, John? How about that?"

"You got me."

John could feel that Bob was losing his head of steam, that he was running low on the energy that came with these bouts of exasperation. He waited to see whether Bob would have anything else to add.

"I'm thinking about calling the MSU extension office, up in Benton Center. See if they can weigh in on the subject."

John Stuckey knew about the extension office for Michigan State University; just about every farmer in Michigan knew where their local MSU extension office was. If Bob was hoping to get some agricultural experts to help him with his problem, that would be the best place to start.

"You know what, Bob? I think that's a great idea. You might be at the end of your rope, but I'll bet they've got longer ropes."

* * *

Michigan State University received, on an annual and recurring basis, funds from the USDA and the Michigan Department of Agriculture, that were earmarked for projects whereby the university would make itself available to farmers in the state who were in need of assistance with problems that the knowledge of the university could benefit. These funds weren't always used for hands-on projects that "put boots on the ground", but they did end up getting spent that way, on occasion.

The university decided to assign Dr. Trent Willingham to the problems that Bob Smithers was having with his fourteen-acre field, down in Knox County, partially because Dr. Willingham was their best available expert, but mostly because Trent volunteered to assist the farmer who'd reached out to the University. Dr. Willingham was the Senior Associate Dean for the College of Agriculture, and had been a professor at the university for twenty-six years. He knew a lot about agriculture --especially mid-western agriculture-- and he usually found it quite invigorating to be out in the field (pun intended), working with real-world problems in need of real-world solutions. Additionally, Trent was a bit of an expert on barren fields, so this project sounded right up his alley.

Trent got the news of his assignment while he'd been catching up on reading so many scholarly articles in the field of agriculture, articles that he'd not had a chance to read while teaching his courses during the spring semester of the academic year.

Trent knew that he'd be on a shoe-string budget, as was often the case with this kind of pro-bono work that the university took, on behalf of farmers in the state, but it didn't bother him much at all. He figured he wouldn't need much in the way of resources to solve the issue. It was probably something only slightly beyond what most farmers understood about the work that they did; Trent imagined a chemical imbalance in the soil or some kind of microbial infestation. It would probably be a simple matter of diagnosing the problem and planning its solution.

Dr. Willingham was planning to ask his summer research associates --interns, really-- to see if any of them would want to head to southwest Michigan with him, or if they'd rather work on any number of projects that he had going on in his lab on campus in East Lansing. He was hoping that the lone junior in his lab --Sam something or other-- would say 'yes' to the opportunity. Trent thought of Sam as a bright kid who might benefit from the field experience. He'd take as many students with him as the university would pay to put up in a hotel for a couple of weeks.

The first series of steps to take, Trent thought, once their team arrived on-site, would be to conduct some in-depth soil sampling.

* * *

Bob Smithers was all set to meet the team assigned to his problem by Michigan State University out on Old Smith Road first thing on a Monday morning in late June. On that particular morning, on his way to the appointment, he was thinking of John Stuckey.

John Stuckey and Bob Smithers had been best friends since grade school. It helped that they lived three miles apart, on the south side of Bangor Springs. It helped that their wives,

Joyce and Tina, were also best friends. The four of them had played four-square and tetherball in the school yard decades ago; these days it was more likely to be euchre or canasta around the dining room table on Thursday nights.

John had always been a deer hunter, was raised to be a deer hunter by his father, whose father had raised him to be a deer hunter. Bob had never intentionally killed an animal, not as a farmer and not as a hunter either, at least not as far as he could remember. Nevertheless, Bob never had a problem letting John hunt his properties. John Stuckey had been hunting Bob's various properties out on Old Smith Road for almost two decades, since they butted up against a small forest, and John knew that there were deer in the nearby forest as surely as he knew how to clean a rifle.

But then, maybe about two or three years back, John and Bob were talking at the Bangor Springs Christmas Tree Lighting, which always happened on the first Friday of December. The Stuckeys and the Smitherses always made it a point to go to the Christmas tree lighting together, as a double-date, mostly to get away from their children.

While John and Bob were standing some distance from the tree and the crowd, Tina and Joyce were staring at the lights, right up close, enamored once again. Each of them were pregnant this year, at the same time as it turned out, Joyce with her and Bob's fifth, and Tina with her and John's second.

John pulled Bob over to the side of the gathering of people, even further away than they'd already been standing.

"I'm going to stop hunting your properties out on Old Smith Road, the ones next to Miller's Field. I wanted you to know, in case someone else asks you if they can hunt on them."

"Oh yeah? How come?"

"Something's wrong out in that neck of the woods. The animals that I see out that way aren't quite right."

Bob looked at John for a moment, trying to figure out if John was just messing with him. John began to explain himself.

"For starters, I've seen squirrels and raccoons and birds of all different kinds out there, even a deer once or twice --never anything I would take a shot at-- and most of them do some funny stuff."

"You mean they tell knock-knock jokes."

"Not that kind of funny, Bob. Funny like bizarre. The coons and squirrels, most of the ones I've seen out there, they'll be walking around like normal, then, all of a sudden, they roll onto their backs and just lay there, for minutes at a time, kicking their back legs out in spasms, flailing around like that."

"Probably just rubbing their scent around on the ground. I've seen our dog do that."

"Our dog does that too, Bob, but this isn't that. It's something different. And then, there's the birds."

Bob paused for a second, then took the bait.

"What do the birds do?"

"Sometimes, they fly right smack into the trees. Other times, they'll just fall out of the sky, mid-flight."

"Well, that *is* bizarre."

"I'll tell you what else..." John started to say, as he began to make his way back toward where Tina and Joyce were watching the Christmas tree. "Last month, I was hunting out there, a few days after the start of the hunting season, and I saw a deer run smack-dab into a tree. It knocked itself out cold. Craziest thing I ever saw. There's something not right out that way, Bob. That deer's hooves, they were glowing when I saw it, laying there unconscious, a dull reddish glow. It spooked me a little bit, to be honest with you, so I wanted to let you know that I'm done huntin' out there. No hard feelings."

Bob Smithers was remembering this event on the Monday morning that he met Trent Willingham for the first time. For all of the trouble that field had given him during his short tenure as its owner, it only really occurred to him that morning that the problem might be beyond the scope of science.

* * *

A couple of weeks later, Bob Smithers had big plans for his July Tuesday afternoon. One of his fields on the south side of Bangor Springs, not too far from his home, had an irrigation system that needed some tweaking. Water wasn't getting to a certain portion of the field, and Bob was going to have to change the path of the irrigation boom if that part of his field had any chance at getting the regular water supply that it needed for maximum yield. With the right tools and a couple of slight adjustments, Bob would hopefully end up with enough time, at the end of the afternoon, to swing on home and head out to his storage barn, at the back of his property, to do an oil change on his tractor before he was going to have to take it out next week to do some pest control spraying.

Unfortunately, all of those plans changed when Bob got a page from his wife, Joyce. He stopped by the house to retrieve the message that she had for him. It was a message from Dr. Willingham, asking if he could come out to Miller's Field as soon as possible. So, just after lunch, he headed out that way, rather than doing what he had been planning to do with his afternoon.

"I came as soon as I could, Dr. Willingham."

"I appreciate it. I know how busy farmers can be during the growing season."

"So, what have you called me out here to see?"

"Well, as you know, all of the soil sampling that we've been doing for the past couple of weeks has come back with inconclusive results."

"Yes, I remember you saying that you were disappointed by the outcome."

"Right. That's why we're going to head in this direction instead." Dr. Willingham extended his hand to point at a wheeled cart at his side. The cart had large, thin wheels with knobby tires, for getting through rough terrain, and a low, flat shelf near the bottom. The underside of that shelf rode so close to the ground that Bob wondered whether or not it had enough clearance to cross the broken soil of Miller's Field.

"I've never seen anything like that before. What is it?" Bob tried to express his curiosity without coming across as an ignorant country bumpkin.

"Well, it's called a GPR device. GPR stands for ground penetrating radar. We're going to try to use it to get a sense for what might be underneath the topsoil of your field, here."

"And what are you expecting to find?"

"To be honest," Dr. Willingham began, "we're not really sure what we might find. Of course, we are hoping to find some answers. I wanted to have you out here today so I could keep you up-to-date on the developments."

Bob fought hard to keep from rolling his eyes. He didn't want to be disrespectful, even though he wondered whether or not Dr. Willingham and his team were going to be able to find anything at all, answers or anything else of the sort.

"If anything turns up, you know how to get a hold of me. Just call the house and leave a message if I'm not in." Bob replied before turning to leave.

* * *

In the few short weeks that Bob had come to know Dr. Willingham, he would have told you that he'd seen most of the facial expressions that Dr. Willingham was capable of. But, the expression on his face after the GPR findings came back was an expression that Bob hadn't seen before, an expression of complete confusion.

"I've never seen a GPR yield results like this. We've been using GPR for more than a decade now, and the results have become pretty familiar to me. These aren't like any results I've ever seen before."

"Well, maybe the machine's busted." Bob interjected.

"We thought that might be the case, too. My intern assistant, Samuel, actually suggested the same thing. As it turns out, this is actually the fifth GPR device that we've run across your field." Dr. Willingham absently pointed toward the cart as he stared at the sheets of printed scans, and Bob realized that the GPR cart was a different color than the one he'd seen last week.

"You mean to tell me that you've had five GPRs create the same messed-up results?"

"What I mean to tell you, Bob, is that it's not the machines that are 'messed-up'. It's your property."

"On that we can agree. I know the property is messed up. I've been trying to grow stuff on it for five years. Tell me something that I don't know!"

"I intend to, Bob. I am just going to need some more time."

* * *

The snooping around that was going on at Miller's Field was not going to be able to continue. There was too much at stake, were the answers to be discovered. Mr. Dire's organization had invested, over a very long period of time, far too many resources and far too much time for the likes of Bob Smithers and his collegiate associates to uncover their secrets.

Mr. Dire would have to put a stop to it, one way or the other.

For now, he knew that it was best to keep an eye on the situation --from afar-- monitoring the progress of the investigative team, to make sure that they didn't get too close to any real discoveries.

If things started to spiral out of control, Dire would take matters into his own hands.

* * *

"This is just crazy. Do you understand what this is going to cost?!?!"

Dr. Willingham turned to face the undergraduate associate with a glare that seemed to have an actual physical force to it.

"Samuel, I don't need you to remind me of who you are, and I *know* that I don't need to remind you of who I am. You will address me properly."

Samuel Heath withered visibly under the intensity of Willingham's scowl, and Trent recognized what was happening as he was watching the young student. He got really close to feeling bad for being so intense with the kid.

Then, Sam gathered himself to speak.

"I apologize. But, with all due respect, I think that you'll end up discovering absolutely nothing from this approach. It's a shot in the dark. Do you really think the university is going to approve an expense like this?"

Trent relaxed, recognizing how close he was to the edge of rage and frustration.

"It might be a shot in the dark, but I'm starting to run out of ideas. Unless you have any theories as to why an entire piece of property might be entirely incapable of growing any chloroplastic cells at all?"

Trent paused, to wait for Sam to make any suggestions that he might have. Sam was a very smart student, and the only one to volunteer to assist him on this project. He had a promising future in ag science, pending his future graduation from State. However, Sam didn't end up having much to say.

"We've been here for more than a month, and we are no closer to having any answers than we were when we first got here. So, we will choose several small 'sites' all over the property to excavate. Excavations will begin first thing Monday morning. I actually requisitioned the excavation equipment a couple of days ago, and it should arrive later this afternoon. It can sit over the weekend."

"Sure thing, Dr. Willingham. Anything you say."

"Once the excavation equipment arrives this afternoon, and you've signed for the receipt of the equipment, you can leave for the day, Samuel. I am going to go see Bob Smithers before I call it quits for the week."

* * *

"I called you guys in because I'd reached the end of *my* rope. You're not telling me you've reached the end of *your* rope, are you?" Bob Smithers was clearly frustrated, and Trent Willingham could understand why. At the end of the day, most farmers reached out to their local agricultural school for assistance when the answers were hard to find. Trent was supposed to have the answers. Most times, he did.

"I'm nowhere near the end of my rope, Mr. Smithers. Don't get me wrong. I have a lot more tricks that I could try. I'm just telling you that, one, I don't often have to go this far to get answers and, two, the way those GPR readings turned out was very abnormal."

"Abnormal how?"

Trent thought for a moment, calculating the words that he would choose to explain the situation to Bob.

"So, the radar works by sending signals into the ground that different materials of different densities then reflect back to the radar in different ways. Since different materials in the ground will absorb the signals at different levels, the GPR device is able to read the reflected signals to make decisions about what's likely in the ground."

"But why didn't that work in this situation?"

"Well, to look at the readings that the GPR devices took, the devices each reported that everything in the ground is so dense as to not absorb any radio waves at all, which is physically impossible."

“Which is why you tried out multiple different devices?”

“Right, Bob. We wanted to rule out the possibility that any one of the devices was malfunctioning.”

“So, what other explanations are there for five GPR devices failing in the same way?”

“Those devices weren’t failing, Bob. I had each of them tested back on campus in my office, after the fact. Each of those devices was working perfectly.”

“And so?”

“My next plan is to start some digging. I’ve contracted for some excavation equipment to come in. As a matter of fact, the equipment is probably being delivered as we’re here talking to each other. I want to choose multiple sites, all over the property, to start some controlled digs, to see what we can find.”

Bob looked somewhat relieved to know that Trent still had a plan.

“Whatever you say, Doc.”

“Bob, please understand that I’m not going to stop until we have some answers. And I’ll tell you this: when we have our answer, it is going to end up explaining how those GPR devices could mis-report on the density of every molecule in your dirt.”

* * *

The heart of downtown Bangor Springs, as much as Bangor Springs could even be described as having a ‘downtown’, for as small as it is, lies at the intersection of the two busiest streets in town, Merrifield Avenue and

Front Street. Front Street, being an east-west road, crosses Merrifield Avenue, a north-south road, to create an intersection with four corners: two of the town's four gas stations, Patrick Hodge's hardware store, and a local park featuring a duck pond populate the corners of the intersection. In a town like Bangor Springs, everyone learns what to do when the ducks cross Front Street to loiter in the parking lot next to Joe's Gas and Grab. It's a full traffic stoppage until the crossing is complete, of course.

The last person in town to hit one of those ducks on purpose hadn't been able to buy basic groceries anywhere in Bangor Springs for half-a-year. Bob Hamlin, president of the local chamber of commerce, had seen to that.

The town only has four traffic signal lights, all told. Three of the four occur on Front Street, at different intersections, and the fourth is on Merrifield Avenue, north of the downtown as you're heading out of town, at the intersection of Merrifield Avenue and Easterly Way.

As Front Street heads to the east, heading out of town, it climbs a rise into the neighborhood of town known simply as 'The Heights'; as Front Street heads west out of town, it climbs a similar rise into the most historical of the neighborhoods in Bangor Springs. The change in elevation, in either case, is probably only about a hundred feet; after all, this is Southwestern Michigan, so any "heights" don't really amount to much.

It's about a two-mile drive, heading east from the intersection of Merrifield and Front, for someone to get to the east edge of town.

Another two miles beyond that will bring you to the closest major north-south interstate highway in the area, M-192, which actually runs north through all of Knox County. To the south, 192 runs down into northern Indiana, before too long. Near the intersection of Front Street with 192 and its on-ramps, the only hotel to speak of in Bangor Springs sits, waiting to welcome travelers from far and wide. The hotel is appropriately named, The Holiday Inn - Bangor Springs.

Trent Willingham has been in town for almost six full weeks --three weeks longer than he expected for the assignment to have taken-- and he's been staying at the HIBS, as the locals refer to it, during the business week, ever since. On the weekends, Trent normally would head back to East Lansing, to spend time with his family. This weekend, however, Trent decided to stay in southwest Michigan -- his wife wasn't going to be home anyway and there wasn't much point in heading home just to spend time with the family Shih Poo.

Unfortunately, Trent's decision to stay in Bangor Springs for the weekend ended up having two negative consequences. The first was that his wet bar bill got to be a little bigger. Up to this point, his per diem allowance from the university had been able to cover his expenses --liquid and otherwise-- but Trent needed to find the answers to the questions surrounding Bob Smithers's field, and soon. He wanted to be able to get at it first thing come Monday morning, so staying in the area would allow for the least commute and the most action once the weekend was through.

The second negative consequence, however, was much more significant. And, as it turned out, Dr. Willingham never even ended up getting to watch any of the backhoes he'd requisitioned.

* * *

Hannah Flores had been the night-time manager at the HIBS for about six months. It was a good job for a girl just out of high school, and she knew how lucky she was to have it. But, hotel management has its share of challenges, and there'd been plenty of times in the last few months when she'd thought that this wasn't the job for her.

Primarily, she stayed for the pay, which was significantly higher than minimum wage and she knew that she was lucky to be making so much, having so little to offer. Truth be told, it was her Uncle Rick who'd got her the job in the first place; Uncle Rick told her that he knew the owner of the hotel, and that she'd be a shoe-in for the spot.

Most of the strange stuff that happens at hotels happens at night, at least that's what Gabe Durham told her. Gabe was the afternoon manager, noon-to-eight, and Laura saw him almost every weekday, as he was finishing his shift and she was just starting. Gabe often told Laura that there wasn't enough money in the world to pay Gabe to move from afternoons to nights. Laura knew, however, that if she offered to sleep with Gabe, he'd swap his days for her nights in an instant.

She'd seen it in his eyes. The way that he looked at her sometimes.

She wasn't *that* desperate to get away from the nightshift. Yet.

It turned out –however– that Gabe was right about that whole "the weird stuff happens at night" thing.

A perfect example of the craziness of the night shift occurred just last Saturday night, in Room 204, where that fancy farming scientist from Michigan State had been staying. She'd received a call at the front counter just after ten o'clock. The lights on the switchboard had indicated that the call was coming from 204.

"Good evening. This is Hannah, at the front desk. How might I assist you this evening."

"Well, Hannah. I'm calling to alert you to a little bit of a situation down here in Room 204."

Hannah looked down at her registration log and saw that the room was registered to a Dr. Trent Willingham.

"Is this Dr. Willingham, I'm presuming?" Hannah asked.

"No, it's most certainly not." the caller answered in a calm and nonchalant tone.

A little red flag went up deep in Hannah's mind. Before she could get the chance to formulate her thoughts into a cogent question, the caller continued.

"I'd like to speak with the manager, if I may."

"Well, sir, it just so happens that I am the manager, Ms. Hannah Flores. What can I do for you?"

There was a pause on the other end of the line. It suggested to Hannah that the caller was formulating their response on the fly.

"Hannah, the first thing that I want to make clear is that you are *not* to come down to this room. It's not going to be the kind of place that you want to be. Rather, I need for you to call the police, dialing 911 to do so, for this is most definitely an emergency."

Hannah was nonplussed.

"Who is this? Who am I talking to?"

"Not that it matters much, but..."

The caller identified himself to Hannah.

* * *

Trent checked the alarm clock on the nightstand next to the bed when he heard the knock on his hotel room door. It read 9:44 in large red numbers that were designed to be easy to see from anywhere in the room. The knock on the door seemed odd because he wasn't expecting anyone and he thought it was a strange hour of the evening for a random visitor to show up unannounced.

Trent went to the door and looked through the peephole.

He saw a man in a dress shirt and tie, with slacks on, all of it beneath an overcoat and all of it darkly colored. Trent thought the overcoat was peculiar, considering it was late summer and the temperatures in Michigan in August, while not outrageously hot, are usually accompanied by the kind of sticky humidity that often makes being fully-clothed and out-of-doors uncomfortable, to say the least, even this late into the evening.

Trent spoke through the door, in a voice loud enough to be heard.

"Who is it? I'm certainly not expecting a visitor at this hour of the evening. Would you please identify yourself?"

"I apologize, sir, for the lateness of the hour. I don't mean to alarm you. I have information about Miller's Field --out on Old Smith Road-- and I understand that you might be interested to know more."

The part of Trent Willingham's mind that should've been able to register an objection to the fact that someone outside the door knew who was in the hotel room --who Trent was, what he was doing in town, what his interests and motivations might be-- and that such an advantage on the part of the person outside might not be the best news in the world, that part was swallowed up by the part of Trent's mind that thought that it was a true stroke of luck that someone was there to assist him in solving the riddle - a riddle that, up to this point, he'd not had much luck with on his own.

Trent opened the door and welcomed the gentlemen, who proceeded into the room and ended up taking the chair at the hotel room desk. Trent thought that the man looked to be as old as he was, maybe slightly younger, and the stranger was bald, with a long, gray, triangular beard and rimless glasses. In finding a place to sit, Trent settled for a seat on the edge of the bed he intended to be sleeping in later.

Trent could hardly contain himself.

"So, Mr…"

"Dire. You may call me Mr. Dire."

"So, Mr. Dire, what can you tell me about the farm property out on Old Smith Road, currently owned by Mr. Bob Smithers?"

"Well, for starters, I can tell you that I wish he'd never purchased it. That's for sure."

Trent thought that it was a strange way to start the conversation off, but he wasn't really in a position to dictate the course of the discussion. Trent paused for long enough to allow for Mr. Dire to continue on.

"I don't really want to take up too much of your time, Dr. Willingham. What I came here to tell you tonight is pretty simple. Miller's Field has secrets, and they are secrets that would best be left alone. I understand that Mr. Smithers wants answers, and I understand that you want to give him those answers, but I'd like to have you understand that the answers aren't worth the price of admission. To put it bluntly, Dr. Willingham, I came here tonight to tell you to quit this project."

As he was formulating a response in his mind, Trent recognized his fear -- newly arrived and taking up space in his head. The bald man had come to convince Trent to quit his mission, and Trent recognized that people often went to extremes to convince others to be obedient. As part of Trent's mind was thinking of what he should say to this Mr. Dire, a different part of his mind was trying to calculate escape routes from the room.

"Mr. Dire, I am a man of science. I'm a man of knowledge and wisdom, and I came here, to this most southwestern corner of our fair state, to use these tools to try to help a farmer in need of assistance. Without any additional information from you, as to what secrets I should be endeavoring to protect, what information I'm about to uncover, and why it would be bad for me to uncover it, I am going to do what I came to Bangor Springs to do. Convince me to stop my scientific investigation, or understand that I will not yield."

For just a moment --the slightest of instants-- the bald man seemed to be considering Willingham's response. But then, in a sudden burst of fury and effort that seemed almost unreal, Mr. Dire was on him, so quickly as to prevent the professor from even having a chance to protect himself. Trent Willingham was probably dead within a few seconds of the start of Mr. Dire's attack.

The rest of what Mr. Dire did --following the murder of Dr. Willingham-- was for his own enjoyment.

* * *

Officer Frank Moody and Officer Andrew Billings, of the Bangor Springs Police Department, were dispatched to the HIBS at 10:11 p.m. on the evening of August 7th, to investigate the 911 call placed by the night manager at the hotel, one Hannah Flores. The dispatch officer, Mya Hopkins, working at the Bangor Springs police precinct, sent Billings and Moody over to the hotel as they were finishing up a domestic disturbance call that they were refereeing at the Pine Ridge apartment complex on the west side of town. If not for the fact that Bangor Springs is as small as it is, it might have taken longer for the two officers to go from one side of town to the other, but as it were, they made it to the HIBS in short order. First item of business was to question the manager while waiting for their backup to arrive -- two duty officers from the Knox County Sheriff's Office.

Mya hadn't been able to prepare them for what they were heading into -- having very little information to give. As Moody and Billings made their way across town to the HIBS, Frank was wondering what they were getting themselves into. Not much information to go on, from the 911 call, according to Mya, but she did make it sound like an active crime scene. And, since Mya was the sharpest of the dispatchers working for the BSPD in those days, she decided that the event, as described by Hannah, was just weird enough that backup might be necessary -- Mya had placed a call to the Knox County Sheriff Dispatch straight away.

Mya's last words to Moody and Billings before disconnecting on the radio call were, "Expect anything."

As Frank made his way to the front door of the hotel lobby, he knew what his first question to Hannah Flores was going to be, aside from the preliminary questions that would need to be asked. Frank wanted to know why it was that Hannah had thought to follow the advice of the caller from the hotel room --this Mr. Dire-- why she'd decided to stay in the front office area of the hotel and call the police, as she'd been told to do.

If it had been Frank, the curiosity would have certainly overcome him.

Hannah Flores was waiting for them behind the front desk, the host ready to receive yet a couple more guests on this strange evening.

"Good evening, officers. Welcome to the HIBS. I'm Hannah Flores."

"I'm Officer Moody. This is Officer Billings."

"Hello, Ms. Flores." Andy chimed in.

""How may I assist you in your investigation? I've been instructed by the hotel's upper management to cooperate in any way that I can."

Frank thought it pretty wise of the night manager to call her superiors and seek their advice, apprising them of the situation.

"Let's just start with a basic understanding of what you know."

"Well, aside from what I told the lady on the 911 call, which I'm assuming that you've already heard, I know that the guest in Room 204 was a professor from Michigan State University. He was in town, working with Farmer Smithers on a piece of land that was giving him trouble.

Frank knew who Bob Smithers was - everyone in town knew Farmer Smithers. Frank also thought he knew which field was giving Smithers some trouble - probably Miller's Field. When Frank was a kid --back in the days when everybody called him Franky-- he'd hit a wild turkey with his very first car near Miller's Field out on Old Smith Road, a very strange turkey indeed. So, needless to say, he knew about Miller's Field; bizarre stuff going on out in that neck of the woods.

“Come to think of it,” Ms. Flores continued, “there was another person staying here from MSU, I think.” Hannah started shuffling through the pages in a log book in front of her, searching for something on one of the sheets. “Here, we go. Room 208. Samuel Heath. Listed here in the notes, it says that Mr. Heath was an associate of the professor.”

“Well, we’ll be sure to investigate that lead.” Andy responded.

Just then, a squad car belonging to the Knox County Sheriff’s Office pulled up outside. Frank saw it ease into a parking spot right alongside their own patrol car.

“Looks like our back-up is here.”

* * *

The amount of blood in a person is usually somewhere between a gallon and a gallon and a half, depending on the person’s size. That’s the equivalent of somewhere between thirty-two and forty-eight half-cup servings, just FYI. And, if you’ve ever seen those kinds of paintings where the artist has just taken smatterings of paint and flung them onto a canvas -- a half-cup of green paint here and a half-cup of blue paint there, with a half-cup of purple paint on top of it all, then you can start to get a picture of what Room 204 looked like when the officers opened the door to it.

Blood flung everywhere. Red on red on red.

The Knox County sheriff deputies, alongside Officers Moody and Billings, were surprised by the mess of the scene, and it usually takes quite a bit to surprise a police officer. Andy excused himself almost immediately, to see if Samuel Heath was in Room 208, perchance. Frank knew that his partner wasn't the kind of officer that took to scenes like this one.

For a moment, Frank and the two deputies just kind of stood in the doorway of the hotel room, trying to figure out how to even begin processing a crime scene like this. There didn't appear to be a body anywhere, from what they could see from the doorway, and there didn't appear to be any other signs that a crime was in progress. What had happened here was now over, by the looks of it.

The deputy that Frank would've thought of as the oldest of the three of them spoke first, as they were all three just standing there, overcome by the ghastly gore.

"Well, we are either going to have to call in for a crime scene investigation team to do this the right way --and who knows how long that could take-- or we are going to have to take the initiative, having agreed that it was the proper course. The Sheriff's Department has a crime scene team that we could call down here, but I'm not sure it would help, judging by the mess."

"How would we even start this?" Frank asked, honestly wondering if either of the deputies had any notion as to how to take the first step, and then the second and third steps, into the room. "I'm having a hard time even imagining how a forensic team is going to manage to do this."

The silence among them resumed for an additional moment, as the three of them continued to look around. Then, the younger of the two deputies pointed to the wall above the bed's headboard and said, "What do you make of that?"

Frank hadn't even noticed it, overcome by the rest of the scene as he'd been. But, sure enough, someone --presumably, the perp-- had drawn something on the wall, in the blood of the missing professor.

"I hadn't even seen it until you pointed it out, Deputy," Frank replied. "Some sort of a symbol, I guess?"

"Not like any symbol I've ever seen before," the other deputy said. "Some sort of gang sign or something?"

Just then, Andy returned. He didn't quite come all the way up to the doorway before making his report to the three of them.

"There doesn't appear to be anyone down in Room 208. On a Saturday night, could be that a young college kid found something better to do than to hang around while his boss was getting murdered?"

"Could be." Frank agreed, and the two deputies nodded as well. "I'll call down to the front desk and have the manager hold him down there in case he shows up."

"Roger that." the older deputy confirmed.

Frank stepped away from the three of them, down the hall a few paces, to call the front desk on his flip phone.

"Hannah? This is Officer Moody, upstairs, investigating your 911 call?"

"Yes, Officer Moody. How can I help?"

"Well, it seems that Samuel Heath isn't in his room, and we were hoping…"

"Officer Moody," Hannah interrupted, "he's standing right in front of me. He just came in the front door of the hotel not more than two minutes ago. I was holding him here until I could figure out how to get a hold of you."

"Fantastic. Thanks, Hannah."

Frank disconnected the call and told his fellow officers that there was a lead at the front desk. The deputies stayed at the hotel door, to secure the scene, while the Bangor Springs officers went down to talk to Sam.

* * *

Samuel Heath was standing at the front desk, dressed in the apparel that one would have expected a college kid to be wearing at 10:37 on a Saturday night. Frank assumed that he'd probably been in Bangor Springs, trying to find a social scene that approximated what he was used to back in East Lansing. Frank also assumed that he'd been unsuccessful in doing so; Bangor Springs has about as much in common with East Lansing as a German Shepard has in common with a Chihuahua.

Moody tried to begin the interview, but Samuel got the jump on him.

"Why is it that I'm being kept from going to my room? Is there a problem, Officer…?"

"Moody. And this is my partner, Officer Billings. The fact of the matter is, Mr. Heath, there's a big problem."

"What sort of a problem?"

"It would appear that something criminal has occurred in your boss's hotel room. When was the last time that you saw him or spoke with him?"

"It was yesterday afternoon, at the end of our work day out at the Smithers field on Old Smith Road. What do you mean, 'criminal'?"

Frank didn't particularly appreciate being asked as many questions as he was asking, but he understood the concern and curiosity on Sam's face.

"Mr. Heath, it would appear --from our initial findings-- that your boss has been murdered."

Sam's face lost its color so quickly that Frank was concerned that the kid might pass out and drop to the floor. He prepared himself to catch Sam in case he ended up folding like a lawn chair.

"I don't know what to say. This is horrible. Yesterday, when he told me to stay on-site to accept delivery of some excavation equipment, he said that we were going to be using it on Monday to continue our work for Farmer Smithers. I guess that won't be happening. I've got to contact the university. The dean of the department is going to need to know."

Frank wrote down a note in his notebook to be sure to contact the Michigan State University School of Agriculture.

"We'll contact the university." Frank assured Sam.

"You didn't happen to see him at all today?"

"Nope. Most weekends, Dr. Willingham would go back to East Lansing, to be with his family for the weekend. I think he'd decided to stay in town this weekend to be able to get an early start on Monday morning."

Frank thought it was odd that the professor might have been murdered in a place where, and at a time when, he wasn't normally expected to be.

"Mr. Heath, we are going to need to get contact information for you, in the event that we need to get a hold of you during the course of our investigation. As for tonight, I can't think of any reason why you wouldn't be okay to stay in Room 208."

"Of course, Officer Moody, I'll provide you with any contact information that you might want. But, as for staying in that room tonight, I can't imagine anything I'd like to do less. I will pack my things and head back to campus, if it's all the same to you."

Frank Moody had no reason to think of Samuel Heath as a suspect in this investigation. He, therefore, couldn't think of a reason to constrain the kid to remain in the area.

"That's a two and a half hour trip, son. Are you sure you want to make that trip in the middle of the night?"

"I'm pretty sure that I don't want to stay in that hotel room, a dozen yards from a crime scene. If that means that I've got some driving to do, I hope that you will let me do it."

And so, Officer Moody got Sam's contact information --dorm room phone number, dorm address, home phone and address, etc.-- and then, he let the young man go his own way.

* * *

And that's pretty much how that went. The two local cops and the two county deputies decided to process the crime scene themselves, doing their best to preserve as much evidence as they could. Officer Billings mostly offered moral support during that process. Additional interviews were conducted --Bob Smithers, a couple of the cleaning staff at the HIBS, one or two other people around town-- in the days following the incident. Michigan State University was contacted immediately, and their interest in having the murder of one of their professors solved kept the investigation going longer than it may have otherwise, considering that the people of Bangor Springs, and their police force, weren't terribly interested or concerned about an outsider who met his end at a hotel located halfway to Chester.

The investigation eventually went cold, and the body of Dr. Willingham was never found, as it were. Additionally, no one was ever able to locate this "Mr. Dire" character - the man who allegedly called the front desk from the hotel room.

The process by which Michigan State University was attempting to assist Bob Smithers with the problems he was having with his fourteen acre field in Bangor Springs ended with Trent Willingham's life. Sam Heath and the rest of Willingham's research team went back to their campus. Bob Smithers eventually got a report from the university, co-written by Heath and some professor that had never even been to Bangor Springs, and the summation of the report was "Sorry, but you're out-of-luck."

Mr. Dire had his way, for the most part, or so it seemed. After that summer, Bob Smithers never attempted planting Miller's Field again, mostly out of frustration but also out of some sense of respect for the life of the professor who'd tried to help him out. Bob's only solace in having bought the property ended up being his ability to drive across it --hither and yon-- while he planted and harvested the surrounding fields.

However, truth be told, Mr. Dire's dealings in Bangor Springs --out on Old Smith Road-- during the summer of 1993, weren't his first interactions in that particular neighborhood. These days, though, ol' Dire was just trying to stay on top of a continuing process of damage control resulting from his first-ever project for The Scion some sixty plus years previous -- a project that hadn't gone as expected.

The End & The Beginning

Santa Fe - One

Kathryn Santos had been working at the Casa Paz Assisted Living Facility in Santa Fe, New Mexico, since the start of 2014 -- for almost four and a half years now. During that time, she'd come to know many of the residents of the facility quite well. She'd come to care for many of them in a way that is unique to the truly gifted workers in the healthcare industry. Sometimes, they'd open right up to Kathryn, these elderly inhabitants -- as starved as many of them were for attention. Others had been tougher nuts to crack, but Kathryn worked on the tough nuts, too, showing them a genuine charm and concern that was eventually persuasive. Even for the toughest of nuts.

Except for the man in Room 204.

It didn't seem as if anything would ever be able to crack that man.

He was one of the most depressing residents of Casa Paz, and all of the employees would tell you so. Kathryn was the only nurse that seemed to even try to spend any time around him.

Kathryn liked being around him because he was quiet -- most of the time. In Kathryn's mind, too many of the residents of Casa Paz talked too much or made too much noise. Of course, some of that talk and noise was to be expected -- after all, nursing homes aren't meant to be silent. In Kathryn's mind, however, the only thing worse than too much talking was the incoherent babbling, moaning, and screaming of some of the residents; those noises were somehow significantly worse, almost creepy.

Kathryn liked the man in 204 --everyone called him John, even though it was understood that 'John' wasn't his name-- primarily because he didn't make any sounds at all. Kathryn had always been drawn to people who talked less, the introspective types. Granted, no one had been able to establish that John was even able to talk, much less that he was choosing to not speak on purpose. Nevertheless, there's something that Kathryn has always appreciated about those who would communicate if it were necessary, but who are just as fine with not.

At one point, as Kathryn was explaining her appreciation for the quiet man in Room 204 to Nora Lietz, the old battle ax who ran the corps of nurses at Casa Paz, Nora told the story of the man's most recent speaking splurge.

"It's been almost five years since he said a thing to anyone here in Casa Paz. Kathryn, you've only been working here for four years, right?"

"Well, four-and-a-half next month."

"So, his silence predates your arrival here. No one has heard a peep from him in all that time. Of course, when you get to be that old, what is there left to say?"

Kathryn thought about this for a moment, and then Nora continued on.

"It was the very early morning hours of October 21st, 2013, in the dead of the night. I'll never forget it, not as long as I work in this place, and probably not as long as I live. He woke up, from a dead sleep, sat up straight in his bed, and screamed the name 'Patsy' repeatedly for just over ninety seconds. Over and over again, just screaming that name."

"No he didn't!" Kathryn was stunned.

"He sure did. After that, he slipped into a coma that lasted for twelve days. And all of that started at 1:19 a.m. For some reason, those numbers have always stuck with me --1:19-- as if there was something about them."

Kathryn remembered Nora's telling of that story just about every time that she stepped into Room 204. Of all of the patients in the Casa Paz Assisted Living Facility, some that Kathryn liked more and some that she liked less --and some that she liked very little at all-- she thought that John was one of the only ones that she actually enjoyed being around -- which wasn't to say that every day was a day when you wanted to be around the man. Sometimes, she would sit at his bedside, watching him as he would stare out the window or up at the ceiling. Occasionally, they would look at each other, just enjoying each other's company. Kathryn felt comfortable around him, and the truly crazy thing about it was that she had no reason to feel comfortable. She knew nothing about him -- nothing about his past or his experiences or his sins. All the same, John was what she imagined her grandfathers must have been like, grandfathers that she'd never got to know.

But the story that Nora Lietz had told her was always in the back of Kathryn's mind.

* * *

Casa Paz wasn't the greatest nursing home in the Santa Fe area, but it was one of the cheapest. And, for being one of the cheapest, the place didn't look run-down or dilapidated at all. In fact, from the outside, one would have thought that the nursing home was a very fine facility indeed. The interior design left a little to be desired, but getting potential customers in the door was more than half the battle. Considering how well the nursing home was able to fare with the pittance that they received from each of the residents of the home, a thrifty and intelligent someone had to be managing the affairs correctly.

That someone was Daniel "Butch" Alvarez. Butch was probably one of the most frugal nursing home managers in all of New Mexico.

As the sole manager of the Casa Paz Assisted Living Facility, Butch Alvarez was in charge of all things, well, managerial. Butch had been called 'Butch' ever since he was a kid, when he turned out to be the only boy in his neighborhood to favor a nice, tight haircut, while all of the other boys he grew up with wanted hair that was long and flowing, in deference to their cultural heritage. Butch had always been like that -- neat and orderly. A place for everything and everything in its place.

This level of organization and discipline made for a man with great managerial skills.

He ran the nursing home, as much as it would allow itself to be run, like he ran his life.

A place for everything and everything in its place.

He also had a soft spot for veterans, and this had an effect on his management of the home, as well. He thought it was one of the absolute crimes of American society that soldiers who came home from war overseas were not treated with the utmost honor, respect, and courtesy available, in consideration of their service.

For this very reason, Butch was harboring seven veterans in the Casa Paz nursing home, even though their ability to pay was significantly less than what was expected, even for one of the cheapest nursing homes around. Once Butch factored in the coverage that your average geriatric veteran was liable to get from the V.A., and you added that to the Medicare coverage for nursing homes like Casa Paz, it should have been enough for any veteran to be able to be provided for in their golden years.

This, often, wasn't the case.

Butch normally found that it was so tedious to jump through the hoops that the V.A. set up in order to be able to get the funds that these national heroes had coming to them. It shouldn't be so hard. But, as anyone who has ever worked with the V.A. can tell you, their systems are mostly broken and inefficient, and that made it hard for Butch to make sure that these fine men and women got what they needed.

Butch was smart enough to understand how to arrange for the 'shortages in monies' from these seven veterans by 'moving numbers around'. You borrowed from this bucket as you filled that bucket and, if you did it right, no one had any questions to ask about any of it. He, in his mind, was doing what was necessary. Butch thought of it as his civic duty, doing what he was doing, to make a place for these people in his facility.

Of course, there were probably others who would've felt differently, since Butch was violating several state and federal laws to make all of this work. But, Butch thought that it couldn't hurt if no one knew about it. He didn't really feel like he was doing anything wrong; rather, he felt like he was doing what was right by these national heroes.

Of these seven veterans --really, of all of the guests of Casa Paz-- Butch was up-to-speed on their individual situations, and this was to be expected. In the medical field, especially in the field of geriatric medicine, you worked a lot with families and patients on their individual issues, and in doing so, you soon got to know them all on a deeper level, a more personal level. But, if there was one patient at Casa Paz that Butch knew very little about, it was the John Doe in Room 204. As far as anyone knew, he'd been born a geriatric; there was simply no one to provide any information about that man anywhere in the United States, to Butch's knowledge.

* * *

Early on, when Kathryn was first starting to ask some questions in her own mind about John and his back story, she went to talk to Butch.

"So, what can you tell me about the man in 204, Butch? I feel like I need to know a little bit more, to be able to try to relate to him."

Butch leaned back in the chair behind the desk in his office. The move was partially an attempt at giving himself a moment to contemplate the question and his answer, but it was also just a move to become more comfortable.

"You already know almost everything there is to know. The truth of the matter is that we got the man from Christus St. Vincent Hospital back in 2010. He'd been a patient of theirs for some time --a stroke patient, if memory serves-- and his amnesia and lack of identifying papers had made him a 'John Doe' for them, as well."

"Did you ever do any follow up with them?"

"Well, the whole thing was before my time." Butch answered. "I started in 2011, and John was already here. At that point in time, I had one mission and one mission only -- make sure the place didn't close. I didn't have any time to go tracking down the back story on a mystery man."

"I see." Kathryn replied.

Butch turned to one of the file cabinets behind his desk. There were three of them, each black, standing about four and a half feet tall, each of them with four drawers. Butch keyed his way into the one on the left, top drawer, and found a file folder. He pulled it out, shut everything back up, and returned to his desk.

He handed the file folder to Kathryn.

"This is all we've got on the guy. Have at it. Find out what you can. Dig up what you may. In the seven years that I've been here, you're the first person to seem to give a damn."

Bangor Springs - One

Clint and Tami Shumer, of Modesto, California, were being relocated -- to Michigan, of all places. Clint was excited for the opportunity to gain control of the entire Midwest sales region, but Tami thought that this move was going to be the end of life as she knew it. They'd established a life in Modesto, one that she'd grown very attached to. She had her favorite things to do in Modesto -- she loved Graceada Park in the summertime, and the farmer's market in Modesto never ceased to amaze her, and the San Joaquin Valley between Fresno and Sacramento was a place of so much abundance and beauty. Tami was just having a hard time imagining how things in Michigan were going to compare to things in central California.

And, if it had been even five years earlier, she would have refused, and she would have used the kids as an excuse. But now, the kids --Ted and Allyson-- were in college in Oregon and Texas, respectively, and Clint and Tami were empty-nesters living in a house that was about two thousand square feet too large. These days, all of her excuses for staying in Modesto would have seemed like rain on Clint's parade, in light of the opportunity that was being presented to him. And so, Tami hadn't even bothered to put together any arguments.

Clint began almost immediately, making promises to build her a new home where the two of them could enjoy a change of pace and an escape, where they could try small-town life. Tami, trying not to be sucked in by the cunning ploys of her husband, did secretly think that a new house might just be worth a change of scenery. While Clint was looking for nice little towns to settle in, and for pieces of property to build on, Tami secretly found herself getting excited about the possibilities, despite herself.

Clint had recently narrowed in on southwestern Michigan as a likely destination, for a number of different reasons: close enough to Chicago and to northern Indiana, not too far from Indianapolis and Detroit, land and housing prices that were very cheap, by comparison to what they'd seen in California. Clint seemed particularly interested in a little town called Bangor Springs, Michigan. Located in the most southwestern of all Michigan counties, it bordered Lake Michigan, which was --by all accounts-- a very beautiful lake. According to Clint's research on the internet, the people of western Michigan called their coastline on Lake Michigan "the gold coast".

Tami was hoping that their move to the midwest would end up being 'golden'.

* * *

In a town the size of Bangor Springs, at least in the modern day, there aren't many mysteries anymore, what with the invention of the internet and all. Most information is available with a few keystrokes on a computer, and people who know how to find that information can solve a lot of mysteries from the comfort of their own home and couch.

But, even without the internet, when it comes to a small town, you just get the sense that there's a closeness. That everybody knows everybody. And it's this very way in Bangor Springs. And, even when there is a person in town who doesn't know someone else, they at least know someone who knows that other someone. In a small town like this one, there's an interconnectedness that makes it hard for people to keep secrets, and it makes it even harder for there to be any situation, any particular mystery, that no one knows anything about.

Often, if one is looking to find some information on a topic of local interest, you would just ask a local business owner who could point you in the right direction. In Bangor Springs, they always seem to have the inside scoop. Without too much work --or delicacy-- you can usually unravel any 'mystery' with five or six well-placed questions, and their resulting answers.

In Bangor Springs, the closest thing that there has recently been to a significant mystery is Miller's Field, not that it's that significant, really.

If you did decide to go to Beth Silva, the head librarian here in Bangor Springs, she wouldn't be able to explain the mystery of Miller's Field to you. If you went to Michael Hodge, who runs the local hardware store like his father before him, he wouldn't be able to explain the mystery of Miller's Field to you, either. If you went to Monica Humphrey, the part-time secretary at the First United Methodist Church of Bangor Springs, or Maud Patton, the owner of the Sunoco gas station in town, neither of them would be able to explain the mystery of Miller's Field to you. Even the town's self-declared expert on Miller's Field -- Paul Brachman, the local newspaper reporter-- hasn't been able to do much to explain the mystery.

Miller's Field lies northeast of town, out on Old Smith Road, about two and a half miles away from downtown, as the crow flies. It's not a field that most people come across during their daily business in town, unless you happen to take Old Smith Road into or out of town regularly. Oddly enough though, despite few people from town having reason to come across it very often, everyone in Bangor Springs has at least heard of the mystery of Miller's Field.

Old Smith Road is one of the quicker -- albeit more obscure-- ways to head into the northern part of Knox County, toward Benton Center or Clearwater, if you're heading in that direction. But, there are other roads to take to get to those places, faster roads and more direct ones, like Merrifield Avenue, for example. People tend to use those roads.

It suffices to say that most people don't have any reason to travel on Old Smith Road.

These days, Miller's Field lays smack dab in the middle of a much larger crop field. Every spring, for at least the last couple of decades, Bob Smithers would plow and plant the crop fields surrounding Miller's Field --some years with corn, and other years with soybeans, maybe wheat every once in a while, if there was a market for it-- always being very careful to plow and plant around Miller's Field in the middle. In fact, in late-April or early-May, when whatever Bob had planted would start to pop up out of the ground, the barren outline of Miller's Field would become obvious to anyone driving down Old Smith Road, heading out of or into town.

For you see, that's the mystery: no one alive in Bangor Springs, Michigan can remember the last time anything grew on Miller's Field.

No crops. No weeds. Nothing at all.

Oh, and Bob Smithers --the farmer who'd owned Miller's Field since 1988-- died last month.

FROM BRACHMAN'S FILE #1 -- July 13, 1979

Franky Moody was a seventeen year old boy living out his adolescence in small town America in the last year of the 1970s. As such, Franky really only wanted to do two things, as a teen boy -- spend time with his girl and go fast in his car. Whenever the opportunity to do them both at the same time, or at nearly the same time, presented itself, Franky was as happy as a puppy with two peters.

Amanda hated being in Franky's car when he got to thinking about driving faster than he ought to, and the way that she rode him to get him to behave himself was a real downer for Franky. He learned, fairly early on in their relationship, that he was best served when he did what she told him to do, when he behaved how she wanted him to behave. To deal with the unpleasantness that Amanda dished out when Franky misbehaved had never been worth the trouble.

But, there was always the drive to pick her up for a date. And there was always the drive back to his house, after dropping her off, at the end of a date. Those were opportunities for some speed.

On July 13, 1979, just about a week after his seventeenth birthday, Franky was on his way home after a particularly enjoyable date with his girlfriend. It had been particularly enjoyable because Franky had made his way to third base with Amanda, and the feeling of her skin under his fingers was on his mind -- probably would be on his mind for days.

And, as if Franky even needed an excuse for driving fast, his entire nervous system seemed to be on fire with the excitement of being so aroused -- Franky was doing twenty miles an hour over the speed limit within the first mile's worth of road leaving Amanda's house, at 7338 Old Smith Road, headed south and back into the town of Bangor Springs.

The turkey came out of nowhere, right as Franky was passing by Miller's Field on his left side.

If Franky didn't know better, he would have sworn that it simply materialized in front of his car a split second before he smashed into it with his front end. But, of course, such things aren't possible. The loud smash prompted him to pull over, just to be able to inspect his ride for damage. In the initial, he wasn't even really sure what he'd hit.

Anyone living in southwestern Michigan has probably seen a live turkey once or twice in their time, so recognizing one when you see one isn't that hard -- assuming that they look like turkeys are supposed to look. What kept the turkey, stuck in the front of Frank's '76 Maverick, from looking like a turkey were two sets of things. The first set of things, of course, was the damage that the accident had done to the bird. That made the turkey look pretty disgusting, in and of itself. Half of the bird's rib cage had split and pierced through the right side of the bird -- small boney white jagged shards dripping wet, dark blood onto the chrome of the Maverick's grill. The turkey's left foot had almost broken off, suspended --by just a couple of sinewy tendons-- from falling onto the asphalt below.

The other set of things that kept the turkey from being easily identifiable was the mutations.

If the accident itself hadn't managed to kill Franky's record-setting good mood, leaving Amanda's house, it was the mutations that kept young Master Moody thinking about that turkey for weeks thereafter. The crazy thing had two heads, Franky saw, as it hung almost lifeless stuck in the grill of his car. Two heads meant four glazed over, dying eyes looking up at him when he first saw it stuck there, square in the middle of his grill, equally spaced in between the left and the right turn signal lights.

Almost lifeless because it was still twitching with the final electrical impulses coming from its brain, attempting in vain to signal muscles that were in no condition to do much more than just spasm.

Frank's initial disgust and revolted ire got the best of him for the first few moments, but then he realized that he was going to have to take some action. Frank walked off the side shoulder of Old Smith Road and grabbed a thick stick from the brush. Returning to his car's front end with the lever in hand, Frank pried the turkey out from his grill, breaking the stick a couple of times in the process -- each time sacrificing a little bit more distance between his working hand and the carcass of the bird. Finally, the turkey fell to the ground with a bit of a wet plop.

Done with the deed, Frank wasted not a single moment in getting away from that particularly nasty scene. Before he left though, Frank kicked the turkey into weeds off the side of the road -- equal parts improper burial and vented frustration. He finished his drive home, checked his Maverick's front end once more underneath the lights inside his garage, and then beat a path to his bed for the night.

He didn't end up sleeping, however. Every time he closed his eyes and tried, four dead turkey eyes were there, staring back at him.

July 11, 1932

"I'm just not sure how we are going to be able to make it through, Norma. This is turning out to be the worst year yet."

Tom sat across from his wife, Norma, just about every night lately, at the small kitchen table where they took their meals with their two children, Patsy and little Jim. They would sit, late into the night, long after the kids had gone to bed, trying to figure out a way to make everything work. They would sit that way until it became so dark in the house that it was impossible for the two of them to see each other across the kitchen table without lighting a lamp. At that point, with no new, brilliant ideas for saving the farm, they'd go off to bed, once again.

"Do we have anything that we can sell? Anything that will get us enough money to be able to make it through until the harvest season this fall?"

Norma was usually great for having ideas, and Tom had always loved her for being so smart, for being such a great help to him. So far, though, none of the ideas that Norma or Tom could come up with seemed like a good fit for the quandary they were in.

"I've already sold just about everything that we can sell, everything that we don't need for farming or for keeping you and the children alive. It would be different if we'd recently had a decent crop, but the problem is that we are facing the worst year yet in a series of bad years. We just don't have much in reserve to be able to lean on."

Norma knew how serious the situation was -- Tom didn't keep these facts from her. Still she seemed newly concerned every time he mentioned their financial woes.

"Do we not have anything in the bank? Nothing at all?"

"I spent so much money on corn seed in the spring to plant the field, it pretty much drained us. It's just that the weather isn't cooperating -- too little rain so far this year. I don't know how much of a crop I'm going to have by harvest time."

Norma knew the old adage -- corn should be knee high by the fourth of July. Unfortunately, that hadn't happened. Without the necessary rains, the crops had just stopped growing. If the lack of rain kept up, the crops would start withering soon. The long green leaves on the short corn stalks would curl in on themselves, length-wise, shielding their moisture from the harsh summer heat.

She reached out her hand, across the table, to lay hold of her husband's. She wanted to comfort him, to reassure him that everything was going to be alright. Tom smiled at her in response, but it was a defeated smile, weak and lacking in enthusiasm.

"I suppose I could head into Bangor Springs, to try to find some additional work, for pay. The problem with that is, manual labor will leave me less time for minding the crops. That work will have to get done sometime."

"Well, the kids and I could help with that, to try to ease your burden a little bit. We're not useless, you know."

Tom squeezed his wife's hand, gently.

“I know you’re not, and I appreciate the offer. Providing for this family is supposed to be my job. I won’t have my wife and my children burdened with the work that’s supposed to be mine to do.”

Norma disengaged from that discussion -- partly because they’d had it so many times before, and partly because she knew that it was a losing fight. She sat quietly, waiting for Tom to continue.

“Maybe we should just go. Sell the house and the farmland and move away from here. Try to find some other place that is easier to farm than this. We could head back to Illinois, back to where my family’s from. Sometimes, I think that this farm is just cursed.”

Norma didn’t entertain this idea with so much as a response. She knew that he didn’t really mean it, and she was pretty happy where they were at, all things considered. Tom was only really half-heartedly suggesting it to begin with.

Little did Tom or Norma know that 1932 was about to get a lot more cursed, for them and their family; much more cursed than just having some problems with dry soil.

July 14, 1932

Tom didn't like the options that were lying in front of him, but he liked the thought of his family starving even less. Of course, they weren't likely to starve --not really-- because farmers can always just eat the food that they're raising. But, whatever they ate from the fields or from their barnyard was food that they wouldn't have available to sell. The trade-off was a tricky one to try to maneuver.

He'd heard of so many of the farmers in the Bangor Springs area selling off their property, acre by acre, just to have enough money to be able to 'get by', but Tom tried to be an optimist - he believed that things were eventually going to get better. How those farmers were going to be able to pull themselves out on the other side of this, without the land that they'd all sold to make ends meet, was a mystery that he didn't intend to ever face.

But, the thought of selling off some of his land was mighty tempting.

But then, just the previous Saturday, Tom was approached by a man in town, while he was in Bangor Springs on farm business. The man appeared to be an older gentleman --in his early sixties, were Tom to hazard a guess-- and he was definitely someone that Tom had never seen around town before. The man was dressed fairly formally, for a man just walking around Bangor Springs, in a shirt, a tie, and dress slacks. Tom noticed he was bald on the top of his head, but the size of his gray, triangular beard countered his hairless pate.

He came right up to Tom as Tom was leaving the general store, addressing him through glasses that were seated on the end of his nose.

"Are you Tom Miller?"

"Depends who's asking."

"My name is not important, because we are never really going to get to know each other much. What you should know, Mr. Miller, is that I have something that you are going to want to hear."

Tom looked around, up and down the sidewalk on Front Street, to see if anyone was noticing him speaking to this unusual character.

"If you'll excuse me, sir, I'm not normally in the practice of conversing with people who are wholly unfamiliar to me." Tom started to walk off, wanting suddenly to get back home to his family. But, the bald man wasn't done talking.

"Mr. Miller, it's like I said -- you're going to want to hear what I have to say. I've got an offer for you, an offer that could help to keep your wife and kids from feeling any of the negative side effects of what is looking like it might be a bad growing season. You can walk away if you want to, but don't you at least want to hear what I have to say?"

"What harm could there be in just listening?"

Tom wanted a way to make it through, without having to sell off his land, but this strange development stunk to high heaven. Good fruit doesn't come from bad trees, and Tom knew that from the Good Book.

"I suppose I can at least listen to you."

"Good. So, here's the deal."

Tom walked with the man a few hundred yards, away from the relative bustle of Front Street, away from the eyes and ears of prying neighbors, over to an alley behind the lumber mill. It was there that the man told Tom about the offer. If this odd man ended up delivering on his promises, the cost to Tom would be minimal, and the gains would be enough for him to be able to provide for Norma, Patsy, and Jim for the rest of the season and well into the next season.

If he played his cards right.

July 15, 1932

Mr. Dire had been going by the name 'Mr. Dire' for seven years. Born John Lee Direckson in 1865, he should have been sixty-seven years old in 1932.

But he wasn't.

For seven years, Mr. Dire has been a member of The Scion.

For just as long, Mr. Dire has been stuck at the age of sixty.

When Mr. Dire got to thinking about the implications of not getting any older, his mind started to race. Would he live forever? Was there any limit to the future for him? Would immortality end up being a blessing or a curse? Could he be killed? What exactly had he been getting himself into when he joined up with such as these? For seven years, Dire had been working to try to come to terms with his new reality. But, as with anything, there were advantages -- when he got to wondering too much, he thought about the perks of membership with The Scion.

For seven years, Mr. Dire has been learning the ropes, coming to understand the ins and outs of his new business. For seven years, he's been assisting others in the organization with *their* work, making sure *their* goals were met. While it certainly made learning about The Scion a natural process, Mr. Dire hadn't found it quite as rewarding as he would like his work to feel.

But, just a couple of weeks ago, Mr. Dire received word from The Scion that he was going to get his first *solo* project. The project was going to require a farmer, and that's why Mr. Dire had approached Tom Miller. Mr. Miller was in a position of relative need, and Mr. Dire had learned over the course of his life that you could manipulate those in need when you required something of them.

Mr. Dire had a need, as well. He needed for his first project to be a success. He needed to show The Scion that he'd been a proper choice as a new recruit. Mr. Dire was going to try his best to see to it that this project proved his value to the organization.

Like many of the projects that The Scion is involved in --from Mr. Dire's limited understanding-- this project of his involved some plants.

July 21, 1932

Tom Miller and Mr. Dire only ever saw each other twice, all told. The second time was the night when Mr. Dire brought the seedlings to Tom, the seedlings that Tom was expected to plant, to hold up his end of the deal. The bald man --as Tom was starting to refer to him, in his mind-- brought the seedlings, ninety-nine of them, to the Miller property on Old Smith Road, after nightfall, in ten wood flats, in a horse-drawn buckboard wagon. Mr. Dire had requested that they meet after sundown - he seemed more comfortable being out in public after sundown - and Tom was fine with that. He wasn't necessarily excited about the idea of anyone seeing the two of them consorting with each other, either. In Tom's mind, there was something not quite right about the bald man.

The Miller farm sat on fourteen acres of property northeast of Bangor Springs, and the homestead was on the closest three acres to the road, leaving the remaining eleven acres to the east for Tom to farm the crops. On the front three acres, the Miller family home stood on the southern half, opposite the stable on the northern half. The two of these buildings were separated by a barnyard where the chickens and goats ruled the roost. While the house was slightly closer to the road than to the farmland, the animal barn was closer to the farmland than to the road. This left the barnyard between them somewhat catawampus with respect to Old Smith Road.

On that fateful, summer night, the ninety nine seedlings --lit up only by the two oil lamps that Tom Miller had brought out to the barnyard to meet the bald man-- seemed normal enough, and Tom had no reason, looking at the harmless things, to feel uncomfortable about them, or about this arrangement, much at all.

"Remember the instructions." Mr. Dire told Tom. "These need to be in the ground in the next two days. They need to have plenty of space between them, and you shouldn't have to do much else to them. They're really hardy."

"What about rain?" Tom asked. "It's been a while since we had a decent rain. The ground is pretty much dried up. It's part of the problem that I've been havin' with my regular crops."

"I wouldn't worry about that too much." Mr. Dire chuckled. "From what I know, they will do just fine if you get them in the ground and you give them enough space. I will be back in November, just after the first frost, to collect the fruits."

"*After* the first frost? Are you sure you want to wait until after the frost?"

"It'll be better that way, according to what I've been told by my associates."

"Are you expecting me to harvest those 'fruits' for you?"

"No." the bald man warned, quickly and sternly. "You won't need to bother with these plants much at all after you've got them in the ground. Just keep an eye on them from time to time. One day, late this fall, you'll notice the fruits are all gone, and pretty soon after that, the plants will die away and our business together will be finished."

“So,” Tom confirmed, “plant them, keep an eye on ‘em, and get paid in the fall?”

“That’s correct, my good sir.”

Mr. Dire turned back toward the wagon, to start unloading the flats. Tom stopped him, lightly grabbing his forearm, and Dire recoiled from the physical touch. Tom noticed that the bald man’s skin seemed to be feverish and hot. Although it was a warm July evening, the heat on the bald man’s skin seemed oddly excessive to Tom.

“My family is going to need to have some money before the fall comes. We won’t make it all the way till then.”

Mr. Dire handed Tom an envelope, thick with paper currency.

“This is the only advance. Your only other payment will be in November.”

The two men worked silently then, unloading the seedlings into the grass at the back edge of the barnyard.

Santa Fe - Two

Kathryn Santos started on the research right away, using her break times at work, and she started with the Christus St. Vincent Regional Medical Center, where the man in Room 204 had come from. While some of the other nurses were in the staff lounge, gossiping about their spouses or each other, Kathryn was hunkered over in the corner, on her cellphone, making calls.

She talked with the emergency room staff -- the ones who'd actually been on staff eight years ago-- to try to find out some information about John. After such a long time, only two people were left who had even been there back then. Of the two, the one who remembered John as a patient still wasn't able to be much help.

Kathryn contacted the Health Information Management department of the hospital next, to ask them what they could tell her about the incident, back in 2010. As she was able to provide information regarding her medical need-to-know, as one of the man's current healthcare providers, she was able to get further than your average nosey joe on the street might get. Nevertheless, the medical records department wasn't able to provide much more information than the emergency room staff had provided - no more information, really.

What they did provide Kathryn with was an idea. An idea involving her brother, Dean.

* * *

Corporal Dean Santos was an investigator with the Santa Fe police department, and he was a sucker for his sister's crazy requests for assistance, especially when she gave him the sad, beagle eyes that she used to get her way around him. As her big brother, Dean had always felt responsible for making sure that Kathryn was protected, looked out for. Even when they were kids, Dean was always making sure that his lil' sis was under lock and key, as much as he'd been able to make that happen.

Dean remembered plenty of times when he'd done right by his sister. That one time in college when she got mixed up with a boyfriend who liked to hit, Dean showed the boyfriend how getting hit actually felt. When Kathryn had been in the sixth grade, and Dean in the tenth, he'd made sure that the older brother of the girl who'd been bullying Kathryn took it upon himself to reign in his sister so that Dean wouldn't have to.

Dean was always working to try to provide for the security that Kathryn deserved.

You would think that Dean would've eventually gotten to the place where he stopped feeling the compulsion to say 'yes' to her, every time that she called with a favor to ask.

"Santa Fe PD Dispatch Desk, may I help you?"

"Yes, I need to speak with Corporal Santos, please."

"May I ask who's calling, miss?"

"This is Kathryn Santos."

"I'll put you through to his desk right away."

Kathryn waited on hold for a few seconds, before hearing the gruff deep voice of her older brother.

"This is Corporal Santos."

"Hey, it's Kathryn."

"Hey! What a pleasure to hear from my kid sis! What has you calling to speak to me while I'm at work? Is everything all right?"

"Everything's fine, Dean. But, I was wondering if we could meet up. I've something I need to talk to you about?"

"Sure thing, Kate. Why don't you come over for dinner on Thursday night? Maxine is making her Southwest Meatloaf. And she misses seeing you."

Kathryn Santos liked her brother's wife as little as she liked it when he called her 'Kate', but she was desperate for his assistance and she was willing to go through just about anything to get it. She knew that her brother would have access to investigative resources that were unavailable to normal citizens. If she was going to be able to get him to use those resources to help her find out more about the man in Room 204, spending some time around her sister-in-law, eating her awful cooking, was part of the price to pay.

* * *

Maxine's meatloaf was horrible, and no combination of chili powder, cumin, and paprika was going to change that fact. But, on Thursday night, Kathryn showed up for dinner and she ate the meatloaf, and she pretended to like Maxine --the woman who'd taken her brother away-- just so she could get to the point where Maxine would carry away the dishes and busy herself in the kitchen, leaving little sister and big brother to talk privately.

"You really don't fake liking her very well. You could try a little harder."

"Dean, it's complicated. Ever since Mom died, you're the only family that I got, and I've never been particularly good at sharing."

"No kidding. I still have a scar on my knee from that time when I took your bike for a ride and you knocked me off it just so you could have it back."

"I'm trying to be serious, Dean."

"And so am I, Kate. Max has really tried hard to get you to like her, and I don't want to have to choose between seeing my sister and keeping my wife happy. Like it or not, Max is a part of my life now, a big part. I may have loved you first, but don't try to force me to decide who I love more."

Kathryn sat there, for a moment, thinking of the implication in her brother's last sentence, wondering if it might be possible that she was losing him to Maxine. The thought infuriated her, and she wanted nothing more than to get away from it.

"Dean, I hate to change the subject…"

"No, you don't"

"...but I need a favor. I need you to help me."

"Well, I'll tell you what, Kathryn. Let's make a deal; I'll help you out if you'll start trying to make Max feel like you care."

And, as she agreed to the bargain, wondering what it was going to cost her, she was hoping that her brother's access to investigative means was going to be worth it, in the end.

* * *

"I heard the two of you talking out there, through the open kitchen window." Maxine said to her husband when he came inside after his long conversation with his sister. Kathryn had excused herself for the evening, having accomplished what she came to her brother's house to do.

"I thought you probably could, since I could hear you in here clinking dishes around in the sink. As soon as I heard the dishes, I knew the kitchen window was open. When I realized the kitchen window was open, I knew that you were most likely listening."

"Look at you! It's no wonder they made you a detective. I think I'll start referring to you by the name 'Holmes'."

"Ha ha. Very funny. Nevertheless, I doubt if Kathryn noticed that you might be eavesdropping. Her powers of observation leave a little to be desired, most of the time."

"Oh, I wasn't eavesdropping, not really, anyway. Truth be told, I only caught a tiny bit of your conversation -- meatloaf doesn't leave a whole lot of dishes that need to be hand-washed in the first place."

"Well then, what part of the conversation did you end up hearing, if I may ask?" Dean inquired.

Maxine looked at her husband, paused for a moment, thinking of the correct words.

“You don’t have to defend my honor with your sister, you know. I don’t need you to stand up for me.”

Dean grabbed the towel that hung from the handle of the oven door, to prepare for the drying of the dishes that Max had finished washing.

“Well, Max, as it turns out, I am going to stand up for you, whether you want me to or not. You’re my wife. Besides, Kathryn is going to, at some point, have to come to terms with the fact that she is not the most important woman in my life anymore.”

“Is that so?” Maxine chuckled. “If she’s not the most important woman in your life anymore, then who is?”

“Oh, I think you know.” Dean snapped the hand towel playfully at Maxine’s back side, and she skittered out of the kitchen as she fled.

* * *

Kathryn ended up telling Dean everything that she knew about the man in Room 204 -- which wasn’t much-- a few days later on the telephone. She was primarily hoping to convince him that she knew so little that he had to be willing to help her.

“You know, I shouldn’t even be doing this, Kate. Using municipal resources to aid you in your private investigation is just a bit outside of the lines, if you know what I mean.”

“Dude, have you forgotten that guy I was dating, a couple of years back? Where would we be if it weren’t for your use of ‘municipal resources’ in that situation?”

Dean *had* almost gotten himself fired a couple years back, doing a background check on a new guy that Kate was seeing at the time. Of course, that one hadn't been by her request, but it had been a good thing that he'd done the check -- the man had bench warrants out for his arrest down in Torrance County. They dodged a bullet on that one.

She wasn't always the best judge of character.

"Well, that one was different. I had a bad feeling about that guy, and I turned out being right." Dean responded.

"Oh, come on, Dean. You've got to help me out. I've got no one else to turn to, and not much else to go on." Dean could actually hear the fact that she was using her puppy-dog eyes on the other end of the phone line.

"Well," Dean continued, "as it turns out, the officer who supervises the resource room at the precinct lost pretty badly to me last week in poker, and I can imagine that he'd be willing to look the other way while I spent some alone time in there with a small shopping bag. It would beat him paying me what he owes me, that's for sure."

"Have I ever told you what a great big brother you are?"

"So often --in fact-- that it's starting to sound like a broken record."

A few days later, Dean dropped off his 'winnings' at her apartment.

A fingerprinting kit.

The very next day, Kathryn took it to Butch Alvarez.

* * *

"You know, I thought about doing something like this." Butch said, holding the fingerprinting kit in his hand and noticing the insignia on the front of the kit -- Santa Fe PD. He looked up from his desk chair at Kathryn Santos as she stood in front of his office desk.

"Oh really?" Kathryn replied.

"Yeah, these kits are pretty easily available on the internet, turns out. The problem is, you have to have someone to process the results."

Butch looked at Kathryn knowingly, and Kathryn found it hard to hold his glance. She knew that he knew that her brother was a cop, and she figured that he had that look on his face because he was a step or two ahead of her. Time to call an audible.

"Oh yeah. I hadn't even thought of that part. Where am I going to get this kit processed?"

Butch chuckled, letting the whole thing between the two of them drop.

"Well, I'm sure you'll figure it out. So, what's your plan?"

"Unless the man in Room 204 is out for his Tuesday morning golf match with the Governor, I'll probably go in there and do the kit right now. It'll be interesting to see whether or not he is compliant during the process. Hopefully, today is a good day, and not a bad day."

Butch's ears perked up.

"Have things been getting worse with him?"

"Slowly, yes. It seems like he is, more and more often, stuck inside the prison of his mind. And, while I've never gotten the sense that he'd be combative with me, we're moving into uncharted territory with this." Kathryn held up the kit in reference.

"I can help, if you think you might need assistance." Butch offered.

"I'm not really worried about it." Kathryn countered. "If it's not going to be a good day today, I can wait. The part that has me the most anxious is how to get someone else's fingers covered in ink and then smudged properly onto the paper. It might be a little cumbersome."

Butch waited to see if she had anything more to say. When she didn't seem to, he finished off the conversation.

"Whatever you find, be sure to share with the rest of the class, okay?"

"Roger that." she replied.

In police lingo, no less.

* * *

Kathryn Santos tried not to take her work home with her. She tried to maintain a boundary between the things that went on at work --sometimes horrible things-- and the rest of her life. Like a contamination barrier. She didn't want what was going on at work to have any effect on the way the rest of her life was going.

But the man in Room 204 was different.

Kathryn dropped her purse and keys on the table just inside her apartment door. She felt so exhausted some days, arriving home after her shift at the nursing home, that she could barely make it to the living room. She plopped down on her couch and continued to process her day.

She felt really bad about that man, and about the fact that no one knew very much about him, no one seemed to care. No one inside Casa Paz and no one outside, either. It was such a bummer. After all of these years, no one had come to claim him, to say that he was their grandfather or great grandfather, and Kathryn thought that was ultimately sad.

Admittedly, Kathryn's ignorance about the man's past could mean that he'd been rejected by his loved ones, that he was despised by them -- and perhaps for good reason. The problem was that Kathryn didn't know, one way or the other. If she'd been able to find out that he'd been a jerk to all of his loved ones and they were going to let him rot as a result, then at least she would have her answer.

Her calico cat wandered into the living room, from the kitchen, spotted Kathryn on the couch, and came over to investigate the chances of getting some attention from her owner.

"Hey, Patches. Did you come to get some lovin'?"

Kathryn was young enough and inexperienced enough to still be under the impression that everyone should have someone to love. Someone who loves them back. It must be the case that this man has someone, or perhaps *had* someone, who loved him and whom he loved. Maybe he was alone and uncared for by family and friends because he'd outlived them all? Kathryn preferred to believe in that theory, as opposed to the theory that he wasn't worthy of love and attention. She just had a hunch that he was a likable person. She'd spent enough time in his presence to *feel* friendliness in his demeanor.

If there was such a thing as that.

One way or another, she was soon to find out.

She'd turned the fingerprint kit back over to Dean yesterday. Her hopes were that her brother was going to find out enough about the man to jumpstart her searching. She was looking for even more answers than just a name to go with a face.

Sometimes, Kathryn Santos wondered about how this man's bill at the nursing home was getting paid. She knew better than to ask Butch about something like that, however. Once Butch got to talking about patient billing, he'd throw so much medicare and social security jargon at her, it would start her head to spinning.

As she pet Patches, now prone in front of her on her lap, Kathryn ached to know more about the mystery man. She knew that his silence probably made this worse, made the mystery more unbearable. Kathryn just knew that there had to be someone, somewhere on the planet, who was looking for this man. There had to be a puzzle somewhere that was missing this man as its final piece. Kathryn had put together a puzzle or two in her life, and she knew how frustrating it was to get to the very end, only to discover that there was one piece left to place and zero pieces *to be* placed.

She wondered whether or not she would ever find anyone whose puzzle was missing the final piece lying in the bed in Room 204.

* * *

As he laid in his bed in Room 204, looking out the window that was part of the standard set of features for a room at the Casa Paz Assisted Living Facility, the man assigned to the room was engaged in his favorite activity -- thinking. One of his favorite things to think about was the situation that he was in.

For starters, it wasn't that he couldn't talk. At any point in time, he could break his silence and start talking a blue streak with any of the nurses, or with Butch Alvarez, if that's what he decided to do. He might even bother to talk to that nasty old head nurse, Nora Lietz, but he doubted it. Even if he decided one day that he was going to start talking again, and that was a big 'if', he still would avoid talking to Nora, if at all possible. He didn't like her, because it was clear in the way that she cared for people that she didn't *care* for people.

The one nurse that he liked the most was Kathryn. If he decided to talk again, he'd talk to Kathryn first thing.

You would think that it would involve a serious amount of willpower to not talk, to decide that conversation wasn't worth it and to avoid it. Maybe it would be nearly impossible for someone who was in their right mind, considering how the normal person feels a drive to socialize, even if it's only with certain people at certain times. However, the man in Room 204 wasn't entirely in his right mind, and as such, he didn't find it that difficult at all to not talk; he really didn't feel like he had anything that needed to be said, and he also hadn't recently had anyone in his life worth talking to. After a while, when you've gone a certain period of time without talking, you arrive at a place where you realize how overrated it really is -- at least it seems that way when your mind is half-gone.

Being senile, he was constantly trying to come to terms with the wasting away of his mind. It was like living in a home where three-quarters of the rooms are devoid of life as one is forced to walk through those rooms to get from one place to another in the house. If you can imagine that, then you can start to understand what it was like inside the mind of the man in Room 204. The worst part of it all was that it was in flux. Sometimes, improving, but in general, a downward spiral into darkness.

And of course, he had no reason to believe that it wasn't completely natural, this process of his.

He watched the clouds crossing the sky, for the short period of time that he could track any particular one as it made its way across the momentary stretch of sky he could see through his window. He thought again about his silence -- once you've gone a certain period of time without talking, the people around you kind of assume that you're just going to continue not saying anything, and that kind of takes the pressure off, as far as talking goes. The man in Room 204 had arrived at the realization that talking was highly overrated years ago, and at about the same time, he'd also discovered that most conversation was entirely unnecessary. The majority of people, in their conversations with each other, weren't interested in the exchange of information, anyway. What they more commonly wanted was to be heard.

The man, lying in the bed in Room 204, didn't really want to be heard anymore.

He had thought that it would be hilarious, one of these days --just for kicks-- to start talking, just to get a rise out of whatever medical professionals happened to be on staff at the time. He thought that would be a regular riot. The talk of the nursing home would be his talking. HA! The word on everyone's lips would be the words to come out of his mouth. The thought of one day deciding to talk tickled the man's mind in a way that was soothing, especially when he was --on occasion-- being tempted to talk. Like an itch being scratched.

As funny as it might be to one day just start talking out of nowhere, the problem with his senility was that it was turning the man into a darker and darker character, less interested in smiling, less interested in laughing. On the really bad days, he wasn't even 'aware'. He'd heard the nurses talking, on two or three different occasions, about the things he'd done on the days that he'd missed, when he'd become 'unaware'.

It was embarrassing to hear that he'd behaved that poorly.

It was almost as if a darkness was taking over those rooms that he'd been moved out of --in the domicile of his mind-- and that darkness was getting ready to move him out of the house altogether.

Aside from his vow of silence, which most of the medical staff at Casa Paz believed to be an *inability* to talk, and aside from the fact that he was slowly losing his mind, he was pretty well-adjusted, for someone approaching the century mark. In his ninety-seven years of life, he'd lived to see some good times and some bad times. He remembered being married at some point in the past, although the details were kind of fuzzy. He remembered being at war at some point, fighting as a soldier fights - according to the wills of the generals and the politicians.

Some of the things that he remembered from his time as a soldier were things best left unremembered.

A lifetime's worth of memories, both good and bad, many of them gone --probably most, if he was being honest-- but some still available for recall. Of all of them, only one remained as vivid in its detail, as if it had happened the night before, and that was strange, for it was one of the man's oldest memories. The man in Room 204 was quite certain that he was damned to forever remember that cold October night in 1932 when he'd been just eleven years old.

Bangor Springs - Two

Paul Brachman's cat, Mittens, had two modes, and only two modes. Mittens seemed to vacillate between an interest in Paul that was affectionate and heart-warming, and then, every so often, that same cat would seem completely unaware of Paul's existence and/or his presence in the same vicinity.

If you've ever owned a cat, you probably know how this goes.

On this particular summer Saturday afternoon, Paul was sitting in his small home on South Merrifield Avenue in Bangor Springs, seated at his dining room table, looking out the large picture window at the traffic heading north and heading south in town. And, he was thinking.

Paul had the contents of a file folder spread all over the table in front of him, and while he was taking in the scenery of South Merrifield, he was also looking at all of the material on the table. Trying to look at it from every angle. Trying to see something he'd not seen before. Trying to gain a different vantage.

It wasn't working.

Paul had as much information about Miller's Field as he did because --initially-- he'd done the work of digging a lot of it up himself. When he first developed an interest in the property, there was just something about the place that seemed kind of strange, kind of weird, to him. These days, because it was pretty well known that Paul was interested in the topic, information tended to come his way, even when he wasn't looking for it.

Paul considered himself to be a pretty fine journalist, as far as small town newspaper reporters go. He was able to cover the news in Bangor Springs, and the surrounding areas in Knox County, to the extent that people in town liked the job that he was doing, for the most part. Granted, there were people in town who gave him a hard time, had hassled him for the 'inaccuracies' in his reporting. But, every journalist gets that kind of crap, sometimes. People generally appreciate having a small-town journalist to keep them informed, and Paul had been one of the primary journalists in the Bangor Springs area for well more than a decade, now.

And during that time, Miller's Field had become his 'project'.

Of course, the one thing that any decent journalist can't abide by, is a mystery, especially in light of their apparent inability to shed any light on it. Over the course of his years as a journalist in Bangor Springs, Paul had worked to uncover a few of the mysteries around town, exposing the truth to the light of day and educating his readers, his *community*, to the facts. Paul had always lived in this town, had always loved this town, and he felt an obligation to give back through the use of his talents and skills.

Miller's Field, however, was still getting the best of Paul Brachman, as it had been for some time.

It bordered on an obsession for Paul. He would go back to it from time to time, when the news around Bangor Springs would slow, or when he needed something to distract him from other things. The file that he kept on the property stayed at his home, so he could look over the contents whenever he felt the need. Unfortunately for Paul, the file folder wasn't very thick, and it never seemed to get any thicker, not really.

A significant part of the file that Paul Brachman kept on Miller's Field was a hodgepodge of newspaper clippings, and partial print-outs from police reports, and hand-written napkin notes taken during conversations with people up at the Hilltop diner in The Heights. And while Paul had been around for a while, relatively, many of the pieces that were in the file pre-dated his tenure. The field, it seemed, had quite a history. He'd worked to gather as much of it as he could, as it covered a pretty decent scope of time, all told.

Previously, when Paul had been working to solve mysteries or complete investigations during the course of his work for the newspaper, he'd been in the practice of consulting many different local experts, to try to get additional information. None of those experts had a whole lot to offer on the case of Miller's Field. He often felt alone in his quest for answers on this particular riddle.

What Paul had gathered included stories -- like the one from the local cop, Frank Moody, from back when he was a kid and he hit a turkey out near Miller's Field, on Old Smith Road. Frank told Paul about the experience over breakfast at the Hilltop, a few years back.

He described to Paul the grotesque mutations present in the bird, and how it had freaked him out. Frank said he couldn't close his eyes for a month after that accident without seeing the two-headed turkey stuck in the front end of his car, with eyeballs milky and dead. Frank had insisted, when speaking to Paul, that the mutant turkey had been caused by the curse of Miller's Field.

Another tale came from someone who used to live in a subdivision as a kid about three-quarters of a mile from Miller's Field, down a crossroad that intersects Old Smith Road a little to the south. That person's story involved a glow in the sky coming from the direction of Miller's Field, not very long before Halloween one year. So, a group of the neighborhood kids got together and headed over to the field to investigate. According to the witness --an 'Andy' something or other-- the glow ended up coming from the ground. They said that the dirt at Miller's Field was glowing an angry red, bright enough to light up the sky.

Paul had even heard that there were kids, back in the 50s and 60s, who would challenge each other to spend the night in the old Miller farmhouse, from dusk to dawn, back in the days when the place was still standing. According to the reports, coming to Paul most recently from people on the verge of retirement --recalling their childhoods-- no one ever made it all the way through the night inside.

Paul slid his butt forward on his chair, leaning back at the dining room table, continuing his watch on Merrifield Avenue, thinking.

There were other stories, from other witnesses, of strange events. Some of them amounted to little more than gossip, really. But, you get that a lot in small towns -- "I heard from Sally who heard from Fred, whose cousin is Heather's hairdresser, that Heather…" Paul was smart enough as a reporter to recognize legitimate information when he was receiving it. Many times, he would feign interest in a person's story, only to later throw out the notes because the information was unreliable. Paul didn't want to burn bridges with people by discounting the value of their stories to their faces, because you never knew when it was going to be the case that someone --who didn't normally have quality info-- would be the only eye-witness to something that he was going to need to hear about.

The information in the file was a puzzle, its pieces laid out haphazardly in front of him. Anyone who's ever put together a puzzle knows that the pieces, just to look at them, don't seem like much. It's only when they are assembled into their whole that the significance of the whole picture becomes apparent. Paul didn't understand how it all fit together -- he wouldn't ever, most likely, without some outside help.

Paul thought about the Millers themselves, as a family -- all dead, presumably. Tom Miller, the first man on record who'd ever tried to farm the property, all the way back in the late 20s and early 30s, died in 1966, from a massive heart attack while mounted on a tractor and plowing a field near Vernon, Illinois, where he and his wife, Norma, ended up spending their lives after leaving Bangor Springs, according to public records that Paul dug up. Norma Miller died twenty-three years later, at the age of ninety-one, in a nursing home in Vandalia, IL. They'd had a couple of kids according to birth records, but the children had proved harder to track down for Paul.

In fact, Paul hadn't received any new information about the case since he'd finished interviewing all of the linked family members -- cousins and nieces and nephews and whatnot-- almost two years ago.

In the midst of his despair about the case, Paul was encouraged to see that Mittens was in his affectionate mode; the cat kept winding its way in and out and between Paul's two legs, rubbing itself up against him in a way that the cat only did when he was wanting to get Paul's attention. Frustrated about Miller's Field in general, and convinced that a break in his concentration wasn't going to make a darn bit of difference one way or the other, Paul bent down to pet Mittens along the ridge of his back.

The purring was instantaneous and loud, even louder than Paul was accustomed to hearing from his cat, which pleased Paul just that little bit extra. When thinking about the whole thing critically, Paul wasn't sure why it was so important to him that the cat notice him and be interested in him. Maybe, at the end of the day, Paul just really needed to start putting himself out on the romantic scene. At the end of the day, a moody cat is only worth so much in making a young man feel like he's in a meaningful relationship. Paul chuckled at the thought.

When Mittens had had enough, and wandered away down the hallway to Paul's bedroom, Paul sat back up in his chair, to once again face down the pile of papers. At this point, Paul knew that the puzzle was missing too many pieces for him to even be close to understanding what had happened there, back in the early 1930s. Rather than scooping up the papers and putting them back in the manila file folder though --which is what he normally would have done-- Paul left them on the table, organized in the manner that he'd chosen for trying to group similar pieces of information together. It wasn't as if he was regularly entertaining guests who might find themselves seated at his dining room table. For that matter, Paul himself ate most of his meals from paper plates that he threw away after the fact, more often than not seated in front of the cable news television shows that he'd become accustomed to watching.

On this Saturday, Paul decided that, if he continued to just store those papers away for another day, that other day would never come. Maybe, it was time for Paul to use a different approach. Maybe it was time for him to escalate his attempts to solve the mystery of Miller's Field. Granted, it was a pretty cold case, but as sure as summer in southwest Michigan is sure to pack some heat, Paul wondered if the mystery of Miller's Field wasn't about to warm up a bit.

* * *

Everyone in town knew that the most recent owner of Miller's Field was Farmer Smithers. He'd owned it for thirty years --almost-- at the time of his death in 2018. A smaller, but still quite large, number of people in town knew that the aged farmer had passed away in the spring. However, there hadn't been but a half-dozen people in town who'd been paying any attention to the fact that Miller's Field was up for sale - as a property - within a record amount of time after the death of the farmer who'd owned it longer than any other farmer, according to public records.

In the end, it was one of the town's bar owners who'd been the first to notice the most recent developments.

Bruce Randolph, of 8482 Old Smith Road, noticed it on June 15th on his way into work: two bobcat-style excavators and a big backhoe sitting in the middle of Miller's Field. Bruce couldn't remember if he'd ever seen anything in Miller's Field, for as long as he'd lived down that way. He knew for sure he'd never seen anything like this there.

Nevertheless, Bruce continued on his way into town.

Old Smith Road is a north-south road, and its southern end is also the end of it that is closest to the heart of Bangor Springs proper. As it heads to the north, Old Smith Road continues into the northern parts of Knox County. To the south, towards Bangor Springs,

Old Smith Road dead ends into Easterly Way, which is one of a half-dozen roads that one could use to get into the heart of the town.

In this way, and many others, the town is like so many other small towns in Michigan; it offers roads into and out of town towards all points of the compass, so someone can come into town or head out of town to any of the other, nearby towns. Bruce Randolph, having lived in Bangor Springs for most of his life, was familiar with all of the more significant roads, as well as most of the insignificant roads, too. Knox County had very few roads that Bruce Randolph hadn't driven along, at least once or twice, as a resident of said county.

For the rest of the way into Bangor Springs, which wasn't very far, Bruce felt uneasy, as if the construction equipment might be a bad omen. Bruce wondered if his old friend Paul Brachman might know something about this. He made a mental note to call Paul as soon as he got to work.

But then, he got busy setting up the bar and forgot.

* * *

Paul Brachman and Bruce Randolph got together on the following Saturday --the Saturday after Bruce had noticed the construction equipment on Miller's Field-- for nine holes at the Bangor Springs Country Club, where both Bruce and Paul were members. The country club was on the northwest side of town, on the same road that would eventually lead a person over to Sawyer.

Golf was a pastime that the two of them each enjoyed individually, and they'd been enjoying the experience of golfing together ever since Bruce had returned from Afghanistan. They never kept score, or even paid attention to who was able to hit the ball farther or more accurately. If you're going to drive around on a golf course in a golf cart, the expectation is that you're going to play golf while you're doing it, and it was probably that expectation that kept them hitting the balls around with the clubs. They fought more over who got to drive the cart than who was doing better on the fairways.

"So," Bruce began, "I was meaning to ask you, do you know what's going on at Miller's Field, out on Old Smith Road?"

"No. I didn't even know that there *was* something going on. What do you know that I don't?"

"Well, late last week, I was driving by on my way into work… a week ago yesterday, it must've been, and I noticed a couple of pieces of construction equipment on the property."

"Really? That's odd."

"What's odd about it?"

Paul filled Bruce in.

"Well, it's Miller's Field -- so it's been owned for the past thirty years by Bob Smithers, the farmer. But, he died back in March, and I'd heard that the family had put that field in particular up for sale right away. But, there isn't a person around here who would buy that property, because of its history." Paul paused for a moment to think. "I wonder what the deal is?"

"Dude, you're the newspaper reporter. I'm sure you'll figure it out."

"You're darn right I will."

They continued to play, but Paul was distracted for the rest of his time with Bruce on that Saturday. If something was developing in the mystery of Miller's Field, he needed to be on top of it. When they were done with their golf, Paul headed into the offices of the newspaper where he worked. He wanted to strike while the iron was hot, and --when it came to Miller's Field-- things tended to get cold pretty fast.

FROM BRACHMAN'S FILE #2 -- November 18, 1990

John Stuckey often got his first deer on the first day of deer season. He was a pretty good hunter, after all. In the years --the hunting seasons-- when he didn't get a deer on the first day of the season, he usually got one on the second day.

Back in 1990 though, John had ended up skunked going into the fourth day. It was on that occasion that he'd decided to switch up sites, heading over to the woods near Miller's Field, hoping for some luck.

He'd been sitting, on that fourth morning, up in a tree stand, with his .30/06 rifle across his lap, at an hour of the morning when people with brains in their heads were all still in their beds. John was waiting. At that point, he wasn't waiting for the perfect shot, and he wasn't even waiting for the perfect deer. He just wanted *a* shot on *a* deer.

That morning --John Stuckey suspected that he would always remember the exact events of that morning, for as long as he drew breath-- he'd been in the tree stand for just over an hour and he hadn't seen another living thing in all that time. He knew better than to switch from the field that he'd started out the hunting season at, over on the other side of Bangor Springs -- since you learned more and more about a field the longer you sat on it; that information could make the difference in being successful.

Desperation can make you do some goofy things sometimes.

Fear of another morning with nothing to show for his efforts was starting to overwhelm him when he spotted a deer running in his direction, at a full sprint. John quickly moved, from his seated position, onto his knees to watch the deer's approach. He had about three or four seconds to try to understand what he was seeing when the deer ran headlong into the tree in which John was perched and kneeling. The thud that the deer made, headplanting into the tree, shook the tree enough that John could feel the vibration in his knees and shins.

Then, John heard the second thump.

He leaned out over the edge of the treestand, to get a view of the ground beneath him, up near the trunk of the tree. There, he saw the deer, lying on its side. John could tell that it wasn't dead, because its breathing was still pretty obvious -- little puffs of warm, moist exhaust escaping its nose and condensing in the cold mid-November morning air. John tried to wrap his head around the fact that he'd just watched a deer knock itself out while at the same time trying to decide what to do next.

The obvious solution to the problem of having gone four days without bagging a deer was lying unconscious on the ground beneath him. From his current position, it would take no skill at all for him to put the deer out of the misery of the headache it was going to end up having when it awoke. One and done and the end of his streak of bad luck would be here. He could seal the deal right now. But, John knew, it wouldn't be right.

Instead, he decided to climb down to see what he might be able to figure out about what had just happened.

On his way down the trunk of the tree --he'd installed a few steps that were meant to help him go up to and come down from the tree stand-- John did his best to keep his eye on the deer. There was no way of telling when the thing was going to wake up. Halfway down, John noticed that the deer was twitching, even as it laid there on its side. John was familiar enough with the muscular twitching that you often saw in animals --twitching that could serve all types of different purposes-- to know that this wasn't any of that. Rather, it almost looked as if the deer was having some sort of a seizure. Considering how hard it had just knocked itself on the noggin, John would've thought that a seizure was a totally conceivable outcome in this situation.

On the ground once again, and standing next to the deer, John got an even better sense of the size of the beast. One of the first things a deer hunter will do in the presence of a male deer - a buck - is to count the number of tips, or points, in the deer's antlers. John noted, almost without conscious thought, that the deer was a twelve-point buck, or rather, it would have been if it weren't for the fact that it had broken three or four of its tips off in the process of running into the tree. Judging by its girth, John was guessing that the deer would probably field dress at about a hundred and sixty pounds.

John thought one more time about just shooting it and laying claim to the prize. But, that was when he noticed something exceedingly strange.

The deer's hooves were glowing.

It seemed almost imperceptible, at first, but John was sure of it all the same. It was a dull red glow, almost mistakable as a figment of the imagination or a trick of the light of the dawn that was just now beginning to break in the east. But, the more that John looked, the more convinced he became that the hooves were glowing.

John knew enough to know that you don't normally want to eat things that glow. In his mind, it settled the question of whether or not to shoot himself an unconscious twelve-point buck, even if doing so would end his four-day drought. That, and the spasming that the deer was continuing to do, made him wonder about the quality of the deer as a possible future meal.

Rather, he decided to just go home.

John Stuckey always remembered the events of that morning when he thought about Miller's Field, and about whether or not Bob Smithers had made a mistake buying the property. John never did hunt that property again, because he knew something out there wasn't right.

August 9, 1932

Tom Miller planted the ninety-nine seedlings within the timeline that he'd been given by the bald man. Then, in the days and weeks following, Tom kept an eye on the plants.

At least until it got too disgusting for him to continue.

At first, they seemed to be pretty normal plants. Tom didn't notice any 'fruits' on them until halfway through September, which is pretty late in the season for something growing a fruit to start its process. Up till that point, there'd been nothing worthy to note in the development of the plants.

Not long after he was sure that the plants had taken hold, and that there was going to be a process in front of him, he'd mentioned the plants to the rest of his family.

Sort of.

"I've got some farming experiments going on in the northeast corner of the yard, between the barn and the corn. I don't want anyone going near that part of the property for the rest of the growing season. Stay on this side of the barn, please, all of you."

"Farming experiments? Dad, what kind of farming experiments are we talking about, here?"

Tom Miller stared down his daughter, Patsy, with the stare that he reserved for situations when he intended for the seriousness of his decrees to be known by his children.

"Never you mind what kind of work I'm doing back there. It's none of your concern. What is your concern is the whoopin' that'll be coming your way if you don't mind me, Patsy Mae."

She withered under the sheer force of his glance, and averted her eyes from him. Instead, she looked over at her brother, little Jim, with a grimace that let him know how uncomfortable she was to have been so sternly spoken to.

"All of you at this table know that I mean what I say, and I wouldn't tell you to mind me if I didn't have a good reason. No one is to go back there without my permission, and that's the end of it."

But, it wasn't the end of it. Patsy and Jim saw to that.

August 14, 1932

Jimmy didn't exactly understand how his father ran the family farm; at the age of eleven, there was a lot that Jimmy didn't understand.

One thing that Jimmy *did* understand was his father's stern side. He could always tell by the look on his dad's face, whether or not it was a good idea to push him on something. When Tom Miller was serious, his brow would kind of scrunch up and furrow and his eyes would get really big in their sockets. And then, whatever he said next, you'd better be sure and pay attention. When his father did that forehead-eyeball thing, you knew that he meant business.

Last week, Jimmy's dad did the forehead-eyeball thing, right before he warned him and his sister, Patsy, that no one was to go near the back side of the farm property for the remainder of the growing season. Patsy and Jimmy were standing side-by-side, next to the kitchen table, when their father handed his edict down, and they both knew that crossing their father would be a big mistake. On the two or three occasions that Jimmy had managed to make his father very mad, he'd paid for it dearly. Since those times, Jimmy'd learned that it was very important for him to listen to his father.

Especially after the forehead-eyeball thing

But, in Jimmy's mind, it was also very important to find out what his father had going on at the back edge of the farmyard. Curiosity is a funny thing in the mind of an eleven-year-old boy -- it can lead one to great discoveries just as surely as it can lead to great disasters.

The difference between the discoveries and the disasters was often just a simple twist of fate.

September 10, 1932

Patsy was three years older than Jimmy, which made her the perfect older sibling in Jimmy's mind. She was enough older to be of some use to Jimmy --she had experience and knowledge that Jimmy could benefit from-- and Jimmy had certainly been the beneficiary of having an older sister many times during his life.

Patsy was especially brave, for a girl, and Jimmy found this to be one of his favorite things about his older sister. Whenever Jimmy wasn't sure that he wanted to do something alone, or whenever Jimmy needed the advice of someone who wouldn't be afraid to make bold choices, Jimmy looked to Patsy for strength.

So, of course, Jimmy naturally asked his sister to help him find out what their father was doing with the crop at the back of the property.

Patsy was initially uninterested.

"Jimmy-boy, you saw the look on our father's face just as clearly as I did. You know that he only gets that certain look on his face when he's dead serious. I think it would be a magnificently bad choice for us to go back there, snooping around."

"I know. But, what if it's something that he needs our help with?"

"He never needs our help, Jimmy. In case you haven't noticed, even when he says that he needs our help, he's just saying that to get us to help him with things. He's an adult. Adults don't need the assistance of children. That's just the way the world works."

"Okay. So maybe he doesn't *need* our help. But, aren't you just the tiniest bit curious about what he's got growing back there?"

"Any interest I might have had was squashed when he stared me in the face and told me to mind my own business. I suggest that you let your curiosity die, as well."

But, for little boys, curiosity is a hard thing to kill.

Santa Fe - Three

"We got a hit, Kate. His fingerprints came back from AFIS. Turns out he's a military veteran."

Kathryn was excited to hear the news from her brother, sitting in the break room at the Casa Paz, talking on her cellphone. She hadn't been expecting to hear from him so soon after she'd given the fingerprint kit to him. She'd half expected that it was going to take weeks or months to find anything out.

"AFIS? What's AFIS?"

"Well, that's the Automated Fingerprint Identification System. The fingerprints of military veterans are in the system, so they're available to be searched. The whole search took about four minutes."

"Four minutes?!" Kathryn was stunned.

"I've had them come back a lot faster than that even. It probably took as long as it did because it was an old record in the system."

"So," Kate was interested in getting some of the details much more than she cared to hear about how the fingerprint system worked, "what do you know about my guy? You must know a ton, right?"

"No. Not exactly." Dean answered.

"Then, what *can* you tell me?"

Dean's answer was quick, and Kathryn noticed him speaking in a hushed tone.

"I'd rather not talk about it over the phone. Let's meet for lunch. Are you free?"

Kathryn looked at her watch -- it was just a quarter after ten in the morning.

"I should definitely be able to clear up a space to sneak away and meet, in maybe an hour or so."

Kathryn talked with Nora Lietz, to let her know that she was going to need a longer lunch than her usual. Nora allowed it.

* * *

They met at The Ranch House, which was the closest restaurant to the police department that wasn't likely to give you indigestion after the fact. It was pretty busy, for lunch hour on a Tuesday, and Kathryn would have sworn, as they were walked to their table by the hostess, that half of the other patrons in the restaurant were in a police uniform of some kind. Many of them waved at Dean, or nodded in his direction, as they walked in. Dean ordered the baby back ribs, and Kathryn the salmon tacos.

It was then that Dean pulled a manila file folder from the attaché case that he'd walked in with. He handed it to Kathryn, and she opened it to find two sheets of paper, stapled together.

"This is it? This is all that you found? I thought you were a detective."

Dean chuckled -- apparently, he'd failed to realize that Kathryn was somewhat upset.

"It's not like a fingerprint search returns a person's life story, a complete list of all of their known associates, and the passwords to their social media accounts. I don't know what you were expecting, sis, but I've gotten a lot less when it mattered a lot more. Don't forget to be thankful."

Kathryn sneered at her brother as she pulled the stapled sheets out of the manila folder and set the folder down on the table. She glossed over the details on the first page, and then turned to the second -- hoping for more on the second than what had been on the first. She was quickly disappointed.

She put the papers down on top of the closed manila folder with a pout on her face. Dean had seen it many times before.

"You're further down the investigative trail than you were a week ago."

"I know I am, and I'm thankful for your assistance, believe me. I guess I just had unreasonable expectations."

"You know what you could try?" Dean offered, trying to cheer her up, "You could try one of those DNA match services. I'm sure you've got access to his DNA in the nursing home environment, one way or the other."

"Yeah. I thought about trying that, too. I'm just not sure at what point I'd be crossing a line, invading this man's privacy."

"Well, you said he's a vegetable, right."

Kathryn's dramatic response belied her true level of indignance.

"I most certainly would *not* have said such a thing. He's not a vegetable -- he's a human being."

"You're right, you're right. I'm sorry. Mea culpa. But, what I was going to say was, if he's not exactly the most communicative person in the world, you might have some latitude to make a decision about harvesting some DNA without his *express* permission."

Kathryn thought about it, in the back of her mind, while the conversation drifted on toward other topics. Dean mentioned that he and Max were thinking about getting a dog - figuring if they could keep a dog alive for a little while, it might be a sign that they were ready for a kid down the line. Kathryn mentioned some vague details about a guy that she'd met at a bar over the weekend. Dean told her how much he disliked the fact that she was about the business of meeting guys in bars.

Basic brother and sister conversation, and all the while, Kathryn was really thinking about three little letters.

DNA.

* * *

The office adjoining to Butch Alvarez's office would have been perfect for an administrative assistant to the general manager, were there a budget for such a thing at the Casa Paz Assisted Living Facility. Instead, the office had many of the things that you'd find in a secretary's office -- just no secretary.

Kathryn stepped into the office to use the copy machine when she arrived back from her lunch. She copied both pages of the report that Dean had given to her, and took the pages next door to Butch's office. Discovering him absent, she laid them on the chair behind his desk -- surely he would find the papers there the next time he went to sit down.

Then, she checked back in with Nurse Lietz and resumed her responsibilities. While changing bedpans and checking on the medication schedules of several of the residents, Kathryn kept thinking about the possibility of collecting a DNA sample from the man in Room 204. '*From Jim.*' she corrected herself in her mind. It's not like getting the DNA would be a difficult thing to do. But, she just wasn't sure that she was ready to go in that direction.

And then, before she knew it, she was at his door. Looking in on him as he was lying in his bed, staring out the window. Kathryn wondered what he was thinking about, wondered if he was thinking much at all.

Jim.

The announcement on the PA system startled Kathryn out of her daydream about her mystery man – as of today a little bit less of a mystery. She couldn't remember the last time that Butch Alvarez had used the system, and that was part of what startled her.

"Kathryn Santos, please report to the director's office. Nurse Santos, to the director's office."

She made her way to his office.

"So, I appreciate getting the copy. Have you had it for very long?"

Kathryn looked at her watch and then back at Butch.

"About forty minutes."

Butch chuckled like she'd said something funny. Kathryn waited for him to say whatever he'd called her to his office to say.

"Former military. Looks like a World War II veteran."

"Yes, sir." Kathryn replied.

"Well, I'm sure that you're aware -- hell, I'm sure everyone in the place is aware -- that I have a soft spot for veterans. To discover that the man in Room 204 is a veteran of 'The Big One', double-u, double-u two," --that was the way that he said it, spelling it out like that-- "I am honored that we have such a hero in our midst. And we wouldn't have even known about it if it weren't for what you did."

Kathryn started to relax a little bit, becoming more and more comfortable with the notion that he wasn't upset with her at all.

"Thanks, Butch. I'm happy that you're happy to have the extra bit of information."

He held the two sheets of paper in the air between the two of them.

"You're damn right I'm happy. With this, I'll be able to petition the V.A. for assistance from them in the care of our friend. But, considering how old he is and how long it takes the wheels to spin at the V.A., we'll be lucky if they even respond to our initial requests before the man's passed on."

Kathryn smiled enough to let Butch know that she was happy that he was excited, but not so much that he'd get the impression that she was as interested in funding as he was.

"What about you?" Butch asked. "What are you going to do with the information? Will it spur you on to continue to investigate?"

"You see, that's the thing." Kathryn began. "I was just thinking about that when you paged me down here. Part of me is thinking about grabbing some of his DNA and sending it off to one of those biogenetic search companies. But, I don't know how I feel about crossing that line. Taking his fingerprints was one thing, but a DNA sample without his permission makes me feel a little icky."

"It doesn't seem probable that he'll vocally grant you permission anytime soon." Butch responded, a sarcastic smirk on his face.

"I know. But it doesn't make me feel any better about going ahead with it, all the same. Maybe I'll try searching some other way." Kathryn pointed at the two-sheet report in Butch's hand. "I saw, when I first went through it, a last-known-address. Maybe I'll start with that."

Butch set the papers down on his desk and looked Kathryn in the eye.

"In any case, I wish you the best of luck, Kathryn. You're going to need it. After all, that name's like a shot in the foot. So generic. It certainly would have been an easier search for you, had his name been 'Merkin Muffley' or something like that."

Kathryn giggled.

"I know, right?! I don't know when I last heard a name as vanilla as 'James Miller'."

* * *

Maxine Santos took one look at her husband, and knew that something was up.

"What's wrong, babe? Long day at work?"

Dean looked at Max and thought about how wonderful it is to have someone who knows you well enough to know if you are upset, just by looking at you. That same person, then reaching out to try to help you with whatever you're dealing with, is an amazing thing. He was so very grateful --just then-- to have her as his wife.

"No, that's not it. Work was fine."

"So, what's got you so upset? I can tell by the look on your face that something's bugging you."

Dean sat down at the kitchen table, while Max continued her work at the counter, prepping for dinner.

"It's this favor that I'm doing for my sister. She came over here a couple of weeks ago to ask me to help her find someone."

"What?! You mean she didn't come over here because she loves my Southwest Meatloaf recipe?!"

"Ha ha. Very funny. No, she's got it in her head to do some research on one of the residents at the nursing home where she works. A guy by the name of James Miller."

"Wow," Max replied, "talk about a generic name."

"It certainly doesn't make things any easier. But, we didn't even know his name until I was able to find him through a fingerprint search. I had lunch with Kathryn today and gave her the AFIS results. She was telling me that this guy is mute, and they suspect that he's not all there, mentally speaking."

"That's so sad." Max answered. "Sometimes, I don't even understand how your sister is able to work in a nursing home without crying herself to sleep every night."

"Agreed."

Max continued chopping vegetables.

"So, what's the problem, then?"

"The problem is that I've uncovered more than I ever wanted to. And a lot of it is not good."

"About James Miller?"

"No. About the nursing home."

Max stopped her chopping, setting the knife down on the cutting board and turning toward him. Dean could see that she was processing what he'd said.

"So, what did you find?"

"I think the director of the nursing home, Kate's boss, is financially mismanaging the place. Most likely illegally so. I came across some information while I was digging around, investigating this James Miller person."

"Oh no." Max responded. "That's not good. Question is, then, what are you going to do about it? Are you going to take the information to your sister?"

"I don't think that makes the most sense. I'm actually leaning toward talking to the director myself. Since the dirt is primarily about him."

Max moved from the counter, over to the table where Dean had been sitting. She got down on her knees in front of him, down at the same level. She embraced him in a hug of comfort and support.

"I know you'll end up doing the right thing."

Dean loved his wife for the emotional reinforcement that she provided in his life.

Bangor Springs - Three

On June 23rd, after Paul Brachman finished golfing with Bruce Randolph, he headed into the newspaper office to try to figure out why it was that Bruce had seen construction equipment on the property of Miller's Field. Most of Paul's investigative tools were in his office, so that was where he needed to be.

The official headquarters of the town's one and only newspaper was, fittingly, pretty near the center of the downtown, located in the second-story office space of a three-story building. This made it one of the tallest buildings in Bangor Springs, and it was owned by one Zak Morgan, who just so happened to be one of the three co-owners of the town's newspaper.

Zak Morgan was as close as one was likely to find in Bangor Springs to a real-estate magnate, and he'd experienced as much success in being such as you might expect was possible in a town of less than five thousand people. While the other two owners of the Bangor Springs Gazette --Joe Horton and Kathleen Morgan-- each had a presence about them that exuded confidence and leadership in a way that made them seemingly more worthy of respect as Paul's superiors, Zak was just somehow less respectable in Paul's mind. Probably because of the video store.

The video store had been on the first floor of Zak Morgan's building, just below the offices of the newspaper.

In the twilight years of the Bangor Springs Video store, many moons ago, Zak Morgan had refused to come to terms with the fact that video rentals were becoming a thing of the past. Netflix, and other video streaming opportunities, had been ringing the death knell for Zak's store for some time. Truth be told, he ran the video rental store for probably four or five more years than he really should have -- as far as businesses go, it never pays to overstay your welcome.

The great thing about the video store as a business, in Zak's mind, was that there wasn't much overhead at all for him to have to worry about, especially since he owned the building that the video rental store was in. If overhead had turned the business into a money pit when sales slumped, he would have closed a decade prior. But, when you own the building, you've got much more financial freedom.

Of course, all of this was several years back. Zak's video rental store had been the last one to close its doors in Bangor Springs. No one really batted an eye when it happened. Paul had written a small piece about the closing for the Gazette, more out of deference to Zak --co-owner of the paper-- than as a tribute to a store whose time had come and gone.

When the three of them --Zak, Kathleen, and Joe-- had come to own the paper, years ago as a joint venture, Zak had been able to provide very little in the way of capital toward the purchase of the business, as wrapped up as his assets usually are in real estate all over town. The one truly consequential contribution of Zak Morgan's one-third ownership of the paper was that he had provided the office space for the Bangor Springs Gazette.

The building itself --Zak's building-- was a very old, very tall structure, and part of the historic center of town. On the third floor of the building, Zak had a couple of walk-up apartments for rent. Beneath those apartments, the newspaper office, and beneath that, the shuttered video store.

Zak's building happened to be right next door to Hodge's Hardware and on the same side of Front Street. Across Front Street from the video store was Bucky's Bar, and across Kennedy Avenue from the video store was the Bangor Springs Public Library. Kennedy Avenue teed into Front Street one block to the west of the stoplight at the intersection of Front Street and Merrifield Avenue.

Paul loved the location of the newspaper office – where he had his desk, an answering machine, and a few other tools of the investigative reporting trade -- because, as a newspaper reporter, it paid to be near the heart of things. As he spotted a parking space on Front, near his office building, Paul waved to Patrick Hodge, who was rotating his selection of propane grills out in front of his hardware store.

* * *

Before Pioneer Construction began their process of building at the Shumer site --at Miller's Field-- Krieger Excavating was called in to prepare the site. While most of this work was just a process of leveling out the site, pushing the 'too much dirt over here' to the 'spot over there with too little dirt', they did end up removing seven tons of spoil from the property, mostly as a result of digging the foundation for the new construction. Dane Krieger, owner of Krieger Excavating, sold that spoil to the Bangor Springs Gravel Pit, which paid him a pittance compared to what they were going to make from the process of breaking the dirt down into its subcomponents, to sell at a mark-up to their own customers. Dane knew this, but he didn't care. He more than anything just wanted the material out of the way so his company could finish the process of preparing for the beginning of the construction project. As a subcontractor, Dane knew that he was responsible to the general contractor for his part of the project.

The Krieger Excavating company used an International Paystar 5000, one of seven such trucks that the company owned, at the Shumer build site. Dane loved International, and he tried to buy their trucks whenever he could; his father and grandfather had both owned IH tractors on their farms. This particular Paystar 5000, with a capacity to hold about twelve tons of dirt, moved all of the spoil in a single trip, a trip of eight and a half miles, one way, from Miller's Field to the Bangor Springs Gravel Pit, out on Highway 12, south of town. The truck had on it fourteen Falken GI-378 tires, which each stood about three feet tall.

During the contamination investigation that came a couple of months after the practical end of the Shumer building project, conducted by a joint task force including members of the CDC and FEMA, it was determined that each of the tires on that dump truck was probably carrying thirty to forty grams of soil from Miller's Field when it left the property, headed south to the gravel pit. This soil ended up being distributed mostly down the southern end of Old Smith Road, simply because the tires would lose the soil stuck in their treads as the truck gained speed and the tires spun faster and faster. According to the final joint CDC/FEMA report, the contamination impact of the distribution of approximately a half-kilo of topsoil was determined, by the environmental investigators, to be minimal.

But, it's interesting to note that there wasn't a single case of any animal, of any kind, being struck by a car on the southern end of Old Smith Road, not for months after the end of the Shumer building project, such as it ended up being. By all accounts, animals stayed far away from the south end of Old Smith Road for quite some time after all of this was over.

* * *

The first death at the Shumer construction site that summer came quite by accident, but of course, so did the others. It's only after a series of accidents, unfortunately, that one starts to wonder about how accidental several coincidental accidents might actually be.

Jorge Gutierrez, the backhoe operator for the crew from Pioneer Construction, was hit by the bucket of his backhoe on the first Tuesday of July while he was out of the cab inspecting the hole he'd been digging for the future location of the underground natural gas tank. The weight of the bucket, and the force of the impact as the backhoe bucket swung into Jorge, caused massive internal injuries and blunt force trauma that Jorge couldn't recover from. Subsequent inspection of the control stick inside the cab of the backhoe, by the Occupational Safety and Health Administration, had not revealed any conclusive evidence of failure. Nevertheless, it was assumed that the stick had malfunctioned, causing the backhoe's bucket to spin around on Jorge without anyone inside of the cab.

The crew from Pioneer Construction, a company based in nearby South Haven up in Van Buren County, was gone for six business days --slightly more than a week-- from the construction site out on Old Smith Road. During that time, the crew mourned Jorge's death, and the insurance company --alongside OSHA-- inspected the scene of the accident, to try to guarantee that there weren't going to be any more accidents.

Oh my, how that ended up turning out.

Once the construction site was cleared, the crew got back to work, and for a while, progress became the name of the game. They were able to get quite a bit done - all things considered - before the whole thing ended up grinding to a halt.

Doomed from the start, some would say.

* * *

Paul had noted on multiple occasions that, especially in Bangor Springs, when it rains, it pours. Not only was he investigating the juicy gossip going around about the heirs of the Smithers estate and how their process was unfolding, but he'd just heard, through the grapevine, that a construction worker had died at a construction site north of town. Paul only knew of one construction site north of town, and he was willing to bet dollars to donuts that the death had occurred at Miller's Field. A story like that was going to demand his attention.

Bob Smithers had died some four months prior, but his children, heirs of the estate, had been arguing ever since. Bob and Joyce Smithers had had five children, but two of them had preceded Bob in death, as had Joyce, and the three remaining members of the family, a daughter and two sons, were spread all over the U.S.. Only one of them was local, if you would consider being only two hours away as 'local'.

By the time a farmer gets to be the age of eighty-eight, there is much to be sorted out in the estate. The three surviving heirs were prone to arguing about even the smallest of details, each of them jockeying to try to gain as much 'inheritance' as possible. If they weren't arguing about what should be sold and to whom --to pad the coffers-- they argued about which keepsake had more value and to whom each keepsake should be entrusted. They argued about so much of what needed to be sorted out that nothing was getting done very swiftly.

Paul had been keeping his ear close to the rail to be able to glean what he could about what was going on. Who got the combine, and who got the hay bailer, and what was to be done with the farmhouse -- these weren't matters for the public to know. But, Paul knew. Paul knew because he'd driven by the Smithers farmhouse, south of Bangor Springs on Merrifield Avenue, every week since Bob died, waiting for a For Sale sign to sprout on the front lawn. Paul also knew because he was old pals with the local lawyer --Walter Tidey-- that the heirs were using to sort out the estate. Paul was so well-connected, that very little happened in Bangor Springs that he wasn't privy to, if he decided that he wanted to know.

One of the very few things that the three heirs of Bob Smithers had agreed to quickly was what to do with Miller's Field. In the mind of those heirs, Miller's Field had always been a bad decision. Putting it right, finally, was an easy choice.

Miller's Field was up for sale within a week of the death of Bob Smithers. Of course, Paul would have thought that a property like that would be on the market for months, because no one in town was fool enough to want to have anything to do with that field. However, the field was bought in just five weeks, by a couple from California, of all places.

FROM BRACHMAN'S FILE #3 -- October 18, 1981

"Did you see it? Tell me that you saw it?!?!"

Pete and Andy were friends, mostly because Pete felt like he needed friends, and he was willing to be less-than-selective in order to get additional ones. Also, because Andy was subconsciously aware of his obnoxiousness, he was always highly likely to connect with just about anyone who would give him the time of day. And sometimes, that's really all you need as a basis for a childhood friendship.

"Andy, calm down. Take a moment or two to warm the seat up, first. You just got on the bus like three seconds ago. I can still see your house in the rear windows. What has you so fired up this morning?"

Andy intentionally breathed twice --deep breaths meant to slow the blood flow and calm the heart. Pete wondered who'd taught Andy to intentionally breathe like that -- probably his parents or maybe a head shrinker; breathing like that wasn't something that your average nine-year-old took to naturally. Pete could tell that it had worked to soothe Andy, but only somewhat.

"Last night, I was lying in bed, looking out my window to the east. It lit up pretty much the entire sky. You must've seen it."

"Seen what?" Pete finally broke down and asked.

"The glow."

Pete hoped that he would one day be at the place where he had some options as to whom he would extend the hand of friendship. When one has options, you are more free. Until then, he couldn't afford to drop this friend or that one because they were being supremely weird. As the school bus continued to bump and whir its way down the country road toward Bangor Springs proper, Pete decided to take the bait.

"Andy, I didn't see any glow in the sky. I'm fairly sure that you didn't, either."

"No, you see, that's what I thought, too! I thought I must be hallucinating or dreaming or something. But, I pinched myself and everything. I saw what I saw. No doubt about it."

The school bus picked up, from Andy and Pete's neighborhood northeast of town, about a dozen kids who were bound for the school district on every school day. Pete and Andy happened to be neighbors in that little subdivision, but it wasn't that big of a locale, and chances are that --if Andy really saw something-- he wasn't the only person to see it.

"Well, I'll tell you what, my friend." Pete began. "Why don't I just stand up and ask in a loud voice if anyone else saw what you saw. We'll get to the bottom of this in no time." Pete started to stand up from his seat, ready to make good on his proposal.

"Don't you DARE!" Andy grabbed Pete by the windbreaker jacket that he was wearing and pulled him back down into his seat. Pete fell with an animated crash, hamming it up and chuckling to himself.

Pete turned to Andy, to talk some sense to him.

"Listen, Andy. I'm telling you I didn't see a thing. But that doesn't mean no one saw what you saw. What we need to do here is to find out if you've got any witnesses to your story."

Andy nodded slowly, coming to the understanding that Pete was not just dismissing him outright. Pete continued on.

"What time last night did this happen?"

"Well, I first noticed the glowing when it got dark enough that there shouldn't be any glowing, know what I mean? Before that, I thought I was just seeing what was left of the sunset. But, after the dark was full on, the glowing was still there. But only in the eastern sky. I even snuck out of the house to see if I could see where it was coming from. Off to the east somewhere."

Pete ran his knuckles alongside his cheek, the way that he always did when he was mentally wrestling with something. Andy waited for Pete's next thought.

"Okay," Pete began, "here's what we're going to do. Today, after we get back home from school, we'll get together before dinner. You can come over to my house. We'll use the phone in my sister's room, because she'll be at work. We'll call a few of the neighborhood kids, and we'll put them all on stand-by. Everyone watches for the glow. If we end up seeing it, then we can all go as a group to find out where it's coming from."

Andy let himself go limp against the back of the bus seat, relieved of the pressure that he was under. He turned his head and neck to face Pete, sitting next to him.

"That sounds like an excellent plan. I'm glad I thought of it."

“You did not, you little bugger.” Pete replied. He slugged Andy in the arm, and Andy laughed. That’s how they were for the rest of the way into Bangor Springs Elementary School.

September 28, 1932

Tom Miller noticed, as the plants grew, that they seemed to be the same size and general shape of your average tomato plant, three or four feet high by the time they topped out, and a few feet around in circumference. They had leaves that were broad and which came to a point, shaped like spades. The leaves were so broad and so numerous on the plants that they almost completely hid the central stalk and stems of the plant. If you peeled back the leaves to get a look at the inner structure of the plant, even that part looked tomato-plant-like: it was all prickly, with a fine protective hair on the stalk and stems.

Tom was most amazed, in those early days and weeks, by the speed with which they grew. The seedlings, when the bald man had delivered them to Tom in mid-July, weren't much taller than a few inches of green sprout. Within a month, each of the ninety-nine plants had topped out in vertical growth. For a plant that small at the start, to grow so fast --in such a short period of time-- was truly remarkable, especially in the dry growing conditions. Tom wondered, if he had been able to just sit and watch one of the plants, if he would actually be able to watch them get bigger.

It was after that first month of growth that things started to get really peculiar.

Tom made a point to inspect the plants first thing in the morning, every morning, before Patsy or Jim would be awake, so he could keep them from becoming curious about what was out on the back side of the property. About six weeks after Tom had planted all of the seedlings, the fruit --if you could call it that--started to grow. The funny thing about that was, Tom was absolutely sure there had never been any flowers on the plants, no flowers or blooms of any kind.

Tom had never known a fruit plant that didn't start out with a flower or a bloom.

The fruit started out looking exactly like tomatoes, pale green, and small, and almost perfectly round, with a pearly kind of iridescence on their surface. Tom convinced himself that what he had was ninety-nine tomato plants. The question of why Mr. Dire would need someone to secretly grow tomato plants was beside the point in Tom's mind. Six weeks in, near the end of August, Tom was sure that he was raising quite a batch of tomatoes.

Nine weeks in, all of the tomatoes turned black.

Even as they continued to grow larger.

Tom knew that living things, growing things, especially things planted in the earth, weren't supposed to be black. And this was just the beginning of the strangeness to follow.

And it wasn't like the black was a deep purple -- like an eggplant, or a deep green -- like the darkest of zucchinis, or even a dark blue -- like a blueberry on the bush. This was black. Dead black. The kind of black that you saw in charred remains or rotten flesh.

It was a worrisome black.

September 30, 1932

Mr. Dire didn't have much --didn't need much-- but what he did have, he kept in a safe place. Additionally, Mr. Dire tended to reside in places where he was not easily found. As such, he had a pretty reasonable assurance that his treasures and secrets were secure just because they were as hidden as he was.

On this Friday afternoon, Dire was at 'his place', a place that wasn't his in any real sense. It was an abandoned cabin in the middle of some deep woods on the northwest side of Bangor Springs. He was retrieving, from the scant collection of his belongings, the documents that he'd acquired from The Scion when he'd first been notified of his assignment.

Standing alone inside of the cabin where he was hanging his hat these days, he wanted to look over the information in the document, to be sure that he was doing his very best to successfully complete this first assignment for The Scion.

Dire had received his assignment as a set of instructions to carry out, handwritten on plain paper, and also as a set of three pages of information that had been copied onto paper, by someone's hand, from The Compendium. He could tell that it had been the same person -- to give him his written instructions and to give him the copy of the Compendium pages. The handwriting on the two documents was the same.

Mr. Dire knew about The Compendium in the same way that most of the members of The Scion knew about The Compendium: you heard about it through rumor and gossip; you occasionally received information from it, either directly or second-hand; you maybe even occasionally rubbed elbows with someone in possession of one of the original books from the set. For most of the members of The Scion, they knew little about The Compendium because they lacked the requisite power that it took to be a part of the upper echelon in the organization. As someone who'd belonged to the group for only seven years -- a relative blink of a metaphorical eye -- Mr. Dire was not likely to have enough clout anytime soon.

The instructions for the care of the plants that he'd entrusted to the custody of Tom Miller were pretty straight-forward. The specifications for when they ought to be planted, the dictates for what the plants would require in order to grow successfully -- Mr. Dire had read all of these pieces of information a dozen times each. He knew many of them by rote memorization. All that he could be doing to succeed, he was doing.

Dire paced around the insides of the abandoned cabin, thinking and mumbling to himself.

The uncertainty of the outcome, and all that was riding on his success -- that and the fact that he wasn't really doing very well with the notion that it was probably going to be another few weeks, at least, before the first hard frost, before the end of the assignment -- all of these things were causing a lot of stress for Dire. In the end, he imagined that this stress was at least part of what his first assignment for The

Scion was all about. A chance for them to see how he'd perform under pressure, and a chance for him to come to know that about himself.

The bald man heard a rustle above and looked out through the hole in the roof of the cabin. He saw a rook, roosting on a low branch in a nearby tree. Its eyes --of blackest coal-- seemed to be watching the man just as the man was watching the bird. Dire whispered 'boo' under his breath, almost inaudibly, and the bird took to its wings. Dire chuckled, and the laughter brought a little bit of ease to his soul.

He needed to try to stay calm about things. Considering the work that he'd done, and the relative simplicity of the instructions he'd received, there really wasn't much of a reason for concern.

October 1, 1932

Standing in the back section of his farmyard, in between the cornfield --its stalks measly and its leaves withered as they were-- and the backside of his barn, Tom was staring down at one of the ninety-nine tomato plants that were growing in three long rows in that section of yard, hidden from view from the farmhouse and the prying eyes of his young children. Tom was, in fact, looking down at the first of the tomatoes that he'd noticed going black. His mind was racing away with thoughts of various kinds.

Tom knew, as every farmer worth their salt knew, that anything black on a plant was bad. So, Tom's initial reaction last week to the black tomato-like fruits, and the fact that they were continuing to get larger despite having turned black, was a reaction of panic. He thought for sure that he was going to end up on the wrong side of the bald man. If something went wrong, and he wasn't able to deliver on his part of the deal, he didn't seem like the kind of guy who was gracious and merciful.

Tom bent over and reached for the black fruit, holding it in the palm of his hand while it hung from the stem of the plant. It seemed warm, warmer than he would have expected it to be on an autumn morning.

He couldn't wait for the frost to come, not just because his family was definitely getting closer and closer to needing the second payment, but more so, he just wanted the whole thing to be over with. He was also worried about whether he'd even get a second payment at all -- after all, what if the fruits weren't supposed to be black and Tom had done something wrong?

But this morning, as a chilly morning breeze blew across the barnyard with warnings about the coming winter, the coming frost, Tom looked across all ninety-nine of the plants. It had been less than a full week since he first noticed the first tomato turning black. But now, all of them were fully turned, fully black.

However, the fruits were continuing to grow, which didn't make any sense to Tom, either, although it was an encouraging sign. So, maybe this was how the process was supposed to go. It wasn't as if the bald man had given Tom any detailed instructions about this part of the process. He hadn't even given Tom his name. If the bald man had intended that Tom was to be involved in some sort of tending of the plants, wouldn't he have given Tom more information along those lines? Rather, Tom had received almost no instruction at all. So, that must mean that it wasn't really anything that he needed to worry about.

But, worried he was.

Tom had donned a jacket this morning as he was leaving the farmhouse to come out and check on the plants. As the breeze picked up around him, seeming to come from all different directions, Tom pulled the fabric of the coat tight around him, to protect him from what he couldn't control -- the wind and also the strange circumstances developing around these plants.

Of course, it might not have been so bad to watch the fruits turn black, had it not been for the other development. The other thing that started worrying Tom Miller about the plants was the smell that they started to create. At first, it wasn't so bad, and it wasn't bad at the moment -- although Tom knew that the smell wasn't bad at the moment because of the wind. Yesterday, on a calmer and warmer September morning, the stench had been so bad that Tom had decided to wear a kerchief around his mouth and nose as he went out to check on the plants, not that it had helped much.

When you paired the blackness of the plants with the smell, it was a harbinger.

The omen that the sight and the scent combined into in Tom's head was a vision of death. As he stood alone --so alone-- in the chill of that first October morning, he wanted more than anything to be able to talk about this with someone. The problem was that Tom didn't have anyone that he could talk to about any of this -- while he hadn't exactly hidden this from his family, he had been quite clear that the topic was verboten. He'd done this partly for their protection, but also because he wanted to mask how desperate he was to keep putting food on the table, ashamed for having to stoop so low as to make a deal with a man like the bald man.

Tom turned from the plants, from the stiff wind, from the entire scene, deciding instead to head back into the farmhouse.

Even Norma, the person that he normally would have gone to, was now off-limits because of the way that he'd approached the situation. Trying to talk with her about the weird things that were occurring --the sights and the smells-- would just lead them eventually into talking about money, and then he'd get frustrated about being incapable of providing for his family as a farmer. His pride and his shame had disconnected him from his entire family.

Norma was usually really good at helping Tom make sense of things. He could take his ideas and put them in front of her and she'd see them for what they were, and she'd normally be able to help him look at things differently, to gain new perspectives. He was missing that particular skill of hers right about now. Without her assistance, and without anyone else to go to for help, Tom felt more alone than he'd ever had in his whole life.

He would be happy when the whole darn thing was over. He'd be happy when he had the rest of the money that the bald man owed him for his trouble, and then, they would be able to make their way through winter, to a year that would hopefully be better than 1932 had been.

October 5, 1932

Jimmy had used the age-old approach of nagging his sister, to wear her down. Her initial reluctance lost its strength under his persistence, and then --before long-- he had her at least somewhat open to the idea of some investigation.

After that, they waited, biding their time. Jimmy mentioned it to her every couple of days, to keep the idea from ever really leaving her consciousness for very long -- and it certainly helped for him to continue to remind her that he wasn't going to let the thing go. What they needed was an opportunity when their father wouldn't be around. They needed enough time to be able to investigate things properly.

Jimmy and Patsy both knew that the morning wouldn't work, since no one in the family got up earlier than their dad. They knew that the daytime wasn't going to work, since they were normally at school during the week and their father could often be anywhere on their property without anyone knowing where he was or when he might stick his head around the back corner of the barn and find them there.

On the evening of Wednesday, October 5th, Patsy and Jimmy were in the backyard, checking the chicken coop for any eggs that needed to be collected.

"So, when are we going to go take a look-see?" Jimmy asked, motioning with his head toward the back part of the property. He was hoping that Patsy would end up having an idea that hadn't occurred to him.

"I'm still not convinced that it's a good idea."

"Come on, Patsy. You told me you'd think about it."

"I can't help thinkin' about much else, you keep bringin' it up all the time. It's gotten to be that a girl can't think of much else these days, what with you pestering me about it all the time.

Jimmy fought to keep a grin off his face, for he surely didn't want to upset his sister by showing her that he was proud of himself for having been quite the nuisance on the subject.

"In any case," Patsy continued, "I think we should go at night."

"That won't work. Mom and Dad are often up late in the evening. I hear them in the kitchen talking sometimes, after we've gone to bed."

"Well then, we'll go later."

"How much later?"

"We'll go after they've gone to sleep."

The idea was so far outside of what they normally would have done --how they normally would have behaved-- that it just might end up working. Jimmy had always thought of his sister as a smart one, but sometimes, her ability to think of things in a different way was downright impressive to him.

Santa Fe - Four

Inside the mind of Jim Miller --the man in Room 204-- there were rooms that had been emptied by his growing senility, but then there were still some rooms that had fared much better, still mostly furnished with the reminiscence of a lifetime. Little did anyone suspect --not even Jim-- that, as the construction site in Bangor Springs, Michigan grew --the future home of Clint and Tami Shumer-- James Miller in Santa Fe, New Mexico was losing more and more of his mind.

Whether or not these changes were correlated, who can say?!

While Jim was disadvantaged to have lost so many of his memories to the ravages of progressive cerebral failure, natural or otherwise, there were still some significant parts of his past that he could lie in his bed and ponder. Through some sick and twisted development of fate, one of the big parts of his past still available to him mentally were thoughts on his father. So Jim would often lie there in that bed in that nursing home in Santa Fe, New Mexico, and he would think about dear old dad.

There had been no love lost between James Miller and his father. In the years that followed Jim's sister's death, Tom Miller and Little Jimmy built up walls between each other that would never come down. Tom partially blamed his son for Patsy's death, even as he wrestled with the knowledge that he was the one who was truly responsible. James became Tom's scapegoat, for it was easier to blame him than it was to face the reality of his own responsibility.

As unfortunate as this ended up being for Jimmy --blamed by his father for something that wasn't really his fault-- he suffered even more because of the distance that grew between the two of them. The relationship between a father and his son is an important thing, and men who don't get to benefit from the full power of a healthy connection to their father end up the worse for it. James faced his grief over the death of his only sister, mostly without his father. James became a young man, mostly without his father. James went off to war, mostly without his father.

By the time that James got back from his fighting in World War II, his parents had left Bangor Springs and moved to southern Illinois. That didn't bother James one bit; he certainly wasn't headed back to Bangor Springs either, regardless of whether or not his parents had been there. But, James was also very much aware that he didn't want to be near them, anyway. When James got back to the states, he wanted to be about as far away as one could get from The Midwest. From farming. From barns. From trying to eek out a living at the mercy of whatever Mother Nature decides to give to you, that fickle wench.

How much further can you get, from The Midwest, than New Mexico?

Jim Miller turned onto his side, and looked out the window of Room 204, remembering.

As it turned out, the last time that Jim Miller saw his dad, in person, was the day that he left for boot camp in 1941. Tom had seen him off from the bus station in Sawyer, Michigan, right near the interstate highway, I-94. Sure, they'd talked on the phone, from time to time, throughout the years, but that was mostly because Norma forced the two of them to talk. None of that talking on the phone had ever amounted to much, anyway.

The damage had been done.

James and his mother had continued to stay in touch, because as tragic as it is for a man to lose the connection to his father, it's even more detrimental for him to lose connection to both of his parents. Through the years, Norma would keep Jimmy up-to-date on the things that were going on in their world, and James would do the same for them.

As an old, dying man, Jim often wondered if he would've been better off disassociating himself from his parents altogether. They say when you get stabbed, pulling the knife out can cause you to bleed to death. But, you also can't live your life with a knife stuck in you.

* * *

Kathryn liked to be lazy on Saturday mornings. Considering the work that she did, and how hard it was, she felt like she'd earned it. She believed that making it through the work week should come with some kind of perk. On this particular Saturday, she was enjoying her second cup of coffee with Patches on her lap and the Jim Miller manila folder next to her on the couch cushion.

Having had the chance to think about it for a few more days, she'd decided that she wasn't going to get a DNA sample from Mr. Miller to try to answer any of the questions that she still had. She just couldn't get over the idea that doing so would be crossing a line, somehow. Instead, she thought she might be able to use some of the information from the fingerprint search results to get further down the investigative trail. Kathryn reached over to pick up the manila folder with the hand that she'd been petting her cat with, and the cat jumped down off of her lap, recognizing that it wasn't going to get any more attention at the moment. Kathryn scanned through the report again, for perhaps the hundredth time since getting it from her brother.

The more she thought about these other possible avenues, she realized that it wouldn't be a bad idea to try to work with Butch, since he was most certainly going to be doing some investigating of his own, with Veterans Affairs. Anything that he might uncover could assist her.

The results from the search in AFIS --the two page report that Dean had given to her at lunch last week-- had had more to say about Jim's military history than it had about much else. Sifting through that information as she read the report, Kathryn was looking for something that she might be able to use to try to find someone that would be able to speak to her about Jim as a person.

The one thing that kept popping out of the report was 'last known address'. Looking at it in detail for perhaps the first time, Kathryn recognized the address right away, on Monterey over in the Casa Linda neighborhood.

* * *

Thirty minutes later, Kathryn drove by the small, single story home --former home address of James Miller-- not necessarily because she expected that she would get any useful information by just passing in front of the place, but rather because she kind of just wanted to see what kind of a home Jim had lived in, previous to his stroke. It was quaint and homey, and Kathryn could imagine him having lived there, once upon a time, perhaps with a wife and a family of his own.

As she drove by, she noticed a couple of young children playing in the front yard, in the shade of a fir tree at the corner of the house. Kathryn puttered by the house at a speed that was so slow that she was in danger of backing up traffic behind her, were she not careful. She wondered about what would have happened to the property, when Jim had ended up in the hospital, mentally compromised as he was. It was probably pretty likely, according to her brother, that the premises would have ended up back in the possession of the municipality, with no one to keep up with the property tax payments, and such. Most likely, after that, the property had been sold by a real estate developer, perhaps to the family that was in the place now.

As curious as she was to find out more, Kathryn pulled a u-turn down the block a ways and came back by the house from the opposite direction, just to get another peak.

* * *

On her fourth time by the house -- back and forth, and then back, and then forth again -- a man stepped off the front porch of the place and out into the road, blocking her from proceeding down the small neighborhood street. As he made his way around to the driver's side --to her side-- of the car, she rolled down the window to facilitate a conversation.

"Listen, lady. You've driven by my house, coming from both directions, a half-dozen times in the last half-hour, and I just need to know what your deal is. My kids are playing out in the yard, for heaven's sake. You're not some kind of perv, are you?"

She almost corrected him on the number of times, but she didn't. As a nurse, she'd learned to read people -- she knew that it wasn't going to help de-escalate things for her to get technical with the guy. Instead, she came clean.

"I'm sorry. Let me pull over to the side, into that parking spot up there, and I'll explain everything."

"Alright." the man said.

He followed her up to the parking spot, still pretty much standing in the road as he did it, and when she stopped, he came to stand outside of her window again. He was clearly attempting to keep her from exiting her car, in case she was a nutjob -- smart move.

"So," he continued, "what's your deal?"

"First off, I don't mean any harm, so you needn't be concerned about that. I'm curious about your house because I'm curious about the man who lived in it before you, a number of years back."

"Well, my wife and I have been in the place for five years come next month, so I can tell you that no one has been in this house except for us in at least that long."

"Well, my name is Kathryn Santos, and I'm a geriatric nurse at a local nursing home. We have a man in our facility that I am doing some research on --out of curiosity-- and I think that he may have lived here just before you."

The man stared at Kathryn, trying to determine whether or not he believed her story, whether or not he was going to trust her. In the end, he stepped back from her door enough for her to be able to open it and get out.

"In that case, I think I have something that you might be interested in taking a look at."

* * *

The man was huge, so big that he could have been a decent football player at some point, college or the pros, but his two small children, playing in the yard as he and Kathryn walked to the front door of their home, were so small as to create a disconnect in Kathryn's mind. 'How could a man so tall and muscular ever have children so small and dainty?', she thought to herself as they passed by the children and into the home.

"We bought the place from a flipper, and he told us all of his tales about the fixes that he made and the repairs that had been done. Said that he'd picked up the property in an auction and that it had been vacant before that."

'Dean had been right.', Kathryn thought.

Once inside, the man closed the door behind them and he seemed, somehow, to be even larger inside than he had outside. In the enclosed space of the inside of the building, he was almost grotesquely large.

He caught her wheels turning.

"Is there a problem?" he asked her, in a defensive tone.

"I'm being rude, and I'm sorry for that. You're just so *big*. I don't know if I've ever met anyone quite as tall and massive as you. I don't mean anything by it."

"It's okay. I often get that reaction from people. I played linebacker at UNM --Go Lobos!-- but my career ended there."

"I bet you would've been a great pro linebacker."

"I tend to think that I'm better off -- from what I hear from friends of mine who went pro, they end up with problems of their own to go along with those big money contracts."

"I've got to admit, you seem pretty well adjusted to your situation, Mr. ..."

"Metz." the man replied. "Carl Metz."

He reached out to shake her hand and his seemed as large as a frying pan -- it swallowed hers inside of it and the grip had a rock-like strength to it.

"Well, let's go see the box."

'The box?' Kathryn thought to herself.

Carl walked into one of the back bedrooms of the single story ranch and Kathryn followed. She watched Carl pull down an old cardboard box off of a shelf in the bedroom closet. He turned and placed it on the bed in the room. He lifted off the lid and the two of them peered down at the contents.

"The flipper said that this was the only box in the house, when he bought it, that appeared to be of any personal importance. He told me that he couldn't bring himself to ever throw it out, since some of the stuff inside looked to be pretty important -- some of it even looked fairly old, maybe even antique. He thought that it should stay with the house. When we closed on the sale of the property, he said that the box belonged to us, or more accurately, to the house."

Kathryn looked at what was in the box, and some of it was easily identifiable as memorabilia of one kind or another -- old loose photos, keepsake brochures and ticket stubs, a couple of pieces of broken jewelry, and old keychain engraved 'JFM'. Additionally, Kathryn saw a smaller box inside of the larger one, a shoebox. She pointed at it and looked at Carl.

"What's in there?"

"It's a box of letters, all in individual envelopes. I could never bring myself to read any of them, felt too much like spying or eavesdropping."

Kathryn stood and looked at the shoebox, her minding racing with the possibilities.

"In my estimation," Carl said, "the box is yours now. You're the only person to have expressed any interest in the history of this home in as many years as we've lived here. I have to go out front and check on the kids. I trust that you can see yourself out."

Before she knew that she was even thinking about doing it, she'd reached her arms around Carl's immense neck and shoulders and was hugging him in gratitude.

"Thanks, Carl. This box means quite a lot to me."

"I'm glad that it does."

A few minutes later, Kathryn was on her way back to her apartment, the cardboard box riding shotgun beside her. She'd make herself some lunch and then she'd get into searching through the box.

Bangor Springs - Four

For ninety-three years, Mr. Dire has been learning, has been coming to understand quite a bit about the organization that changed the trajectory of his life. In that same time, Dire has climbed the ranks. Initially not much more than a grunt assigned the menial labor of the team, he's proven himself on a few occasions and has been rewarded as a result.

To say that The Scion is an unusual group is an understatement only completely comprehensible by those on the inside. What makes the group so unique is partly the strangeness of its mission, but the structure and nature of its membership is also very bizarre.

There are 250 members of The Scion at any one point in time. This number doesn't change; it neither goes up, nor does it go down. If someone leaves the organization --which is extremely rare-- then someone else is brought in to take their place. It hasn't been the case, in at least the last four centuries, that someone has left The Scion without the organization having advanced notice. Ninety-three years ago, Mr. Dire was approached to replace a 'disengagement', as they're called.

All of the members of the group --each individually and all of them as a collective-- are responsible for the mission of the group across the entire planet. So, it averages out, right now, that there is one member for every thirty million people, give or take. While that might seem like a large ratio, it helps to understand what that means, relative to the population of the planet. There are two Scion members overseeing

England, and eleven overseeing the U.S. Half of those eleven have purview over the coastal states, while the other half manage the states of the interior, in consideration of how the population is distributed geographically.

Members of The Scion become members for life, which isn't unusual, per se. But, once one becomes a member, life becomes a bit of a relative term. As an example, as of October 17, 2018, Mr. Dire has been alive for 153 years, a member of The Scion for 93 of those years.

There have only been three disengagements in the 93 years since Dire joined the team, which means that he's still considered one of the new guys. The reasons for which a member might want to disengage are normally outweighed by the nasty drawbacks for doing so.

* * *

Jesse Moyer was the president of the Knox County Audubon Society, and had been such for almost twenty years. If anyone in southwest Michigan knew more about birds than Jesse, he certainly wasn't aware of it.

Besides knowing so much about birds, Jesse knew the best places to look to find particular species of birds in their natural habitat. If you were looking for a tufted titmouse, Jesse knew where in Knox County to look. Jesse could tell the difference, just by listening, between the sound of a red-headed woodpecker and a red-bellied woodpecker. Jesse knew which cardinal was red and which cardinal was brown -- the males are red, of course. Jesse knew that swamp sparrows were much less likely to 'sing' than field sparrows.

In short, Jesse knew a lot about birds.

And Jesse knew about Miller's Field. Because of the oddity of it. Birds did not fare well in the vicinity of Miller's Field.

Jesse himself lived in Newburg, the most southwestern town in Knox County, but he knew the two most active birders from the Bangor Springs area were Jane Li and Connie Sheppard. He knew that the two of them had been very concerned for a number of years about bird life near Miller's Field -- they'd been conducting semi-serious investigations into the life of birds in that area, and then reporting back to the Audubon Society.

The results were not encouraging.

Of all of the pieces of information that Jane and Connie had reported back to Jesse, some of the most interesting ones always stood out in Jesse's mind. For example, Jane and Connie had conducted research into flight patterns around that area, and they had convincing data to suggest that birds avoided flying over Miller's Field if they could. While this wasn't necessarily strange, especially when you consider the flight patterns of different species of birds, the two of them had several hours of video showing birds redirecting themselves --in flight-- to avoid the property boundaries of Miller's Field.

Still no theories on how the birds knew about the property boundaries.

Jane and Connie had also, over the last few years, gathered a lot of information about the nesting habits and birth rates of some of the more common species in Knox County, in the vicinity of Miller's Field. According to the two of them, mutation rates seemed to be significantly higher in the birds born around Miller's Field. Jane and Connie had enough evidence to start to suggest that, the closer a bird was born to Miller's Field, the more likely it was to have mutations of the beak, claws, and/or the structure of the skull. The two of them wanted to try to do some historical research, investigating any information that might exist anywhere about similar discoveries in the past, and they'd very recently asked Jesse if the Audubon Society might be able to help fund, or at least subsidize, such a search.

Jesse was working with regional and national leaders within the Audubon Society to try to get funding for Jane and Connie to do this work. The two ladies were very serious about trying to find out what was going on in that locale north-east of town, and what could be done about it.

When Jesse thought about those two ladies, he often thought of the quote from John James Audubon himself -- "The difference between a bird-watcher, a birder, and an ornithologist is just a matter of dedication." He was proud of the work that Jane and Connie were doing.

* * *

Paul always checked his voicemail first thing when he got into his office -- granted, that wasn't always the same time each morning, but on most days it was at some point in the A.M. In the twenty-first century, most people were slowly working their way from voice telecommunications, but Bangor Springs had its elderly element, like most small towns, people who were still very accustomed to speaking on the phone and leaving messages on answering machines --Paul wondered whether or not there were really any answering machines anymore, with tapes to rewind and such; he doubted it-- and Paul knew that the elderly in Bangor Springs were often the people who were in the know on matters of importance.

On this particular Thursday, the voicemail that Paul got first-thing was a message from Clint Shumer. Paul didn't know the name, but he jotted down the contact information in the message. The first thing Paul noticed about the return telephone number that Clint Shumer left on his voicemail was that the area code wasn't local. Paul swiped into his smartphone and browsed the internet for a couple of minutes, trying to figure out where the '209' area code was in the United States.

According to Wikipedia, the phone call would have come from California.

--It wasn't every day that Paul Brachman got calls from California.

--Hadn't Miller's Field been purchased by someone out in California, according to Walter, the lawyer for the Smithers estate?

Paul set about the business of calling Clint Shumer back.

"Hello, this is Clint Shumer."

"Mr. Shumer, this is Paul Brachman. I had a voicemail from you on my phone this morning."

"Yes. Mr. Brachman. From what I understand, you are the local investigative journalist in Bangor Springs."

"I guess you could say that."

"Well then, I think I have something to ask of you."

"Okay. What business do you have for an investigative journalist?"

"I'd like you to find out what the hell is going on at the site of my house construction on Old Smith Road. From what I'm being told by the construction company, the whole damn place is haunted."

Something clicked in Paul's mind, as the pieces of the puzzle came together in his head. The Smithers estate, the construction site deaths, the California buyers, Miller's Field. Paul realized who he was talking to on the phone, and he realized that he was already investigating --had been investigating for years, as a matter of fact-- the property now belonging to Mr. Clint Shumer.

* * *

Jorge Gutierrez was bashed by the bucket of a backhoe, but after that...

Nick McCoy fell off of the roof of the house while the trusses were being positioned and secured. He landed squarely on his head, shattering his spine at the third, fourth, fifth, and sixth cervical discs, and severing his spinal cord. The safety harness that he was wearing, the one that was supposed to secure him in the event of a fall, "catastrophically failed", according to investigators.

Nick had been the star quarterback of the Coloma High School football team about a decade earlier. In fact, his last football game ever had ended with a neck injury that put Nick in physical rehabilitation for a year. The doctors in the Emergency Room over in Chester, where Nick was taken after his fall from the roof trusses, thought that his previous neck injury had probably been --at least partly-- responsible for the severity of this second neck injury. His death was probably the most painless of the five, according to the doctors that Paul Brachman interviewed after the fact that autumn. Nick was probably dead within a few seconds of hitting the ground.

A couple of weeks later, Luke Lang was electrocuted by a radio with a short circuit while he was standing in a mud puddle. The electricity coursing through his arm, across his chest, and into the puddle of water on the ground, stopped his heart. By the time his heart was revived by paramedics twelve minutes later, the lack of blood flow to his brain caused permanent damage that was beyond repair. Luke was nearing the end of his summer break at the time of his death, the summer break between his junior and senior year at the University of Dayton, in Ohio, where he was finishing up a degree in Criminal Justice. Luke was hoping to become a Knox County sheriff, just like his older brother, Alex.

Emily Carson's death, probably the strangest of all of them, also ended up taking the longest, from start to finish. She cut the tip off of her index finger with a circular saw while she was cutting two-by-fours at the work site. This was obviously not a mortal wound, but she ended up with a hospital-acquired staph infection --the MRSA type-- that spread through her blood, eventually leading to sepsis and the shutdown of many of Emily's major organs from septic shock. She died a week after the initial injury, and she left a husband and a five-month-old daughter behind.

The last of the five deaths connected with the Shumer building project was Dexter Booker. He was the youngest of the crew members that Bill Sandival lost that summer, and was also the crew member at Pioneer Construction with the least experience. He'd been on Bill's crew for only about six months. Dex, as he was known, had a nail gun misfire on him. The nail, rather than going into the particle board that Dex was working on, came out the back end of the nail gun, back toward Dex's neck. It caught him in the side of the throat, piercing his jugular vein. While this wouldn't normally have been a mortal wound, Dex was working alone on a remote part of the Shumer building project, and ended up bleeding to death before he could get help, before anyone else could find him.

* * *

The day before Clint Shumer left a voicemail for Paul Brachman at the Bangor Springs Gazette, he'd reached out to speak with the general contractor building his house -- Bill Sandival.

"So, what can you tell me about the progress on the build, Bill?"

"What can I tell you?!?! WHAT CAN I TELL YOU?!?! I CAN TELL YOU THIS FOR SURE -- IT'S OVER!"

"Whoa whoa whoa, Bill. Calm down, a bit. What do you mean, 'It's over'?"

"I mean that I've stepped foot on that property for the last time, with God as my witness."

"Wait a second. We had a deal. I signed a contract with Pioneer Construction."

"Yes, you sure did. And I would advise you to get your copy of the contract and consult the termination clause section."

"You're terminating the contract?!?! On what grounds? You can't terminate the contract without grounds!"

"Oh, I've got grounds, alright. The first set of grounds that I have is that OSHA is going to have that construction site locked down for weeks, investigating all of the crazy crap that's happened out there. But, to be honest with you, Clint, that's not even why we're backing out. The real grounds are this -- that land is haunted somehow, and I've got the funeral programs from five funerals in the last three months to prove it."

Clint stopped to think for a moment before speaking again. He needed to try to think of a way to de-escalate this conversation.

"Bill, I can't imagine what you've been through, how horrible it's been for you, and I can certainly understand how frustrated and confused you must feel. But, if you quit on this job, how is my house ever going to get finished?"

"Clint, last week I sat through the funeral for a nineteen-year-old kid whose jugular got tore out by a malfunctioning nail gun. That doesn't happen, Clint. It just doesn't happen. Nail guns don't backfire. I've been using nail guns ever since they were invented and I'm not even sure that I can explain how it's possible for one to backfire. I'm *also* telling you --as sure as I am speaking to you now-- that no construction team, from Pioneer or from any other construction company crazy enough to attempt it, will ever finish that building. That project is a doomed one, if I've ever seen such a thing."

Clint heard the click on the phone line that signaled that Bill had hung up.

* * *

As it turned out, Clint and Tami Shumer never officially lived in Bangor Springs. When things started going south with the house that was being built on the property that they'd purchased --on Miller's Field-- the two of them were still residents of the great state of California. Clint was doing a fine job managing the entire building process from a distance and the Pioneer Construction team, before the deaths of their five construction workers, was working alongside him to get the property ready without having to require either of the Shumers to be on-site.

As a regional sales director with more than twenty years of experience in supervising individuals that he might not very often --if ever-- see, Clint knew that it could be done, having someone build you a house from afar. Clint approached the project as he approached the task of managing his subordinates at work -- in situations where you feel like you can trust the people who are working for you, then you grant a certain amount of leeway. Otherwise, keeping a tight leash on things was always a pretty prudent choice.

In Clint's mind, Bill Sandival had been the perfect example of a worker that you could count on... at first anyway. He seemed to initially have a firm grip on what was going to be involved in managing the project with a homeowner that was going to be handling things from afar. Bill seemed like a knowledgeable, experienced, trustworthy kind of guy.

Again, these were Clint's initial impressions.

But, in the eighty-four days between the death of his first construction worker, on July 17th, and the death of his fifth, on October 9th, Clint had been losing faith in Bill Sandival by degrees, even as Bill continued to lose his trusted employees to accidental deaths. By the end of it all, Bill was a raving lunatic in Clint's estimation. The final conversation that the two of them had told Clint just about all he needed to know.

FROM BRACHMAN'S FILE #4 -- March 23, 1963

"Good evening, Officer? Is there something I can do for you, sir?"

As the young man looked up at the police officer, the officer looked back down at the kid --Gerald Hobbs-- with a look on his face that practically screamed, "You've got to be kidding me, son!"

"For starters, you could try explaining to me why it is that you are sitting in the middle of the Pine Ridge Cemetery at 11:38 on a Saturday night. Let's start with that, shall we?"

Jerry didn't really know what to say to the officer. He'd always been told that lying to anyone in authority was a bad idea, so he knew better than to try that. But, Jerry was also pretty concerned with the fact that the truth --once he said it out loud-- was going to make him look like an idiot.

"Well, you see, Officer." Jerry stammered.

"Yes?"

"Well, let me ask you this, Officer...?"

"Dwyer, son. My name is Officer Dwyer."

"Well," Jerry started again, "let me ask you this, Officer Dwyer: have you ever done something to try to impress someone? Like, a girl?"

The officer stood above Jerry, looking down at him as he sat on his blanket in the quickly chilling night air. The kid looked just about as pathetic as you could imagine a teenage kid looking, all pimples and thick glasses, gangly and awkward. Officer Dwyer actually felt sorry for the boy, and decided to play along.

"Well, yes. I suppose that I have, at some point in my life."

"Well, Officer Dwyer, that's what I'm doing here. I'm trying to ask this girl out - her name is Shirley. But she told my friend Ralph that I wouldn't even have a chance with her unless I'd done something really scary before. Something truly impressive."

"What's so impressive about you sitting here in the dark, son? What kind of a girl are you trying to impress that this sort of tomfoolery is going to ring her bell?"

The silence between the officer and the teenage boy grew. During its growth, Officer Dwyer wondered whether young Gerald Hobbs would truly understand the weight of his question. After all, it was Dwyer's experience that the most important people in life weren't the ones that you had to do a whole lot of work to impress in the first place. Young Master Hobbs would --sooner or later-- come to discover that whoever he was trying to impress probably wasn't worth it.

Unfortunately for the two of them, Gerald hadn't come to any such realization previous to taking up a position in the midst of the main cemetery in Bangor Springs on this chilly March evening.

While the officer was pondering these things, Jerry was hoping that he wasn't about to get into any real trouble. As far as he could tell, he hadn't done anything wrong, certainly nothing illegal.

"You know," the officer picked the conversation back up, "there are more impressive places –more spooky places– to hang out than the Pine Ridge cemetery, Jerry, if you're really trying to impress this girl. I've heard one of the spookiest places to spend some time in the dark is just north of town, out on Old Smith Road. The old Miller place."

"I've never heard of it."

"Well, from what I understand, a little girl died out there some years ago and legend has it that her ghost is still haunting the property."

"Really?!?! That does sound spooky! I wonder if Shirley would be impressed to hear that I'd spent the evening sitting alone out there."

Jerry Hobbs got up off of the ground, hastily folding up the blanket that he'd been sitting on. In ten loping steps, he was at the side of his '54 Belair, with the door handle in his hand. Jerry turned back and looked at the policeman.

"Thanks, Officer. I've got a great feeling about this advice of yours. This could be just what I need. One day, Shirley and I will name our first kid after you!"

Dwyer chuckled as Hobbs got in and pulled away.

* * *

Officer Benjamin Dwyer, twenty-six year veteran of the Bangor Springs Police Department announced his retirement from the police force on the following Tuesday morning, two days after the disappearance of one Gerald Hobbs. His mother and father were in the police department first thing Monday morning to file a missing persons report. When Dwyer heard, he almost told his fellow department staff where they could possibly look to try to find the missing teen.

But, instead, he chose not to incriminate himself.

Dwyer's retirement was a short one, as he took his own life less than a month later.

October 18, 1932

The theory of staying up until after their mother and father had gone to bed was one thing, but the actual attempt at doing it was another thing entirely. They failed the first two times they tried, Patsy and Jim, both of them eventually falling asleep long before mom and dad called it quits for the night.

After the second failure, the frustration got them to talking.

"I don't think it's going to happen, Jimmy-boy. We just don't seem to have what it takes to make this work. I'm sorry."

Jim loved it when she called him 'Jimmy-boy'. She was the only person who called him that and it was a special term that she only used when their conversations were of that special, sibling variety.

"I think we could do it. We just have to be smarter about it."

"Well, what do you suggest? she asked.

"What if we tried it in shifts? You know, like I'll sleep for a half-hour, and then you'll sleep for a half-hour. And the whole time, the awake one will listen for signs of whether or not mom and dad have gone to sleep?"

"Well, I guess it won't hurt us to try one more time. And you seem to be so darn interested in what dad is hiding out there."

And so, it was settled. They would try one more time, on Thursday night. But, in his mind, Jim was already committed to trying to convince his sister again after that. He was, in fact, going to repeatedly keep trying, because he needed his sister to be with him on this, and he really wanted to know what was growing back at the edge of the barnyard.

October 21, 1932

Two nights later, Patsy and Jimmy did it. Not long after heading to bed, Jimmy had snuck over to Patsy's room, and it was there that they enacted their plan -- sleeping in short shifts while the other stayed awake, they were able to keep each other awake past the point when their parents went to bed. And, just to be safe, they stayed up even a bit longer, to make sure that they weren't going to end up going downstairs and getting caught by parents who hadn't yet had the chance to fall asleep. With their bedrooms upstairs, and their parents' bedroom downstairs, they knew they were going to have to be ultimately quiet to get out of the house undetected. The first part of this process was the long trip down the stairs to the first floor.

They talked about trying to get out of the house by leaving through one of their bedroom windows, by using a rope or a ladder of some kind. While it might be easier to get out of the house this way, they decided that there was a greater chance that one or both of them could get injured taking the "second floor window" route.

Since neither of them had ever tried sneaking out of the house in the middle of the night before, it wasn't something that they were going to be great at, for the very first time. All they needed to do was be good enough to pull it off. Patsy knew that her father was a heavy sleeper because she used to get bloody noses a lot when she was littler, and when she went down to her mother and father's bedroom to tell them about those emergencies, Patsy could remember times when her father never even woke up while she talked to her mother about her nose.

This evening, Patsy was pretty sure that, if one of the two parents was going to be awoken, it was going to be their mother.

Patsy sent Jimmy down the stairs first, because she thought that, if Jimmy ended up stepping on a stair and causing any creaking in the floor, then at least she would know where *not* to step. As they took three or four minutes to climb down fourteen steps, neither of them ended up making any sounds at all. That was half the battle.

Since the stairs in the house emptied out into the hallway between the kitchen and the dining room, and the back door was off of the kitchen, they only had six or seven steps to take to get across the kitchen and to the back door. From there, they were almost free of the house. But, when Patsy took the lead and moved to open the back door, she found it was locked. She couldn't ever remember the house being locked before, not that she paid that much attention. But, when you lived out in the country, with no nearby neighbors, there wasn't much point in locking your doors. Patsy slid back the bolt of the lock as quietly as she could, opened the door, and the two Miller siblings made it out of the house.

Just as they helped the screen door to silently close behind them, the grandfather clock in the dining room chimed the hour, a single peal for one o'clock.

* * *

It was a full moon, which was lucky for Jimmy and Patsy, because the light from the moon helped them to make it toward the back of the property without them having to carry any oil lamps. Because of this extra light, and because Jimmy and Patsy were as familiar with their own backyard as they were with the backs of their hands, they didn't have any trouble making their way toward the back of the property.

They headed there, past the yard where the chickens would roam in the day, pecking for food, and then even further, past the barn where the horse stalls were, and out toward the very furthest part of the yard. As they got past the barn, the property turned into the acres of farmland that their father farmed, year in and year out. But, between the barn and those rows of feed corn, there was a strip of area, as long as the barn was wide, and only about twenty yards in width.

As Jimmy and Patsy got closer and closer to the space between the barn and the farmland, they noticed two things: the stench and the glowing.

The glowing and the smell were both coming from the plants, specifically the fruits hanging from the plants, and the glowing was a reddish glow. As Jimmy and Patsy got closer, they could see that the fruits were, in actuality, a very dark color on their outer skin --hard to tell exactly what color in the moonlight-- and the reddish glow seemed to have to fight its way out through the dark skin of the fruit.

This gave the glow a smothered quality. Patsy thought to herself that, if it weren't for the dark skin, the glowing of all of these fruits on all of these plants would have been visible from miles away.

The smell was so bad that it caused Patsy to gag and retch a couple of times, involuntarily, the closer that they got to the plants. Jimmy didn't seem to mind it as much, but Jimmy was a boy -- and they seemed to be built differently, especially for the gross stuff.

The smell was cloying and it seemed to be equal parts sweet and rotten. If something could smell as if it were a rotting dead animal, two or three days bloating in the sun, at the same time that it smelled like a fresh loaf of zucchini bread, just out of the oven warm and steaming, these plants had that kind of a stink.

Patsy and Jimmy noticed that the plants were organized into three rows, and that each of the rows stretched as far as the back boundary of the property, as far as the back edge of the barn. Jimmy quick-counted in his head, for he'd always been a natural at mathematics, and thought that the three rows were probably about a hundred plants all together, give or take.

The two of them approached the first of the three rows, and the first of the plants in that row.

"What are these things? And how can they smell so bad?" Patsy spoke in a hushed tone, despite the fact that they were quite some distance from their sleeping parents. She was clearly more disgusted by the smell than she was concerned by the fact that the plants were glowing.

"I don't know, but I've heard about plants that have bad smells before. Mrs. Sheppard, at school, told us once that plants with a bad smell use the stink as a defense mechanism against animals, to keep the animals from eating them."

Patsy didn't know whether or not she believed what Jimmy was telling her, but she could imagine Mrs. Sheppard saying something like that; their teacher seemed to know a whole lot of things. Without a doubt, Patsy would have found it practically impossible to eat anything that smelled like these plants did. She continued to stare intently at that first plant, looking to see what she could see, with Jimmy at her side.

Jimmy was much more interested in the fact that the plants were glowing. As he watched, he noticed that the glowing of the fruits came and went in slow pulses. The fruits slowly grew in the intensity of their glowing, only to then grow dimmer. Jimmy thought the whole cycle, from dimmest to brightest and then back to dimmest, was probably about four seconds. They looked, strangely enough, like little glowing hearts, red and pulsing. Jimmy also noticed that all of the fruits on a single plant throbbed at the same rate -- each of them growing brighter and dimmer in concert with the other fruits on the same plant.

It was then that he also noticed that all of the fruits on all of the plants in each row throbbed in the same unity with all of the other fruits on all of the other plants in the same row.

Panning back further still, Jimmy realized that all of the plants, in each of the three rows, were in synchrony.

While Jimmy was making mental notes about the glowing of the fruits, and while Patsy was trying to figure out how something alive could smell so bad, they both were caught off-guard by the motion that started occurring, inside the fruits themselves.

"Did you see that?!?!"

"Of course I did, Jimmy. I'm not blind!"

"Well, what was it?"

"How am I supposed to know? This is all as crazy to me as it is to you."

To Patsy, the motion inside the fruits nearest them --for the only motion that Patsy could see in any of the fruits was only in the three or four plants closest to them-- reminded her of a lesson that she'd been taught by her father once about chicken eggs.

Tom Miller had once held a chicken egg up to the light of an oil lamp to show Patsy how you could tell whether an egg, having been incubated by a hen, was fertilized or not. Tom showed his daughter that you could see, if you looked closely into the egg, with the light of the oil lamp behind it, the very beginnings of life in an egg. Tom told Patsy that it was important to regularly gather the eggs, before the hens had a chance to incubate the fertilized eggs into chicks. Sometimes, when Patsy would "candle" an egg, as her father had called it, she could see the baby chicks, barely just little bird skeletons, inside the egg.

The lesson, from years ago, when Tom had been teaching Patsy to gather the eggs from the chicken coop, came storming back into Patsy's memory. She watched the movement inside the fruits on those first few plants, because she could see something *alive*, moving inside, just like she'd seen in those candled eggs.

* * *

What Jimmy saw inside those fruits looked strange, for sure, but he didn't think it was strange for the same reason that Patsy thought it was strange. Jimmy thought it was strange because it was something alive and squirming around inside of what appeared to be a fruit or a vegetable. He knew that there was supposed to be a line between plant life and animal life -- these plants were definitely crossing that line.

What Jimmy thought he saw inside those fruits looked just like a skink, tiny lizards that were native to this area.

Jimmy Miller was a bit of a skink expert.

At the northeast corner of the Miller farm property, just across the imaginary line that marked the edge of his father's land, there was a pretty big forest. As a kid, growing up, Jimmy had spent hours upon hours in that forest -- despite his father telling him not to, since it wasn't their property. When Jimmy wanted to get lost, he went to the forest to see what he could see and to be alone with his own thoughts.

In that forest, Jimmy knew where to look to find the skinks.

Skinks liked to lay out in the sun when they could, to get direct sunlight to warm themselves, and in the forest, direct sunlight was sometimes hard to find. You need a break in the tree cover overhead, for the sun to shine directly down. Additionally, since skinks are lizards, they like to stay near water and near the places where there tend to be plenty of bugs to eat.

Since Jimmy knew all of this about skinks, he was naturally very good at finding them in the northeast forest.

While Patsy was doubly upset at seeing something moving inside the fruits on the plants, Jimmy was just trying to figure out how those tiny skinks got stuck inside of those glowing tomatoes. Jimmy got down on his haunches to try to get a closer look at the fruits, without getting any closer to the plants.

"They look like skinks!"

"Aren't skinks usually bigger than that?" Patsy asked. She'd remembered seeing the skinks that Jimmy had been able to catch and bring home, on occasion. She'd remembered them being bigger than what was curled up inside of those fruits.

"Well, maybe not baby skinks."

"Jimmy, how did baby skinks end up trapped inside of glowing fruits on these plants?"

"I haven't figured that out yet."

"Well, they're giving me the heebie-jeebies. All of a sudden, I don't want to be here anymore. I think Dad was right, trying to keep us away from here. We should go."

"But, Patsy, we worked so hard to get out of the house in the first place. Don't you want to do a little more exploring?"

"Nope. I do not."

"Come on." Jimmy jumped up, grabbed Patsy's arm, and pulled her down the row about thirty feet. This put them solidly behind the barn, and out of sight of the house altogether.

Jimmy was amazed.

"Would you take a look at that!"

Jimmy pointed at the plants that they'd just been standing in front of a moment ago, the plants at the start of the row. The lizard-things that had been visibly moving inside the fruits on those plants now seemed to have gone away, gone back to sleep. And, the glowing of those fruits had changed somehow. As Jimmy turned to face the plants nearest them now, about a third of the way down the row, they were now squirming to life. Each fruit, on each of the nearby plants in the first row, seemed to now have a squirming lizard-thing inside of it.

"Isn't that bizarre? It seems almost as if they sense our presence."

"Oh, it's bizarre, alright." Patsy was tense, and getting tenser by the second. She didn't want to stay, and she was trying to get her brother disengaged from all of this. "Jimmy, can we go now?"

But, Jimmy was less alarmed than his sister, probably because, in his mind, there wasn't anything here to be afraid of. Weird, for sure, but not necessarily dangerous. He stepped through the first row of plants, to stand in the space in between the first and the second rows.

"James Frances Miller! You will come back here right this moment. I am ordering you, as your older sister, to obey me!"

But James was barely even listening. He was standing in close proximity to six plants now, three in the second row and three that he'd just walked past, in the first row. Each of those plants probably had about five or six fruits, plus or minus. As Jimmy stood and looked, all six of the nearby plants, and all of the fruits on each of them, came to life with serpentine motion inside them. Jimmy slowly began to spin around in a circle, to get a glimpse of all of the plants.

That was the moment when Patsy decided that she'd had enough of these shenanigans. She stepped into the space between the first two rows, determined to grab her brother and force him to her will.

* * *

"I called you once, Jimmy, and I expect that you will listen to me when I call you."

"But, look at all of them, Patsy! Aren't they beautiful?"

Jimmy was continuing to spin around in circles, looking at the plants and the red glowing fruits and the lizard-things. He seemed to be drifting into some type of euphoric disconnection, almost a trance of some kind. He had a giddy look of joy on his face, as if he'd never been as happy as he was to be standing in this place, among this dark mystery. Patsy grabbed him firmly by the forearm, with all of the force she could muster, to get him to stop.

"Are you joking with me? They are not beautiful, and I'm not amused, Jimmy. I want to leave, and I want to leave right now."

And, that was when it happened.

Jimmy would end up living long enough to replay this moment, over and over and over again in his mind, thousands upon thousands of times. It would, as it turned out, end up being one of the dying thoughts on his mind, many decades later.

The sound that the fruits made when they blew up was a wet, muffled pop. Nearest the two of them, James ended up hearing close to a dozen of those pops, one right after the other.

Right after the pops came the screeching.

As each of the skink-like creatures dropped out of each of the popped fruits, they began to screech; it was a deeply unnerving sound and it had in it a tone that was unmistakably hostile. In the two or three seconds when the fruits started blowing open, the screeching was relatively quiet, but it didn't take long for each additional skink-thing, with its additional screeching, to add its voice to the awful chorus of screeching skink-things. They seemed, for all of their noise-making, to be upset about something.

The skink-things, ten or twelve altogether, each dropped out of their broken shells and down to the ground, near the base of whatever plant they'd hatched from. This resulted in Patsy and Jimmy being surrounded on all sides, in a circle of these little lizard creatures, who seemed for the moment to still be gathering their wits about them. The screeching continued, and it was hard to tell if they were screeching to communicate with each other, or if the screeching was something else. It hadn't occurred to either of the siblings that the sound was going to be loud enough to wake their parents -- for they were somewhat distracted from intellectual thoughts. But, it was at this very moment that Norma Miller started stirring in bed, back in the farmhouse.

As each of the skink-things looked around, craning their tiny necks and getting their bearings, Jimmy noticed that the "fruits" that had popped open to release each of the lizards were dripping their bright red liquid contents onto the ground.

"What are they?!?!"

"As far as I know, lizards don't hatch from plants, Jimmy, so they can't be lizards. Do you still think they look beautiful?"

"Not as much as I did. I liked them better when they were in those little fruit things."

"I think we should get out of here. We have no idea if these things are poisonous or what. We don't even know if they have teeth, Jimmy."

As it turned out, they did have teeth.

* * *

Jimmy Miller took the first steps away from the circle of the lizards, stepping over a couple of them to get out of the space between the first and second row of plants. As he left, on tiptoes for some reason, Patsy followed right behind him. The two of them got about five or six steps away from the skink-things --and they got to feeling better with every step of distance between them and the creatures-- when, for the first time, the lizards stopped screeching.

The silence that fell, when the screeching stopped, caught Patsy and Jimmy's attention, simply because there hadn't been silence for what seemed like a very long time. When the screeching stopped, and brother and sister were about five yards away, Jimmy was slightly closer to the farmhouse than Patsy. Both of them turned to see why the screeching had stopped. What they saw was that all of the little skink-things had turned themselves to face the two of them, the fleeing siblings, each pair of black reptilian eyes focused on the older sister and her little brother.

And then, in an instant --and all at once-- they jumped.

James Miller, in the eighty-six years that passed between that moment and the moment of his death, remembered that moment 31,426 times, truth be told, according to a reliable source. This averaged out to a little more than once per day, for eighty-six years. He thought about whether or not the skink-things would have been able to close the distance between him and his sister in a single jump, had they been further away. He thought about whether he would've died, had he been the closer of the two of them. In the years immediately after Patsy's death, the thought was pretty much constantly on his mind, among other thoughts on the events of that night. As time went by, and the trauma of his sister's death weighed less and less on him, as the mortal grief gave way to aches of guilt and --eventually-- to the less-sensitive scar that commemorated the emotional wound of the loss, James Miller thought about that five yards of distance less and less often.

Because Patsy was closer to them than Jimmy was, most of them landed on Patsy, while only one of them made it all of the way through the air to land on Jimmy. A couple of the lizard-things missed both of them entirely.

It didn't take more than a half-second for Jimmy to feel the one that had landed on him, on his forearm to be exact, since it almost immediately started biting into his skin. The bites of the tiny skink were a lot more painful than any skink bite that Jimmy'd had ever had in real life. When Jimmy looked down at his forearm, under the light of the full moon, he saw that the teeth on the lizard, as tiny as it was, seemed to gleam in the dark. It was while he was noticing the gleaming that he also noticed the little pinpricks of blood that were welling up on the skin of his forearm, each grouping in a pattern of matching upper and lower crescents, resulting from the upper and lower jaws of the lizards. The blood looked almost purple in the muted darkness. Jimmy noticed three or four sets of bitemarks in the split second that he'd had to inspect what was going on. Busy little bugger.

It was just after that moment that Jimmy noticed his sister had started to scream.

* * *

Norma Miller elbowed her husband Tom with the force of a kicking bull, and he woke up in that sudden way that brings a person from deepest sleep to full awareness in very short order. The first thought, after realizing that he'd been awoken by his wife using a level of force that he would have previously thought her incapable of, was that he heard his daughter screaming. The problem with this understanding, as he was processing it in his mind --ever so slowly it seemed-- was that the sound seemed to be coming from further away than the distance between his bedroom and the upstairs bedroom that belonged to Patsy.

Then, Tom thought about the locked back door.

Tom had recently taken to locking the back door of the house. Initially, he'd convinced himself that he was trying to keep the kids inside at night, but the truth of the matter was that Tom was becoming more and more concerned about those plants and what they were becoming. If Tom had been able to be completely honest with himself, he would have been able to admit that the locking of the door was meant to be protection from what was outside.

"Tom?! Are you with me?! I think I hear Patsy screaming."

"Yes, I hear it, too."

"But where is it coming from?"

"I don't know, but it almost sounds like it's coming from outside. Why would they be outside?"

Tom thought instantly of the plants at the back of the property, and then he jumped out of the bed, scrambling to find his slippers. His terror at the thought that she might be out there, and that something may have been happening to his only daughter, caused Tom to move with a speed that was close to superhuman.

Norma got out of bed, as well, to follow Tom wherever he was headed.

Heading out of the house, they were sure that Patsy was outside, because the sound of her screaming grew ten times as loud when they opened the back door to emerge from the house on the farm yard.

They could see Patsy and Jimmy, near the barn at the back of the farm yard, and the two of them seemed to be bothering with something. Patsy's screams were as constant as she could manage, gasping for breaths in between the screams.

Tom ran toward them, with Norma close behind.

* * *

The lizards were pretty easy to wipe off, and Jimmy had gotten rid of his single attacker easily; he then turned to help his sister. As he did this, Jimmy accidentally stepped on the lizard that he'd brushed off. While he momentarily regretted the loss of life, it helped Jimmy to realize what the plan ought to be; they could squish each of those little skinks-things under foot and be done with them before they ended up doing too much damage with their pointy, sharp teeth. Normally, Jimmy would have been opposed to the wanton destruction of life in any form, but the lizards had brought the fight to Patsy and him, so he was going to return the favor.

The problem with this plan, when Jimmy turned to help his sister, was that the lizards on Patsy had squirmed their way under the nightgown she was wearing. He could see the small bumps of them, under the cloth of the gown, twitching and moving about. It wasn't going to be as easy to shed them underneath her pajamas.

Jimmy screamed at Patsy to get her attention.

"You've got to take off the nightgown, Patsy. They're going to keep biting you if you don't."

"I can't." Patsy screamed back at him. "It hurts. Make them stop, Jimmy. Kill them."

"We've got to get the nightgown off."

Jimmy moved to try to help his sister pull the pajamas off over her head, but she was jerking left and right. With every bite, she was responding with tugs and lurches that made it impossible for him to assist her at all, and equally impossible for him to do the disrobing by himself.

"Jimmy, I can't take much more of this. They are biting me all over. And it hurts so bad."

"I'm trying, Patsy. I'm trying."

Santa Fe - Five

Butch Alvarez had always thought that he would most likely get caught, eventually, doing the questionable, illegal things that he did to keep the Casa Paz nursing home up and running. Not that the thought bothered him enough to run things 'properly'. In his mind, the pros out-weighed the cons. For what he was able to do for the vets in the nursing home -- repaying them in part for their service to the nation-- he'd been willing to run some risks.

The last thing Butch expected, however, was that the discovery would end up being made by local law enforcement. Mr. Alvarez imagined that it would be some federal organization, like the IRS or the CDC or the HHS, maybe even the V.A. -- if the V.A. was even capable of investigating such things. Those agencies, interested in the work being done inside of nursing homes and assisted living facilities for various reasons, would be more likely, in Butch's estimation, to be paying attention to what he was doing, to what was going on in the Casa Paz facility.

On the other hand, Butch didn't have any reason to think that the Santa Fe Police Department was ever going to get so bored that they might decide to run around and investigate the goings-on at the local nursing homes in the area.

But, that seems to be exactly what transpired.

Wonder of wonders, Butch heard through the grapevine that some detective on the Santa

Fe police force was asking around about his nursing home. Asking questions about the facility in general, and asking questions about specific people inside of the facility. Butch had heard from his sources that there were even some specific questions about veterans in the nursing home, veterans like James Miller.

The logical conclusion to reach was that this activity was the result of Kathryn Santos asking her brother to process the fingerprint kit that she'd used on James Miller, and Butch kept trying to calm himself with the notion that there wasn't anything to worry about, not really.

Nevertheless, all of this raised red flags in Butch's mind. And, while he'd never really had a reason to put together an action plan for trying to avoid prosecution for his crimes, he also kind of wondered if it wouldn't just be the nobler thing to take his punishment --what he had coming to him for doing what was wrong, despite his choices being the proper ones--and roll with the punches.

Perhaps, Butch thought to himself, sitting at his desk in his office, it would be prudent to make some plans for either of these forks in the road, since things seemed to be heading in that direction.

* * *

There isn't a zoologist on the planet that knows what a saurian is. No photos, no sightings, no DNA samples, nothing at all. Not one shred of evidence that they even exist. No biological study of the animal at all, except --of course-- by The Scion. The Scion have kept the animal's existence a secret.

Just one of their many secrets.

This isn't to say that the saurians have never been studied before. In fact, they've been the focus of a number of different 'scientific' experiments conducted by The Scion over the years, really the last couple of centuries. Most recently in that history, Mr. Dire has come to supervise the research being done.

Dire has come, during that time, to be very interested in the little creatures. The features that make them unique from other creatures on Earth. The possible advantages that having them and breeding them could benefit The Scion. The relationship between them and the other similar lifeforms known to humanity.

But especially, Dire was interested in their venomous qualities.

Of the eleven humans on the planet who'd ever been bitten by a saurian, as far as The Scion were aware, only two of those humans had stumbled into the situation. Truth be told, the other nine people were used by The Scion in experiments with the saurians. Nasty business, some of that experimentation had been, but fully necessary -- in the name of research, of course.

Ten of the eleven people who'd ever been bitten, either singly or repeatedly, by a saurian, had not lived for very long to describe the experience. Or to be available for scientific study. Of course, for the math majors out there, that means that only one person on Earth has ever survived being bitten by a saurian.

Jim Miller --the man wasting away in a bed in Room 204 of the Casa Paz nursing home--is a special man, indeed.

* * *

The contents of the box, as nearly as Kathryn could tell as she emptied it out on her kitchen counter, back in her apartment, was mostly trinkets and knick-knacks. The odd dinner receipt here, the old matchbook --half empty of matches-- there. A couple of printed photographs with no obvious connection to each other, except to say that James Miller was in each of them. One of the photos featured a woman, and Jim looked so young in it. Kathryn wondered if Jim had been married to this woman at some point.

As odd as one might find a box with loose puzzle pieces in it --maybe two or three from each of a dozen different puzzles-- Kathryn was able to make heads or tails of very little of it.

But, beside the oddities in the box, there were the letters, in their own little shoebox. Kathryn pulled the stack of them out of the shoebox and set it on the counter. Then, she took the box, with the box inside, and lowered it off the side of the counter, scooping everything that had been on the counter back into the box in a single, clean sweeping motion.

She figured that, if there was anything to be learned from the box, it would be learned from looking through the letters.

* * *

"Hey, Dean!" Maxine called for him from the kitchen with a voice that had Dean coming to her on the double.

"Yeah? Is everything alright?"

"You said his name was James Miller?"

Dean stopped for a moment, to try to understand her question in his mind. When it finally occurred to him what Max was asking, he continued on.

"Yeah, James Miller. Why?"

"Couple weeks back, when you mentioned the name to me, I thought it sounded vaguely familiar, but I couldn't quite place it."

"You thought that name 'James Miller' sounded familiar to you?" Dean teased his wife. "How does that name sound familiar to anyone?!?! It's the most generic name in human history."

"Yeah, yeah, yeah. Give me a break, will ya?"

Dean eased off, and Max continued.

"How old is this guy? He must be pretty old if he's at Kathryn's nursing home, right?"

Dean pulled out his detective's notebook, the one that he kept tucked in his back pants pocket, usually on the left. He flipped it open, turned a couple of pages, and then squinted to look at his own chicken scratch.

"He's 97."

Max grabbed some paper of her own, and a pen, from the junk drawer next to the refrigerator, and started some quick math on it. When she finished, she turned to Dean with a sparkle in her eye that Dean had rarely seen.

"So, he would have been a kid around the time of the Great Depression?"

"Yeah, I guess so. Max --tell me-- what's going on with all of these questions?"

"I can't tell you until I know more. For now, just let me play detective for once, will you?"

Max gave her husband the playful look that she knew he was powerless to fight. He winked back at her, with a playful look of his own, and headed back to the living-room from whence he'd come.

* * *

Lena Peters was the only surviving daughter of Bob Smithers of Bangor Springs, Michigan. And she was the only cousin, from that side of the family, that Maxine Santos still communicated with. Lena's two brothers were useless jerks, and Max had never been very close to either of them. Additionally, Max had been working for several years to put that part of her past behind her, so it didn't serve for her to go reaching back into the past whenever the mood struck her.

Lena was a big-time accountant at a big-time accounting firm, Plante & Moran, in Chicago. Max called her up to ask her about James Miller.

"Hello?"

"Lena?"

"Maxine! How's my favorite cousin doing?"

"I'm well. How are you?"

"Not too bad. Busier than a one-legged gal in an ass-kicking contest, but I can't complain. Ed understands and he helps as much as he can."

"That's good."

"It's been so long since we talked. I don't know if you heard, but my Dad died back in March."

"I'm so sorry, Lena. I hadn't heard."

"Yes, it seems like my brothers and I have been working to settle the affairs of the estate ever since. You know, I think that, the older my brothers get, the more pig-headed and annoying they become."

Max smiled. Since she'd believed Lena's brothers to be pig-headed annoyances for a very long time, it must have been the case that Lena had built up a tolerance to them, growing up with them as their sister, a tolerance that Max had never had the advantage to develop. Apparently, the tolerance was breaking down, though, or Max's male cousins were developing new skills in obnoxiousness.

"Have you been able to put things to rest?"

"Mostly. We still have a few remaining issues to settle, but the major details have all been worked out. I don't remember it being this difficult when my mother died, but back then, most of her stuff just ended up with my dad. When the second parent goes, it's a lot worse."

"I'm sorry to hear that." Max paused for a moment or two, to allow for a break in the conversation, before she set to changing the topic.

"Didn't your dad farm Miller's Field? Back in the day?"

"He tried, once upon a time. Why do you ask?"

"I've got some questions about the Miller family that owned that field originally."

"Well, then, the person that you need to talk to is Paul Brachman. Do you know Paul?"

When Lena said Paul's name, Max's mind wandered off, leaving the conversation with Lena behind. Paul Brachman was one of the last people on the planet that Max ever wanted to talk to again. Talking to Paul would mean reconnecting to Bangor Springs in a way that she wasn't at all crazy about, after all of the work that she'd done to leave that place in her past.

Max came back to the conversation, and eventually, Lena and Max said their goodbyes, after Max took one last opportunity to offer her condolences to her cousin regarding her father's --Max's uncle's-- death.

Max spent the rest of that evening, sitting next to her husband on the couch while he begged the Colorado Rockies --through the TV-- to give him a reason to watch the postseason. Max couldn't have cared less about baseball, though; instead, she was trying to think things through.

In the end, she'd come to the conclusion that she had a choice to make. She could play her hunch, point her sister-in-law toward Paul

Brachman, and wash her hands of the whole thing. But, considering that it was a long shot, such an approach would go south in a hurry if things didn't pan out -- it would look to Kathryn as if Max had sent her on a wild goose chase.

The other choice --the one that seemed like the right thing to do, the more that she thought about it-- was to speak with Paul Brachman herself. Max didn't want to speak to anyone in that God-forsaken Michigan town, let alone the lead reporter for the newspaper in that God-forsaken Michigan town. And, it wasn't even that he was the town's reporter that made the thought of speaking with him sound like a bad idea.

It was the fact that he was Bruce's best friend.

Bangor Springs - Five

Bucky's Bar is the oldest bar in town; though it has been managed by multiple owners throughout the years, it's been the most popular bar in town since the 1950s. Since Bangor Springs is such a small town, you would expect that the number of bars would also be relatively small. The town council annually doles out five liquor licenses, which is about one liquor license for every one thousand people in town. While this might not sound like a lot, a single establishment -- whether a bar, or a convenience store selling cold beer and pints of flavored whiskey-- should be able to account for several hundred patrons, depending. And then, when you factor in that Bangor Springs has twice as many churches as it has bars, and the accompanying fact that many people in Bangor Springs don't drink at all, you should start to see the issue.

So, needless to say, there's a bit of competition in Bangor Springs for the sale of alcohol.

Bruce Randolph is the current owner of Bucky's Bar. 'Bucky' to only his closest, childhood friends, Bruce bought the bar upon his honorable discharge and retirement from the military, after multiple tours in the Middle East and in Afghanistan. Bucky bought the bar from Don Duran, who'd owned the bar for decades prior -- it's always been a staple of Bangor Springs.

Bucky doesn't ever talk about his military experiences to anyone, except his closest friends, of which he has very few. Because of his military pension --Bucky calls it his 'high-three'-- Bucky doesn't really need the bar to do much more than break even, most of the time. That, and give him something to do to occupy his time. Of course, Bucky's Bar has never had a problem turning a profit, at least not since Bucky took over. On most Friday and Saturday nights, it's packed as tight as sardines in that place.

Bucky's best friend growing up in Bangor Springs was Paul Brachman. They hung out all throughout middle school and high school. They had a third amigo, Cyrus Yates, who died in a car accident just a year out of high school. That morbidly sad event, while Paul was in his freshman year at college and Bucky was making his way through boot camp, and then waiting for his first overseas deployment, tied an indissoluble knot between the two of them. Ever since Cyrus's death, the two of them have been very close.

Two women in the history of Bangor Springs have made attempts at being *Mrs.* Bruce Randolph, and both failed. The most recent of these two was Beth Silva, the head librarian at the Bangor Springs Public Library. Paul --to be completely honest-- had considered that marriage doomed from the start. In the first place, what were the chances that a head librarian, and a man who hates to read, are ever going to go very far?

But, the real reason that Paul had considered Bruce and Beth doomed was that Paul wasn't sure that Bruce had ever recovered from the end of his first marriage.

Paul had a sneaking suspicion that Bruce's heart still belonged to his first wife, Maxine Smithers.

Bucky is single these days, primarily because he is largely unlikable. While this might sound like an indictment of his character, Paul has always found Bucky's unlikability to be quite likable. Paul has always understood Bucky to be who Bucky is, just as Bucky has always known Paul to be who Paul is.

Besides the fact that Paul and Bucky have been pals for decades, they continue to be friends through a few, well-defined, business arrangements, among other reasons. One such arrangement is the advertising that Bucky's Bar receives in the Bangor Springs Gazette. If you want to know when Bucky's is having a "50¢ wings night" --always a popular night for the bar-- or when the bar is having a "two dollar domestic bottles, three dollar shots" night --another popular night for the bar-- you can get that information from the Gazette.

In exchange, Paul gets "the scoop", which is to say that Paul regularly connects with Bucky to get the gossip that he overhears and/or plain gets told by the customers that he regularly sees.

You'd be surprised what a bar patron will tell their bartender that they won't tell the town crier.

* * *

Paul Brachman was sitting at his dining room table --once again-- in front of the contents of the file folder that he'd left sitting out. Pouring over the details. Trying to see something he'd not seen before.

Paul had known, for a couple of years at least, that Jim Miller was the only lead on the Miller's Field mystery. He knew what most people knew, through the grapevine: Tom and Norma Miller, the original namesakes for Miller's Field back in the 1920s and 30s, according to the property records of Knox County, were both dead, as far as he could tell. He also knew that the oldest of their two children, a daughter whose name he'd never been able to discover, would have been about a hundred years old, if she was still alive.

Paul also knew that there were approximately 25,000 men in the United States named James Miller. He knew this the way that anyone would have come to know it in the twenty-first century -- he'd looked it up on the internet. A pretty difficult place to start from, if you're thinking about searching for someone in particular. Paul couldn't do just any old name search and hope to narrow things down at all.

However, Paul was able to search for James Miller more intelligently than just using random name searches, because he had information that he could add to the formula. He knew that James was a WWII veteran, and that helped to narrow the search considerably, especially when the number of surviving World War II vets seemed to drop, year after year. Paul tried to use every piece of information --as few as there were-- to eliminate possibilities in the internet search results.

Still, even with the extra pieces that Paul could put into the puzzle, it wasn't enough for him to be able to get any real results. He'd tried several different approaches to the search for James Miller, but it never really amounted to much of anything.

Paul needed what was referred to in the investigations business as a 'break'. He pushed himself away from the dining room table in frustration, and walked into his kitchen.

* * *

Paul ended up getting the break he needed on the following Tuesday night, October 9th. It came in, initially, as a random text from a random number.

Paul?

-Yes? Paul texted back.

It's Maxine.

Since Paul had only known one woman in his whole life named Maxine, he'd only needed a quick moment to figure out who was texting him.

-What can I do for you? he replied.

Can we talk? I need to speak with you.

He thought about it for a minute, figuring he had practically nothing to lose.

-Yes.

As he waited for the phone to ring, he added the contact number -starting with a 505 area code- to his contacts list as 'Maxine Smithers'. No sooner had he done this, then the phone rang.

"Hello."

"Hello, Paul."

Paul tried remembering when he'd last had a conversation with her. Probably before the divorce, at least.

"Maxine. If someone had told me, at any point during my day today, that I was going to be getting a phone call from the woman who broke my best friend's heart, I would have said, 'Maxine doesn't even have my number.'"

She seemed unaffected by the jab, and instead took a step to explain herself.

"I started by calling the office of the newspaper --the Bangor Springs Gazette-- it's on your website. I almost left a voicemail on your machine, but I heard you, in your voicemail greeting, giving out your cell phone number. If you really don't want random voices from your past contacting you, you shouldn't make it so easy."

"I guess the trade-off for being available for anyone to reach you is that you're available for anyone to reach you."

"Listen, Paul. I didn't call to catch up on old times. And I didn't call to listen to you bark at me like my ex-husband's own personal guard dog. To be honest, calling you, or anyone else in Bangor Springs, is pretty low on the list of things I love to do."

"So, what is it? Why did you call?"

"What can you tell me about the family that originally farmed Miller's Field? Back in the 30s?"

"Out on Old Smith Road?"

"No, Paul. The other Miller's Field." Her tone was snarky and on-the-edge.

"Okay, okay. Take it easy. Geeze. Well, the mother and father were Tom and Norma Miller."

"Did they have any kids?"

"Two that I know of. A boy and a girl. The girl's name has always been a mystery to me, but the boy's name…"

Maxine jumped in.

"Was it Jim?"

"Yes." Paul was a bit surprised. "Yes it was, Max."

"In that case, I think I'll be giving your phone number out to someone who really wants to talk with you. If that's alright with you?"

Paul and Maxine exchanged some additional, necessary information before ending their call on that Tuesday evening. The intrigue was almost more than Paul could handle.

* * *

To be completely frank, Mr. Dire had always been responsible for the curse on Miller's Field, the curse by which the field was completely barren of vegetative life. He'd been harboring a fair amount of animosity against the two Miller kids ever since they'd compromised the saurian harvest he was supposed to have had in hand, all those many years ago. And, while the one twerp paid with her life that fall, the other one had escaped his clutches.

Surprisingly.

And it wasn't as if they'd done that much damage, the two of them, not really. It was the principle of the thing that upset Dire at the time -- still upset him these decades later. That, and the fact that his first job for The Scion had an asterisk next to it.

And so, to keep bygones from becoming bygones, Mr. Dire --with the permission of The Scion-- had dispersed some 'resources', every so often, to keep the land poisoned, as it were.

In the years immediately after the Miller Farm folded, fiddling with the property hadn't even been necessary -- no one was interested in the property to begin with. But, Mr. Dire had been diligent anyway, because it pays to be diligent. That diligence, and the socio-political fallout from the work that Mr. Dire had been doing on the property, every so often for most of the twentieth century, had paid off. The strange occurrences and the odd rumors that circled around Bangor Springs, regarding Miller's Field, had been a bit of dark work, earning Dire the admiration of his fellow Scion members.

But then, that business with Bob Smithers and that meddling ag professor back in the mid-90s -- that had been quite the intrusion.

But Mr. Dire had handled that. Granted, direct intensive approaches weren't normally his style, but drastic times call for drastic measures. Dr. Willingham made his bed in '93. Dire's solution --though harsh-- had been just the ticket.

But, just recently, things didn't seem to be getting much better. What for decades had been the simple matter of just 'seeing to the property' was now becoming something in need of an active plan of attack. And, just as Mr. Dire was getting ready to put something in play, the construction site accidents started happening. While he didn't intend for them to happen, he did suspect that the accidents were pursuant to his 'poisoning' of Miller's Field. He also wondered if the deaths would end up being intimidating enough to stop the construction project *dead* in its tracks.

The problem was that the whole ball of wax was threatening to tumble out of control. These deaths were not inconspicuous, to say the least, and Mr. Dire knew that the more attention the affair drew to itself, the more that The Scion --and Mr. Dire himself-- fell into the danger of being exposed.

Mr. Dire knew that most of the outside world wasn't going to be that interested in a string of coincidental deaths at a construction site, but five in a row was a bit much. He also knew that they *would* attract the attention of the local snoop, Brachman. Mr. Dire wondered if something was going to have to be done about him. Sometimes, when you're trying to keep things hush-hush, there's nothing worse than the prying eyes of a small-town, local reporter.

And he'd crossed paths with Brachman before.

To Mr. Dire, it almost felt like a confluence was forming. He knew that, when certain events came together, it was usually prudent to pay attention and to make the best of the opportunities that such events could give rise to. This confluence, though, had a malignant portent -- as if something could go wrong for him, and for The Scion by extension, if he wasn't able to manage things properly. Before just recently, he'd not had reason to be concerned about that piece of property since Smithers.

Dire thought back to his murder of the professor from Michigan State University, about a quarter-century ago. He'd done what was necessary to make sure that the property wasn't going to fall back into a successful pattern of raising crops. In the end, Dire had been willing to go further to win.

A lot further.

FROM BRACHMAN'S FILE #5 -- January 17, 2017

There's something about being close to one's death that makes people think long and hard about continuing to harbor the secrets of a lifetime. Barbara Bender had been seriously considering divesting herself of some information, and within minutes of showing up at her small home in Sawyer on that blustery Tuesday morning in January, Paul Brachman could tell that he was going to be the recipient of a decent amount of information.

And, as it turned out, he definitely did.

Barbara Bender spoke with Paul for four hours, about all manner of things, and Paul served as her confessional priest, with the patience of a man willing to wade into the deep waters to get what he was looking for.

Eventually, his patience paid off.

"You know, I lost my virginity to that man." Barbara announced, apropos of nothing.

"You mean, your husband?" Paul asked.

"No, I mean Jimmy Miller."

Paul perked up in the chair he was sitting in, at her bedside. The mention of Jimmy Miller was instantly tantalizing.

"Really?" Paul baited her. "Do tell."

"Jimmy was the quiet type, all throughout high school, and I liked the quiet ones. There's something about a guy that can't stop, or won't stop, talking. It's always rubbed me the wrong way. Lucky for me, ol' Mr. Bender was the quiet type, too."

"I see."

"Yes, sir. Jimmy and I probably would have ended up together if it weren't for two things. The first was the war, of course. Jimmy headed off to the war not too long after Pearl Harbor, like so many. As far as anyone knows, he hasn't shown his face in Bangor Springs since the day he left for his military training, December 19th, 1941."

"You still remember the day?"

"I sure do. I was attached to Jimmy Miller, emotionally, for a long time after we split up. I think that's the way it is with a woman and her first love."

"So, if you split up with Jimmy before he left for the war, it must have been the other thing that caused you two to call it quits."

"And so, it was. Well done, Mr. Brachman. You really do make quite a fine investigative reporter."

"Ma'am, you can call me Paul."

"Well, that'll be fine, if you'll call me Barb."

Paul nodded at her, and then he waited for her to continue.

"The reason that Jimmy Miller and I could never have been an item was simple: his heart belonged to someone else."

"Oh?"

"He never told me her name, but every time he talked about her, his eyes were sad, inconsolable. He told me that she'd suddenly died and that's as close as I ever got to knowin'."

October 21, 1932

By the time that Tom and Norma reached Patsy and Jim, little blossoms of blood were blooming all over Patsy's nightgown, in the places where the skink-things had bitten her underneath the gown. Tom remembered thinking that they looked like little rose buds all over the nightgown; that they would have been pretty, if not for the reality of them.

Of course, the matter of getting Patsy's pajamas off was a very swift movement for Tom, in his strength. He grabbed Patsy's nightgown by the shoulders, pulling up on it, to get the thing off of her. The motion pulled at Patsy's arms and Patsy, knowing what her father was intending, cooperated in bringing her arms up so that the nightgown could come off. In a couple of seconds, Patsy was standing under the full moon in the back yard in nothing but her briefs. Jim Miller hadn't seen his older sister in this state of undress in quite some time, since Patsy was of the age of her flowering womanhood, and it was no longer appropriate. Of course, at the moment, there were much bigger concerns than Patsy's privacy.

The lizards were crawling all over Patsy's bare skin, seemingly unaware of the fact that they'd been as exposed as Patsy. Norma immediately started swiping at the things, knocking them to the ground. Jimmy knew what to do once they were down; he stepped on each of them as quickly as he could. They squished under his feet with much the same wet pop with which they'd exited the glowing red fruits of the plants. Along with an added crunch of bones.

In short order, they'd cleaned off and killed all of the lizard-things.

Patsy finally stopped screaming, exchanging her screams for moans that spoke of the pain of dozens of bite marks all over her skin. Tom and Norma wrapped their arms around Patsy's shoulders, wrapping her in the fabric of her own nightgown, to escort her towards the house. Jimmy followed behind them, wanting to get away from everything that had taken place in the last ten minutes.

Halfway to the house, Jimmy looked back at where they'd just been. He could see the bodies of each of the skinks on the ground where they'd each been stomped out. He could see them, not because the moon was bright enough to light the scene --at this point, things had started to become cloudy and overcast-- and not because Jimmy's eyesight was particularly keen, either.

Each of the lizard corpses on the ground was glowing the same red that the fruits on the plants had been glowing. He could see that, as the bodies glowed, they also seemed to be rapidly dissolving into little puddles of bubbling ooze. And speaking of the plants, off in the distance, they were all glowing once again -- except for the ones that the lizards had escaped from. But now, the glowing of the plants was a rapid blinking red that reminded Jimmy of anger.

Jimmy turned away from the anger and followed the rest of his family back into the farmhouse.

October 21, 1932

Norma did her best to address the bite marks up and down Patsy's torso and back, some of them slowly seeping blood, while others seemed to have already clotted somewhat. With a wet cloth, Norma cleaned up as much of the mess as she could, up in Patsy's room, with Patsy sitting on the edge of her bed. Tom stood back a few feet, watching his wife and biting his lower lip incessantly.

Tom had plenty of questions to ask, and he was biting his lip to keep himself from angrily asking those questions. Despite his anger at the fact that the children had obviously been outside to get a peek at what was growing behind the barn, he knew better than to get angry at the children when they were hurt -- since it showed a certain failure in priorities that would make Norma angry with him. Once, Jimmy had twisted his ankle falling out of a tree that Tom had told him repeatedly not to climb, and Tom had lashed out at his son; Norma hadn't spoken to Tom for three days after that.

Nevertheless, Tom was angry that the children had disobeyed.

He was angry at the bald man, as well, for it seemed as if he'd been asked to do something that put his family in danger. 'There ought to be a code,' Tom thought to himself, 'a system of morals, that a man would follow that would keep him from propositioning another man to do something that might injure his loved ones.'

Mr. Dire, come to find out, wasn't that morally upstanding.

Mostly though, Tom was mad with himself. He was mad that he'd taken steps, beyond the normal boundaries, to try to be sure that he would have enough money to feed his family, and those steps had put them all at a risk, apparently. What is it, in a man, that he feels so responsible for providing for his family, that he would put them in danger just to be able to say that he'd accomplished the goal?

Deep down inside, Tom knew what it was. It was pride.

Meanwhile, outside of Patsy's bedroom, her little brother was pacing up and down the upstairs hallway, since his parents had forbidden him from being in the room while they put Patsy to bed. He walked down the hall to his bedroom door, at one end of the hall, and then turned and walked to the other end of the hall, where his sister's closed bedroom door barred his progress. He went back and forth like that, for what seemed to him to be hours.

He could hear, every time he got close enough to her door, Patsy moaning inside.

October 21, 1932

As the Miller family busied themselves inside of their farmhouse, each of them focused on Patsy Miller in different ways, Mr. Dire was standing out in the middle of the farmyard, pensively looking down at the damp spots on the dirt, most of them clustered in a type of semi-circle, around the place where Patsy had been standing moments before. The drying stains were all that remained of the ten saurians that had died in the attack on the two troublesome children. The spots had only the slightest red glow at this point, and they would have been entirely invisible, had the moon been any brighter. Mr. Dire adjusted the glasses, perched on the end of his nose, to see the spots on the ground as best as possible.

He wasn't happy that the children had not kept their noses out of his business, and that The Scion was going to be troubled to hear about the fate that befell the plants that were in Mr. Dire's care. He was going to have to make some decisions on what reparations were due to Mr. Tom Miller.

As Mr. Dire turned his attention from the ground, to the lighted window that looked down on the farmyard where he was standing, he could hear the slightest hint of the pain that the daughter was experiencing. He suspected that she was in for quite a miserable tribulation over the course of the next few days. He knew that the saurian bites were particularly nasty, and she'd had more than her share of them.

The suffering of that little girl --recompense for what she and her little brother had done--

brought Mr. Dire some solace. That solace was all that was keeping him from exacting some revenge on the four of them at this very moment.

While their backs were turned, licking their wounds.

Mr. Dire lingered just a moment longer, wishing that the daughter, and that her meddling brother, would be as disconsolate as possible; they deserved it for what they'd cost him. He turned then to leave, walking out the back of the property, leaving through the small field of the saurian plants. As he stepped closer and closer to them, and then walked through them, they glowed with a crimson intensity that would have surprised Patsy and Jim, for it was far brighter than what they'd witnessed just a few minutes prior.

October 27, 1932

Patsy was dead three days later.

She ended up sleeping, fitfully, for the rest of that first night, with her mother dozing in a chair at her bedside. But, when she woke in the morning, each of the little lizard bites had become inflamed and slightly swollen. By the evening of October 22nd, Patsy was running a fever that continued to climb throughout the rest of her short life. Near the end, the pain from the fever --as it was baking her brain right inside her skull-- and the pain from the raw and stinging bites all over her body, had Patsy writhing in agony in her bed.

She died just after sunset on the 25th. That death, at least, was a release from the torturous torment.

Patsy was buried in the yard in front of the house, because it was the part of the yard that had very little utility in terms of fielding chickens or raising a crop of any kind. Norma and Tom agreed that it was the right thing to do. Tom built a small, wooden cross out of some spare barn siding that he had on hand. The whitewashed cross stuck up out of the ground to memorialize the grave. As it turned out, the Miller family, now totaling three members, didn't stay on the property long enough to need to whitewash the cross a second time.

October 29, 1932

It was more than a decade that the family stayed in the Bangor Springs area after Patsy's death, but that year --1932-- was one of the last years that they lived out on Old Smith Road. Not only could Jimmy's parents not stand to be around the homestead anymore, with so many memories of their daughter around every corner, but they weren't ever again able to raise enough of a farm crop to be able to afford living out on the farm.

After 1932, the growing of crops on that property became pretty impossible.

They ended up moving, as a family of three, closer into the town of Bangor Springs. Tom Miller picked up a job at the mill in town, which didn't pay much, but it allowed for him to be able to pay the rent for the rooms that they were staying in just east of the mill. Things stayed that way for about nine years, long enough for Jim Miller to make it the rest of the way through his schooling in the local school. When he left for his military service the year after his graduation from Bangor Springs High School, Tom and Norma left the area and headed to down-state Illinois, where Tom had some relation who were farming in Vandalia.

That's how the story of the Millers in Bangor Springs ended…

Almost.

Santa Fe - Six

'Max almost never calls me.' was Kathryn's first thought when she saw her sister-in-law's cell phone number come up on caller ID.

"Hello? Max?"

"Yeah, it's me."

"Is everything alright? Is Dean alright?"

"Yeah, everything's fine."

"Well, it's just that you hardly ever call me."

"I know. Odd. And, as it turns out, it's about to get even odder."

"Why? What's going on?"

"Kathryn, I want to talk to you about my past and your present."

"Uh, okay?"

"Dean and I were talking about your mystery guy the other night and he mentioned his name. James Miller."

"Yeah, so?"

"Well, the name raised a flag in my mind and I did some digging into my past, back to where I originally come from."

As irritated as Kathryn had been to take this phone call in the first place, she admittedly was starting to have her interest piqued.

"So what did you find?"

"It's not about what I found. It's about what I think you'll find when you speak to an old acquaintance of mine."

Max gave Paul Brachman's phone number to Kathryn, and they talked a little bit longer about the connection that Max had to Bangor Springs, Michigan. When they hung up, Max was hoping that Kathryn would take advantage of the opportunity. She was also hoping that she wouldn't have to get any *more* involved.

* * *

"Mr. Miller, I wanted to let you know that I've learned a bit more about you lately. As much as I've been able to uncover, anyway. I've been researching because I wanted to understand you better."

Kathryn was sitting as close to Jim's bed as she could, in the chair that she'd pulled over from the corner of the room. Of all of the various times that she'd spoken to him, over the years, she couldn't ever remember getting a response from him, no confirmation at any point that he'd even heard her or understood.

That's what made his response even more stunning.

Jim rolled over in his bed --he'd previously been staring at the sky out his window-- to face Kathryn seated in the chair. His eyes, in rare form, were cognizant and bright. It made Kathryn want to continue.

"I know about Patsy, and I know about your father. I know about southwest Michigan, and the farm out on Old Smith Road. I even know about your high school sweetheart -- Barbara. So much I couldn't discover, stuff I'd love to ask you about, but it helped me to feel closer to you." Kathryn reached down into her purse, seated next to her on the floor, and pulled out the package of letters which she'd tied together with a single piece of powder blue silk ribbon. As she brought the letters into his line of sight, he reached out to have them. She handed them over.

The sound of his voice, when it came out, was barely a rasp, for all that it had been neglected recently.

"I knew that you were different than the other nurses. I knew that you were the one that I'd speak to one day, finally having something to say."

Kathryn became aware that her jaw had dropped only after Mr. Miller was chuckling, an elderly, geriatric chuckle, at her facial expression.

"What are you telling me?" she replied out of her shock, with barely a moment to have thought of what to say to him. "Do you mean you weren't talking this whole time because *you didn't have anything to say?!*"

"Can you think of a better reason for not talking, my dear?" Jim croaked. His vocal chords sounded like a breeze through a wet kleenex.

"Wait till everyone else hears about this! Wait till Nora Lietz hears about this!"

Jim reached over to touch her hand, as it rested in her lap, to get her attention.

"She's not going to hear about this, Kathryn. None of them are. Because you're not going to tell them."

Kathryn looked at him for a moment, concerned that maybe he wasn't thinking clearly enough to understand what she was saying. But then, his lips warmed into a charming smile, a smile unlike any she'd ever see on the face of James Miller.

"I'm dying," he continued, "which you might already suspect is the case with a ninety-seven year old man." He coughed a little bit, but it had no real force behind it, and Kathryn recognized it as more of an attempt by Jim to clear his throat. "The breaking news is that I think it's going to be soon. My mind's been getting worse and worse, and I can't imagine it'll be long now."

Kathryn pushed the chair away from the bed and stood. She suddenly felt like she wanted to be free to move around the room a little bit, to get away from his revelation. This was getting way heavier than she'd imagined it being. She took a few steps away from the bed, then turned back around to face him. As she waited for him to continue, she looked down at him, laying there.

"This little secret is going to remain between the two of us. No one else needs to know, especially if I won't be around long anyway."

"But, what about what I've learned about you? What about your story? What about my questions? You've got such an interesting story and no one is ever going to hear it if you stay mute --or worse-- die too soon."

Jim looked at Kathryn, registering her objection while also holding her with his gaze. The pause allowed him a moment to think.

"Could you get me a glass of water, please? Talking for the first time in years is a dry endeavor."

Kathryn walked over to the sink in the room, pulled a disposable paper cup out of the dispenser next to the sink, and filled it for Jim.

She brought the cup to him, handing it to him before sitting back in the chair next to his bed. Jim drained the cup in two swallows.

They were like that, the two of them, silently in each other's presence for several moments; Jim, gathering his thoughts -- Kathryn gathering hers.

After, he started back up again.

"If you've read all of these," Jim pointed to the letters sitting in his lap, "then you've caught a lot of the highlights. I can answer any other questions you might have as we sit and chat. However, the most important part of our discussion will have to focus on my final wishes."

Kathryn wasn't in a position to argue with the man, so she assented by going to the bedroom door and closing the two of them into the room. Then, she asked her questions and listened to his inclinations regarding the end of his life.

* * *

When they were through, and Jim had drifted off to sleep --exhausted-- Kathryn stood as quietly as she could, numb all over, all the while staring down at him. As she thought things over, she was pleasantly surprised to discover that there didn't seem to be any significant part of her --her spirit or her mind-- that was opposed to his wishes, the things that he'd asked for. The Kathryn Santos of an hour ago would have scoffed at the idea that she might just randomly become the executor for a stranger's estate. But --somehow-- the person that she was now was a different person from whom she'd been earlier that same day.

And so, she smiled back at the sleeping James Miller, warmly, and began developing a plan to do exactly as she'd asked him to do.

* * *

The long-term effects of saurian venom haven't exactly been studied by The Scion, and because *they've* not done it, of course that means no one has. Mr. Dire would have liked to do some studies on the subject, eventually. The problem being, of course, that people don't tend to survive the saurian's bite for very long at all.

But, Jim Miller had survived, for more than eight decades past the fact of his being bitten. Of course, he'd been bitten just the one time, and by an unripe organism at that.

For as long as Mr. Dire had been with The Scion, he'd been studying the little lizard-like creatures, especially the usefulness of their venom. That research had hinted at the fact that the venom had certain neurological and psychological side effects. For as long as Dire had wondered about Jim Miller, he'd wondered about his psyche, whether or not Jim was deteriorating mentally.

From a practical standpoint, Dire had also wondered about the possibility of dosing the venom somehow, or perhaps diluting it, in an attempt to develop it into a toxin -- for The

Scion's use, of course. But, without any research, he had no real proof on the matter.

Jim Miller, however, was the proof. The proof that the venom of the saurian does eventually lead to madness, of a sort.

Separated from Mr. Dire, thankfully, by about 1300 miles, the dying Jim Miller would have been quite the matter of interest to the bald man. Jim's clandestine decision, in the summer of 1945, to settle in a different part of the nation than the part where he'd been born and had grown up, ended up separating the two of them.

Unwittingly, though, they were about to get quite a bit closer. And Kathryn Santos was going to help to make it happen.

* * *

Four days after Kathryn and Jim had their heart-to-heart, Mr. Miller passed away. As nice as it is to hear of the very old and the very tired, quietly passing away in their sleep, James didn't go out quietly at all -- odd, considering how silent things had been in Room 204 for the last five years.

Nora Lietz was sitting behind the duty desk, perched on top of a tall stool, typing away on the computer in front of her, entering medical information into the records of the different patients in the facility, something that she always did near shift-end. By her side, in the other stool behind the duty desk, was Kathryn.

She sat listening to the clicking of the keyboard under Nora's hands and staring at the clock on the desk, promising her that she was only nineteen minutes away from being able to go home and get some rest. Kathryn hated the morning shift --10 p.m. to 8 a.m.-- but she'd traded with Darcy who was in desperate need of someone to step in for her at the last minute. Darcy had even thrown in a pair of tickets to see the Santa Fe Fuego play out at Fort Marcy Park, and Kathryn had figured it was a good deal, helping out a fellow co-worker and getting some baseball tickets.

She was going to have to remind herself, the next time that one of her co-workers asked her to cover the morning shift, how much she hated the morning shift. No matter what incentives they were offering.

Then, out of the morning silence, a scream, more bloodcurdling and loud than one would have imagined coming from a geriatric, came from down the hall. Kathryn looked up from the clock, and turned her head slightly, one way, and then the other, to determine where the sound --the scream-- was coming from. To her, it sounded like it was down the #2 hall. Kathryn instinctively turned to look down the hall. She thought for a split second about the scream, deducing that she was hearing a man's scream.

There was only one man living down the #2 hall.

Kathryn jumped from her seat and was halfway down the hall before Nora even knew what was going on.

When she got there, Kathryn saw James in the bed, his back arched up off the bed, his sternum pointing to the sky and his entire torso being supported by his feeble neck and lower back. The position suggested extreme anguish, and the continued screaming confirmed it. It wasn't as if Kathryn had never seen Jim like this before -- having a physical 'episode'. Truth be told, it had happened as many times as Jim had had his worst days. This time, though, Kathryn was surprised by the extreme nature of his fit. The paramount complexion of this situation caught her off-guard, especially since he'd mentioned to her the other day that he thought he might be dying soon.

By the time that Nora made it to the door of the room, Kathryn was already taking Jim's pulse and getting her stethoscope into her ears, to be able to measure his blood pressure with the nearby pressure cuff. She turned to Nora and uncharacteristically started telling the head nurse what to do.

"He's quite obviously in some sort of physical distress. Probably need a sedative. Maybe diazepam?"

"Not diazepam. Unsafe." Nora replied.

"I'm less concerned about his safety than in the effectiveness and immediacy of diazepam. If you choose a short-half-life benzo, we're going to have to wait too long for it to work. He keeps screaming like this, and his heart will explode."

Nora looked at Kathryn, experiencing a number of different emotions in the moment. Anger at the insubordinate questioning, and the rush of being in an emergent situation, but also a level of pride at Kathryn's assessment of the situation. She thought that Kathryn would make a good head nurse someday. Someone Nora could trust when she eventually decided to step away from things.

"I'll go get the valium." Nora said, and she was gone.

Kathryn turned back to Jim, leaning over him still wracked by agonizing pain in the bed. His eyes were rolled back to whites in his head -- whatever he was seeing wasn't of this world. She placed her hand on his forehead, feeling the heat coming off of it even before her skin made contact with his.

And as she stood there, with her hand on his forehead, and Nora was on her way back to Room 204 with the sedative, a moment or two ticked by. Then, Jim was gone.

* * *

The experience of dying had been much different for Jim, inside of his mind.

For him, the overall impression was one of struggling to wake up. It was an odd feeling, for a man that had spent years wondering what the point of continuing to live was, wanting to be awake. But, just recently, Kathryn --her concern for Jim and her interest in him as a human being-- had convinced Jim that there might be a reason for continuing on, if someone else in the world wanted it to happen.

The problem was, this morning, that Jim couldn't wake up.

The best he could do was to wander around inside his own mind, except that there wasn't much left to see. Fewer and fewer of the rooms inside had anything in them worth visiting. More and more of the rooms were empty -- or worse, they contained the darkness, the evil that had initially only been in a single room, or maybe two.

This morning, though, Jim was in an entirely different place inside his mind, a place that he didn't recognize, not even as a corrupted version of a former familiarity.

James Frances Miller, during the last moments of his life, was wandering down a long hall, with rooms on either side, a hall unlike any that would have ever existed in a residential house anywhere, considering how long it was. To Jim, it looked more like a hallway in a hotel or some other kind of a facility. He noticed that the rooms were numbered, each individually, with even numbered rooms on his left and odd numbered rooms on his right. Where he stood, looking down the hall, Room 192 was closest, Room 193 a little ways down.

As he was noticing the room numbers, he heard a skittering, scratching sound. It seemed to be quite distant, as he could barely hear it at all. So, he walked by the first few rooms on either side -- low and behold, the sound started getting louder. As he continued on, he was sure that he was getting closer and closer to the source of the sound.

Coincidentally, the hallway was running out of distance.

As he continued, Jim could see, upon his approach, a window in the wall at the end of the hall. He could tell from still some distance that it was night outside -- how appropriate. He wondered if it was actually night-time -- would he have seen darkness outside of his window at the nursing home?

As he got closer to the window, closer to the end of the hall, the skittering got louder and louder. Jim, though, had almost lost interest in the source of the sound. Instead, he now felt entirely compelled to get to the window, to be able to look out of it. Something inherent to his soul told him that he *needed* to be at that window.

His steps continued him on his appointed course.

Once at the windows, Jim noticed that the sky was clear, and in that inky sky, a full moon hung, looking down on the whole scene, a single, gaping, gazing eye. Its sullen glow cast everything below in a pale, weak light, the ground and the plants and the structures. After a long moment of recall, Jim recognized the view as that of the barnyard from inside his childhood home. Jim saw the barn, and the barnyard, and the back of the property --where the crops were usually grown-- was off and to his right.

And, there in the middle of the barnyard, underneath the feeble radiance of the moon, James Miller saw a man, staring back up at him.

The shock of it --someone else with him, inside his own mind-- caused him to reflexively step back from the window, the way that you would if you were hoping to not be seen by someone who had most certainly done just that. Had there been curtains on the window, he probably would have grabbed them and snatched them closed, to try to hide himself.

It was then, at that point, that Jim noticed once again the scratching noise, as if it had gone and only just now returned. It was so loud as to most assuredly be coming from the room on his left. Jim turned and pushed open the door, a door that was already slightly ajar.

The number above the door read 204. 'Of course.' Jim thought as he walked in.

Inside the room, there stood the man who --just a moment ago-- had been down in the barnyard. Jim wouldn't normally have been able to tell whether someone he'd only seen at a distance was the same as someone he was seeing up close. Ninety-seven-year-old eyes aren't worth much for accuracy. But, in the dream, he *knew* that they were the same person more than he actually *knew* it. The old, bald man, dressed in black dress clothes, wearing a long triangular beard and rimless glasses, caught Jim's stare the moment that they were fully in view of each other. The man's eyes glowed an angry red, which seemed odd. But, it wasn't the color that was strange, for Jim had seen that color before, decades before.

'Well, that's creepy.' Jim thought.

The bald man reached out a hand toward Jim, beckoning him. Jim continued his entry to the room, walking gingerly toward the old man.

It was only then, once he was inside of the room, that he noticed the lizards -- the skinks. It was the sound of their tiny claws that had made the skittering noise, tens of thousands of claws making a sound that seemed thunderous once he was inside of it. His revulsion normally would have prompted him to leave. They were climbing the walls and scattered all over the floor. The only place that the little lizards weren't congregating was on a slim pathway that seemed to be reserved between him and the bald man.

"Don't you like what I've done with the place?" the man asked as Jim approached. The question, and its implied hostility, didn't stop Jim's motion toward him, although he would have wanted to stop. At this point, Jim was being drawn toward the old man, more than he was willingly approaching him, a vehicle on auto-pilot. This didn't make sense to Jim in the slightest, as he looked down at his legs and feet, willing them to stop. Nevertheless, he continued on, ever closer.

Jim ended up stopping as he stood directly in front of Mr. Dire.

"Room 204, Jimmy-boy. Last stop."

James Miller waited for the bald man to say more, having nothing to say himself. Sure enough, Mr. Dire continued.

"These little creatures sure are somethin', ain't they?" Jim imagined that it wasn't the vernacular that this man usually spoke -- something about the way that he was doing it seemed more artificial than it should have-- and Jim wondered why it was that he was putting on a show. For Jim's sake?

James looked around at the skinks, but he realized that they weren't skinks at about the same time that the memory, from long ago and far away, resurfaced in his mind to *tell* him that they weren't skinks. They weren't skinks eighty-six years ago, and they still weren't.

"Do you want to know the really scary thing, Jim? The truth of the matter is this -- they've been here the whole time. In your subconscious. Ever since you were bitten." Dire looked around the room in almost a full three-sixty, to reference the saurians. "Eating away at the corners of your mind, stealing your memories, eroding your sanity. You see, Jim, you are the only person to have ever lived any significant amount of time after having been bitten by one of these. And, that experience has connected you to them."

Dire reached out his extended right index finger, and Jim flinched, wanting to turn away. He was being held in place in front of the man by some unseen force, like a bug pinned to a mount. As the bald man reached out, the lizards in the room all started to screech, a sound that transported Jim back eighty-six years in an instant. He'd not forgotten that sound, not for a single moment since that night.

The bald man gently, ever so gently, touched Jim in the middle of his forehead, and as he did it, he said, "Somnus mortis". And before Jim had a chance to recall any of the Latin he'd learned in secondary school, eight decades earlier, everything went dark.

* * *

In the end, Butch and Kathryn worked together to do most of what Kathryn understood to be the final wishes of Mr. Miller.

Execution of the intentions of a man with no family to speak of, and no worldly possessions to distribute, was a series of pretty simple matters -- mostly phone calls, really. But, the two of them took extra care in making sure that Jim's plans were honored. He'd been specific in his desire that no memorial tombstone or head marker was to exist anywhere, so there wasn't any work to do there. He'd asked to be cremated, so Butch reached out to the Rivera Family Crematorium out on Rodeo Road -- pronounced just like the barrel-racing and bull-roping extravaganza-- to come to pick up the deceased and perform the cremation. Kathryn called the Santa Fe County Health Department to register the death, a task familiar to a nurse at an assisted living facility.

The two of them worked in tandem to do the things that needed to be done. While they were working on the issues, one by one, they got a call back from Gloria at the crematorium, just before lunch, to say that someone would be out to Casa Paz soon with a hearse. It was at this point that Kathryn excused herself to call her brother.

For moral support.

* * *

Dean arrived at the Casa Paz Assisted Living Facility a few minutes later, in an unmarked squad car, while Kathryn was sitting on a bench near the front doors, outside, waiting for him. The heat of the day, though it was late October, had already started to gather and build. The two hugged, for a moment, and Kathryn found strength and safety --where she'd always found it-- in his arms. But then, she felt him pull away, much sooner than she'd been prepared for. She stepped back and looked into his eyes, seeking an explanation.

"I need to talk with your boss, for just a moment."

Kathryn couldn't understand the request, and she wondered whether or not she was having a hard time because of the grief that she was feeling or because the request didn't seem to make any sense. Before she could come up with an answer, and under the pressure of his gaze, she pointed down the hall, looking for herself to correctly count the doors.

"Second door past the restroom, on the left."

Dean made a bee-line for Alvarez in his office inside of the nursing home. Butch was sitting behind his desk, about to make another phone call related to Jim's death, this one to the V.A.

"Are you Daniel Alvarez?" Dean asked.

"I am. And you must be Kathryn's brother, the police detective." Butch reached his hand out, across his desk and up toward Dean, and the two of them shook.

"Yes, sir. And, I feel like I must take this opportunity to let you know that I came across some strange information when my sister asked me to start investigating Jim Miller. Very interesting findings, indeed. About this nursing home and the way that it's run."

"Is that so?" Butch asked, trying to keep his cards as close to his vest as he could.

"It is. Mr. Alvarez, I think I might have some additional investigating to do, into this facility, when I get the chance. But, for now, I just wanted to let you know that I'm a little bit suspicious about the goings-on around here."

Butch paused, partially gripped by the emotional responses in his mind, but also occupied by the maneuvering of an intellect that was already planning a way out.

"Well, Corporal Santos, we can speak at some point in the future, if you'd like. For now, I think your sister could really use your help. Your support." Butch motioned with his head and neck toward the front of the building.

"Agreed." Dean replied.

"But also," Butch continued on, "you should know that I'm a pretty observant person myself. I still remember --about a month back-- when Kathryn came to me to say that she was going to find out what she could about Jim. Seems like one of her first steps was a fingerprint check. She ever mention that fingerprint check to you, Detective?"

Dean was well-trained enough to mask his physical reaction to Mr. Alvarez's words --never let them see you sweat-- but he was reacting internally nonetheless. For the moment, he thought the best approach would be to stand down.

"Enjoy the rest of the day, Mr. Alvarez. Perhaps we'll speak again soon."

* * *

Dean took Kathryn over to the crematorium --stopping on the way for some drive-thru fast food-- to fill out the final paperwork for the cremation, and to wait for the procedure to be completed. As luck would have it, the crematorium had an opening, so to speak, and they'd be able to process things rather quickly, all things considered. Kathryn told Dean, as they waited, that she was under orders from Jim to receive the dead man's ashes, and she seemed determined to follow through.

Dean knew better than to fight his sister when she had her mind set to doing something.

As the two of them sat next to each other on the reception area bench, each of them bent in half at the waist, heads in hands and elbows on knees, just waiting for the word from the staff, it occurred to Dean that he needed to know more.

“So, sis, what are you going to do with his urn, his ashes, once you have them.”

A second passed, and then two, and then Dean felt compelled by the suspicion growing in his head. He sat up and turned to his sister.

“Kate? What aren’t you telling me?”

Kathryn sat up as well, turning to Dean. She prepared the look that she always used when she needed to bend him to her will.

“You see, that’s the thing. Mr. Miller --Jim-- asked me to take his ashes to his childhood home. To distribute them there. Apparently, his sister died when he was very young and he wants --wanted-- his final resting place to be next to her.”

“So, a road trip?”

“Well, no. Not exactly.”

* * *

In the end, Dean determined that the best way for him to feel comfortable about the choice that his sister was making -- the choice to transport a dead man’s ashes a thousand plus miles across the heartland of the nation -- was for him to be in her company the whole time. But, by the time the cremation had been completed, there wasn’t much daylight left in the day. So, Dean booked two tickets on a flight leaving first thing in the morning, while

Kathryn had been accepting the urn and signing off on the final papers.

They headed out to the parking lot, back to Dean's squad car. Once inside, with the doors closed, he turned to his sister.

"So, it's settled then. We'll leave first thing in the morning, catch the flight to Michigan, follow Jim's final instructions, and be done with it."

"Right." Kathryn replied.

He started the car and began the short trip to take his sister back to her apartment. She sat silently next to him in the passenger seat, with the urn on the floor between her feet. Halfway home, Kathryn broke the silence.

"You've always been there for me, Dean. Always. Every single time that I've needed you, I've been able to count on the fact that you'd be there. I just wanted you to know that I really appreciate it."

"Of course, sis. That's what big brother's do."

"What is Max going to have to say about this?"

Dean thought for a moment, realizing that he'd not even considered that part of the equation up to this point. He started beating himself up for not having thought about his wife at all, but then he stopped, to answer his sister's question.

"She's usually pretty decent about things. I can't imagine that she'd have much to say about it one way or the other."

A few moments later, Dean dropped Kathryn off at her apartment. He watched her let herself into the building, urn tucked under her left arm.

* * *

"So, let me get this straight. Jim Miller's dead. Kathryn promised him that she'd spread his remains on the site of his childhood home, and you're going with --to Bangor Springs-- because you feel like your sister needs a chaperone?"

"Well no, not exactly."

"Then what part am I not understanding correctly, Dean? Why on God's green earth would you and Kathryn be heading back to a part of the country that I worked so hard to escape from?"

Dean took a moment to breathe and collect his emotions.

"This isn't about you, sweetheart. It's not like I'm asking you to come with. This really doesn't have that much to do with you at all. If it seems like a pill that's too hard to swallow, just look at it this way -- I am escorting Kathryn to the birthplace of one of the residents from her nursing home. Nothing more, nothing less."

Then it was Max's turn to try to de-escalate.

"Hey, I'm sorry. I didn't mean to upset you. I've just been on edge ever since I learned of the search that your sister has gotten herself into --has gotten my husband into-- and how it connects to my past."

"Well," he replied, "you couldn't have been that upset about it. Kathryn told me that you connected her with the local newspaper reporter in Bangor Springs, to help her search."

Max's eyes got big, and Dean noticed it. 'Saying that might have been a bad move,' he thought to himself.

"Look, Dean. I've worked pretty hard to bury my past in that place, and I'd rather not have all of that work undone. The thought that you're going to be within a dozen miles of my ex-husband is just hard to digest. But, I've also been trying --for years now-- to find a way into your sister's heart. I thought she might appreciate the help, that it might win me some points."

"No one is going to go digging around in your past, Max. I promise. If everything works out the way that I expect it to, we probably won't even be in the area for a full twenty-four hours. We'll have little to no time for gallivanting around, peeking into closets, looking for your secrets. And I'll be in touch as much or as little as you want me to be."

Max paused for a moment, trying to decide whether or not this was worth continuing to pursue. Dean didn't seem at all willing to budge, and she wasn't even sure that she wanted him to.

"That's fine." she said to him. "It'll be fine, and I'll be fine, too."

They worked together, after that, to prepare dinner. They ate together and watched TV together, but the tension between them never really went away. Not really. Max was having a hard time letting it go.

They ended up sleeping on opposite sides of the bed that night.

* * *

The next morning, Dean got his sister bright and early, and the two of them made their way to the Santa Fe Regional Airport, "connecting northern New Mexico with the world." The terminal looked like some angry god had dropped an air traffic control tower right down into the middle of some poor native's adobe house. Dean and Kathryn went inside, with the urn and some carry-on luggage. Dean had been able to book a flight to South Bend, -- which was as close as you were going to get to Bangor Springs by plane-- and the flight connected through Denver and Chicago. They were scheduled to be in northwestern Indiana in the late-afternoon, local time.

Somewhere over Kansas, as Kathryn was thumbing through the emergency safety instructions she'd dug out of the seatback in front of her, Dean stared out the window at the ground far below. He thought to himself that it ought to be a pretty simple matter to get in, get this task done, and get back to New Mexico.

Hopefully.

Bangor Springs - Six

Paul Brachman had a personal policy against answering his cell when he didn't recognize the number. It was a quirky habit for a journalist, especially when he worked in a business that regularly put him in touch with people with whom he'd never previously spoken. But, in Paul's mind, the benefits outweighed the drawbacks. He never got any of those annoying sales calls, or any prank calls, either. No scammers trying to convince him to tell them his credit card number or his social security number. In exchange for that, Paul was willing to inconvenience people who'd be forced to leave voicemails when he ignored their initial incoming calls.

However, when you know that you're going to be getting a call from someone, it's possible to prepare for that in advance, with a little planning. When Paul spoke with Maxine Smithers, whose new married name was 'Santos', come to find out, he gave her permission to put his phone number in the hands of her sister-in-law, Kathryn Santos. He'd also remembered to ask Max for Kathryn's number, so he could program it in his contacts -- in preparation for her eventual call.

The very next day, Paul was actually sitting in front of his 'Miller's Field' files when his cell phone chirped in his pocket. He looked at the caller ID and it read 'Kathryn Santos'.

"Hello. This is Paul Brachman."

"Yes, Mr. Brachman. My name is Kathryn Santos."

"Yes. Hello. Max told me to be expecting your call."

The two of them exchanged some pleasantries, back and forth, including some conversation about the differences between autumn in the midwest and autumn in the southeast. They marveled about the chances -- as astronomically small as they would seem to be-- that her patient would be a man that Paul had been trying to locate for years.

"So, Mr. Brachman, I'd love for you to be able to tell me as much as you might know about James Miller."

"Well," Paul began tentatively, "I really don't know that much at all. He's a graduate of Bangor Springs High School, class of 1939. His senior portrait hangs in the high school hallway with the other members of his class from that year -- pretty handsome. He enlisted in the war after the attack on Pearl Harbor, December 1941. His parents have preceded him in death. He had a sister, but I've always assumed that she's gone."

"Yes." Kathryn replied. "She died at a fairly young age. What else do you know?"

"Well…" Paul thought quickly, trying to conjure up things to say, as if he was trying to prove his worth as an investigator. "I know that Jim lived in Bangor Springs his whole life, up until his enlistment. Out on a farm northeast of town. Parents were Tom and Norma Miller, but I never knew his sister's name. Had a high school sweetheart that he left behind named Barbara Bailey. Much more than that, and you're bleeding me dry."

"I see." Kathryn answered back. "In that case, it might be that I know more than you do, at least with respect to Jim's childhood. You see, I recently came into possession of some letters, written to him by his parents, and they shed a bit of light. Unfortunately though, the answers I was hoping to get from you may have forever been lost to the passage of time. Details about the death of his sister in particular."

"Ugh," Paul grunted. "I'm sorry that I couldn't have been more helpful to you."

"That's alright, Mr. Brachman. You've helped me out a little bit. Hopefully, this information --yours and mine-- will assist me in trying to get Jim to open up a little bit. He's kind of a hard nut to crack, if you know what I mean. He's not said a word in five years, and the last word he said at that point was his sister's name."

"Which was?" Paul asked, maneuvering for the information.

"Patsy." Kathryn answered. "Turns out, she's buried out on that farm property you mentioned, dead almost eighty-six years."

"Is that so?" Paul said, intrigued.

* * *

It was, in all likelihood, as close as Paul was ever going to get. He knew it, deep down inside, and he was going to have to come to terms with the reality, from the sounds of it. He sat at his dining room table, with the phone and the files sitting in front of him, integrating what he'd just come to know into the narrative that had been in his mind all these years.

The problem was, he couldn't help but feel a little dejected. To have been the person most interested in the history and the situation out on Old Smith Road, for all these years, and then to be largely left out of the most recent developments regarding the Miller family -- it stung, a little bit.

In fact, Paul couldn't remember there ever being a time when he wasn't the person to solve the case, not in more than a decade as an investigative journalist. He'd covered a number of different stories, throughout the years, all of them of less consequence, in the grand scheme of things, than the story of Miller's Field, but he'd been the one each time to 'do the reveal', as it were. Paul had seen enough whodunit mysteries in his life to know that the main character was the person at the end who stood in front of the others and explained the whole scenario, laying it bare for all to understand. Then, the kudos and the accolades came, when everyone was proud of you and appreciated what you'd done.

He wasn't going to have that with Miller's Field, it seemed.

Imagine working so hard on a crossword puzzle, having only a couple of last clues to solve, and then someone else comes by, while you're away, and takes the final steps without you. So frustrating.

Paul sat there, thinking about going down there -- a quick trip down to New Mexico, to find out what he could from James. But, it wasn't as if he was guaranteed anything once he got down there. From the sounds of it, Mr. Miller wasn't exactly the communicative type, and he'd be an arrogant fool to think that someone would just start gabbing simply because he'd entered the room.

Of course, there was still the investigating that he was finishing up with respect to the Shumer building project, and the five deaths that had occurred out there. Something strange going on with that. Just recently, with respect to the deaths of Jorge, Nick, Luke, Emily, and Dexter, Paul Brachman had begun to suspect that Mr. Dire was somehow involved.

This was starting to feel like a 'Mr. Dire' kind of mess.

Because he'd dealt with Dire before, he knew that Dire was as much a part of Bangor Springs as Hodge's Hardware Store was, if not quite a bit less well-known. It honestly hadn't occurred to Paul, however, at any point during his years of researching, to chalk up any of what was going on at Miller's Field to the man in black.

All of Paul's 'Miller's Field' interest over the years should at some point have brought him to the realization that Dire might be involved somehow. But, there'd never really been anything that looked like it might be his kind of workmanship, in Paul's estimation. The closest Paul ever came to thinking that Mr. Dire might be connected was that information that he'd gathered about the work that Bob Smithers did in the summer of 1993. Apparently, the farmer was trying to hire some ag professor from Michigan State University to help him to solve a farming problem on the Miller's Field property. If Paul had ever come to know anything more, like the name of that ag professor, he would have gone fishing at the police department -- to cross reference the existence of any police reports from early August of 1993, mentioning that professor. Paul had heard at some point, from some nameless person, that part of the story had involved the local Holiday Inn.

But, like always, it all turned out to be another dead end. When it came to researching Miller's Field, that's what you usually got.

When Paul Brachman had looked into the ownership records of the property, years ago, he'd discovered that Bob Smithers had been able to pick up the property in the late 1980s at a land auction. Between Bob Smithers --who turned out to be the uncle of his best friend's first wife-- and Tom Miller, no one had ever officially owned the property on Old Smith Road.

After the Millers left town, early in the 1940s, nobody went anywhere near the property -- except for maybe the squatters who were known to stay in the abandoned buildings from time to time. It eventually came to be known as Miller's Field in the 50s and 60s, primarily because of the spooky stories that surrounded the property. But as time went by, the rumors and the gossip --most of it-- died with the people who carried those tidbits with them.

Ownership rights to the property fell back to the municipality, after an extended period of time when no one owned the land, or seemed to be interested in owning it. In fact, at one point in the eighties, the fire fighters of Bangor Springs used the dilapidated and abandoned buildings for fire fighter training, eventually burning both of them to the ground for the sake of the educational experiences of their team.

Paul had come to know so much, over the years, but it hadn't been enough. As many of the puzzle pieces as he'd been able to put together, the puzzle had turned out to be incomplete. Paul had been avoiding, for years now, coming to terms with the realization that the story wasn't his to bring to a close. As long as the case was still 'open', he hadn't been forced to realize the truth. Now that it was closing, though, it seemed like he was being left out of the final act.

With Kathryn Santos and James Miller on the other side of the country, Paul wasn't in the driver's seat, obviously.

He stared at the papers, thinking seriously about putting them all back in the manila folder and putting the folder in the garbage. He was angry, and he realized it, and he knew better than to act impulsively in a moment of fury. Instead, he grabbed his cell phone and walked out to his backyard.

* * *

There's nothing like reaching out to a friend when you're feeling down, getting some encouragement from a trusted source. However, Paul felt like he also had a confession to make.

"Bucky's Bar. Bruce speaking."

"Hey, Buck. It's me. Paul."

"How many times do I have to tell you -- I might be the last business in Bangor Springs with a landline, but that doesn't mean I don't have caller ID. I saw it was you before I picked up."

"Well, I guess I should be encouraged that you saw it was me and still *decided* to pick up." Paul was wearing his despondency on his sleeve.

"Dude, I can't imagine not picking up when I know it's you... unless you've done something that I ought to be mad about."

"Not really. I mean, I don't know why you'd be mad. It wasn't really that big of a deal, now that I'm looking back on it."

Bruce's tone ticked up a notch in its hostility.

"Paul, what did you do and how angry am I going to be?"

"I talked to Max yesterday."

Bruce Randolph paused for a long moment and Paul could actually hear the gears whirring inside Bucky's head.

"Okay? And...?"

"In my own defense, she called me."

"No reason to be mad yet. Keep going."

"We didn't even really talk for that long."

"Paul, I don't care how long you talked. What did you talk *about*?"

"Her sister-in-law."

"Well, since she's an only child, I'm going to deduce from that statement that her new husband has a sister."

"He does. Just got off the phone with *her* a few minutes ago."

"Alright, now my temperature's starting to rise. You mean to tell me that you've spoken with both my ex-wife *and* her new sister-in-law? In the past twenty-four hours? Next you're going to tell me that you're golfing with her new husband this weekend."

"Not quite. Take it easy. All this has to do with a story I've been working on."

"A story?"

"It's about Miller's Field, Buck. Your ex-wife's new husband's sister works in a nursing home where the last living member of the original Miller family is a patient."

"Wow," Bruce replied. "Talk about your major coinky-dinks."

FROM BRACHMAN'S FILE #6 -- June 24, 1982

These things take on a life of their own -- they start out as rumors or gossip, and then they develop into legends and lore, given enough time. It's been more than fifty years since anyone lived on the property out on Old Smith Road. Generations have come and gone during the time that the rumors and gossip about what happened on Miller's Field have germinated into stories and myths.

Now, the whole thing is a little out of control.

The farmhouse that Jim, Patsy, Tom, and Norma lived in while they were living out on Old Smith Road was, in 1982, in serious disrepair, to say the least. The fact that it was standing at all was either a testament to the people who'd built the original structure, Tom Miller included, or a witness to the fact that most people didn't ever have any reason to trespass on the property --or in the house-- at Miller's Field. Maybe, because it'd been left alone, it was able to survive.

But, not all of the citizenry of Bangor Springs knew well enough to stay away.

* * *

"I can't believe that we agreed to do this."

Sandy Molleston looked at Pam Tolliver with a sneer of contempt on her face.

"Pam, you need to relax. It's not like you shouldn't have seen this coming. The cheer squad has been using this little 'initiation challenge' for years and years. It's most likely the case that all of the girls on the current squad had to do this same thing, and they must have all made it through successfully. Just calm down and make the best of the situation, why don't you?"

"I just don't know, Sandy. Have you heard the rumors about what happened on this property, all those years ago?"

"Be real. This isn't anything to worry about. Just imagine that you are spending a single night in the worst hotel you've ever been in."

The two young women try as best they can to settle into the environment. Sleeping the whole night through in a dilapidated, abandoned house, in the middle of a field in the middle of nowhere, in the midst of swirling hearsay and wives tales about the place, wasn't going to be easy. But, it was the task that lay in front of the two of them --as freshmen recruits to the cheer squad at Bangor Springs High School-- so they each took the supplies that they'd brought with them, sleeping bags and pillows and bug spray and such, to try to build a place for themselves to get through the night in these unusual surroundings.

"My mom is probably still trying to get over the news that I am spending the night with Pam Tolliver." Sandy volunteered, after the two girls had finally squared themselves away.

"What is *that* supposed to mean?" Pam retorted.

"Well, nothing, other than we've never been friends. If I hadn't convinced her that it was a cheer thing, she probably wouldn't have believed me at all."

Pam retracted her claws.

"The whole thing should work out just fine. I told my mom and dad that I was staying at a friend's house, as well. Assuming nothing happens that would require them to find us at the places that we told them we'd be, they probably won't ever suspect a thing."

Sandy looked around the place, sitting on the sleeping bag that she'd laid out on the bare wood floor. In order to get the supplies that she thought she was going to need to make it through the night, she'd lied and said that Pam had invited her to camp out in her backyard. Then, packing sleeping bags and lanterns had made more sense to her parents.

"You know, it probably won't be much longer that this house is still standing. By the looks of the place, it's probably not even structurally safe enough for us to be in."

"Well," Pam replied, "I'd imagine that is part of what makes the initiation task such a challenge."

Sandy peered up through the large hole in the ceiling above where they were, a hole that continued on the second floor, up through the roof of the place. She could tell by the color of the evening sky, through that hole, that it wouldn't be long at all before it was full dark outside.

Pam saw Sandy gazing up at the hole.

"I wonder what made a hole like that."

"I saw a partial tree trunk outside when we first came in, not far from the house. My guess would be that a branch fell through the roof at some point. Then, the exposed floor on the second story would have eventually rotted away for having been open to the elements."

"Makes sense." Pam said.

Sandy turned and fumbled with the battery-powered lantern that she'd brought with her. She'd conned her father into letting her bring it, even though it was his favorite lamp, and he wasn't eager to let her take it. Its large lantern battery made it too heavy to carry around, but Sandy thought it would make a good nightlight, if the battery lasted all the way through the night. She turned it on and its brightness lit the gloomy room, casting long, drawn-out shadows that climbed the walls in all directions.

"So," Pam began again, "what's the game plan, here? How are we going to make it through the evening?"

"Well, in my mind, it's pretty simple. This time of year, the darkness of the night only lasts for about eight and a half hours, according to my encyclopedia at home. So, I'd say we just go to sleep. By the time each of us has had a full night's rest, the sun will be rising and we will have slept through the scariest part of this whole thing."

Pam seemed a little skeptical of Sandy Molleston's plan.

"How do you expect to be able to fall asleep? I don't know about you, but I don't think I'm going to be *able* to sleep, considering these surroundings."

"As for me," Sandy answered back, "I never really have a hard time falling asleep."

Sandy Molleston laid back and wiggled her way into her sleeping bag. Inside of five minutes, she was asleep and snoring. Pam thought that, even if she had a snowball's chance in hell of falling asleep, Sandy's snoring might not help the cause at all.

As she was laying, waiting for sleep to take her away from these strange circumstances, she thought of how she'd gotten here. Cheer seemed like the right choice for a girl looking to pad her resume for an eventual college application process, especially if you couldn't run or handle a basketball. And she knew, as most girls did, that cheer was a great way to catch the eye of any of the football players or basketball players or baseball players, if that's what you were wanting to do.

Not that *she* was wanting to do that.

That evening, they'd been picked up, each of them, from their own homes by an upperclassman (upperclasswoman?) on the cheer squad. Pam's mom had been so delighted at the prospect of her daughter getting a place on the squad as a freshman that she was in no place mentally to be hyper-critical of the flimsy story.

* * *

Mr. Dire had been spending his evenings, when he happened to be in the area of Bangor Springs, in the dilapidated ruins of the Miller farmhouse out on Old Smith Road, for at least the past few years. The house was abandoned, and as such, it afforded him the kind of privacy that was hard to get through other means. And, Dire thought it was somewhat poetic for him to be on the inside of the house, having been left out in the cold on that particular night in October, so many decades ago.

On this evening, however, upon his approach to the building, he noticed it was lit up from within. 'Somewhat odd', he thought. 'It would appear that I have uninvited guests.'

* * *

A few moments later, Pam Tolliver was attempting to convince herself that what she'd heard outside was the wind, or some wild animal. Then, the doorbell rang.

As bizarre as it should have seemed to Pam for a doorbell to ring in a house near collapse and without any electrical connections to speak of --the inability to be hyper-critical during emotional stress was apparently an inherited trait-- Pam's first mental response was one of fear, rather than one of intellectual curiosity.

She looked over at Sandy - still asleep. The doorbell hadn't disturbed her in the least. As Pam was trying to decide what to do, the doorbell rang again.

'Better answer it.' Pam thought to herself.

Opening the front door of the house had been quite the trick when they'd arrived about an hour and a half ago, since the door wasn't hanging on its hinges quite square. Once again --this time alone-- Pam struggled to get the door open, this time from the inside. Upon doing so, she found a man standing on the front porch in a black dress shirt and slacks, with a coat draped over his forearm, and a blood red tie untied around his neck, its two ends sticking out from underneath both sides of his buttoned-down collar. As if this wasn't a peculiar enough look for a man standing in the dark on the dilapidated porch of a dilapidated house, he wore around his neck, on a long length of twine, a circular emblem made out of some shiny metal. The emblem itself looked like a plus sign with fingers radiating out of the left and right tines.

"Good evening." the man began.

"Who are you?" Pam cut to the chase.

"I was about to ask the same question to you, miss. What are you doing here?" Mr. Dire looked over her shoulder at Sandy, still asleep in her sleeping bag on the floor behind.

"To be honest, it's kind of a long story."

"And, as much as I love a good story," he replied, "let's get down to the heart of the issue, here. You see, this happens to be my property, so to speak. And that makes you and your friend over there trespassers."

"I'm sorry. We didn't know that this place belonged to anyone. It's not like you've been keeping up with the maintenance."

"Whether or not I've been keeping up with things isn't the point." the man said. "The point is, you're going to need to leave. You can't be here."

Pam, in a moment, considered Sandy, considered her belongings on the floor. But, for the longest part of that moment, Pam was thinking about the cheer squad. She really wanted to be on the team, and she didn't imagine that some story about a scary man chasing her off the property would serve as an excuse for why she didn't complete the initiation task. She needed to make it through the night in this house, and she wasn't necessarily ready to give up on that. For all she knew, someone from the squad had sent this man to scare them off, ruining their chances. With a newly cemented determination, she replied to Dire's demand.

"Sir, with all due respect, we have to stay the night here. We're not going to be leaving."

Mr. Dire looked at the girl, and he thought about just ripping her head right off of her neck. He knew that he had the strength to do it. One clean jerk and half the problem would be fixed.

But, killing a young girl would draw some attention, and the fact of the matter was that there might be a few people who knew that the girl was on this property. When she didn't show up tomorrow or the next day, his situation would be worse off, not better. In this instance, at least, he needed to be more diplomatic.

Mr. Dire looked at Pam Tolliver, and his eyes started to glow an angry red that helped him to make his point, as he repeated himself.

"You're going to need to leave."

You've never seen a high school freshman run so fast across an old farm field.

Watching her leave, Mr. Dire figured to himself that it was one down, and one to go. He turned and headed into the old Miller farmhouse to deal with the sleeping girl.

October 21, 2018

Dean and Kathryn landed at the South Bend Regional Airport, which was just a stone's throw from Bangor Springs, across the Indiana state border, at 4:17 p.m. local time, that Sunday afternoon. After connecting flights in Denver and Chicago, the two of them were happy to have arrived at their last stop for the day. Dean had made arrangements for their rental car during the short layover in Chicago, while Kathryn had called Paul Brachman to say that they were on their way to his neck of the woods. Paul had recommended the only hotel in Bangor Springs, a ten minute drive from the airport. They were sure to have openings available, according to Paul.

Jim Miller's request --that his ashes be dispersed near the grave of his sister and that this be done as near to sunset as possible-- seemed like it was going to be totally doable, and probably with some time to spare. Kathryn was excited as she put her carry-on in the back seat of the rental car and then sat in the front passenger seat. It felt good to be accomplishing the last wishes of a man who had reached out to her, confided in her, the last communication of a tired and mortal soul.

"So, I'm thinking that we'll head up to the hotel. What did your contact say the name of it was?"

"The Holiday Inn - Bangor Springs."

"Right. Makes sense. We'll head up there." Dean took a quick moment to search the hotel's location on his phone, plotting a course to it and checking on the distance. "Should be there about a quarter to five. Looks like it's a straight shot to the north. We'll check in, dump our stuff, find a place to eat in town, and then head out to this property."

Kathryn nodded as Dean started the rental car.

"I'll text Paul and ask him for a restaurant recommendation. And, just so you know, sunset is right around seven tonight."

"Copy that." Dean acknowledged.

* * *

Mr. Dire made it a point to be in the Bangor Springs area every year when the anniversary came around. Every October 21st, and usually for a few days before and after, the bald man with the triangular gray beard stayed in the vicinity of Miller's Field - mostly out of reverence for the loss of life that had happened all those decades ago.

Saurian life.

Never before, however, had he been treated to such wonderful accommodations. The last time he'd actually had a place to stay on the property itself was decades ago, before the old Miller farmstead was destroyed by some of the locals. Even at its finest, though, that place was quite a dump, compared to what this new construction would have ended up being, had the whole project not suffered such a series of unfortunate accidents. This place, by the looks of it, would have ended up being one of the finest homes in Knox County, all things considered. Their loss was Dire's gain.

He was going to enjoy the perks while he had the chance.

He and his friends.

They'd get a chance to enjoy the glowing from a pretty fine location indeed. The glowing was, after all, his favorite part.

* * *

But, of course, things were different on this particular anniversary afternoon, considering all that had happened in the past couple of days. Mr. Dire was feeling something that he hadn't felt in decades, an awareness that he'd almost forgotten was possible. He drilled down into the sensation, deep inside his mind, to confirm it - and there it was, in the recesses of his intellect.

Jim was getting closer. Had been getting closer for hours.

Wrestling with the limited number of ways in which a dead person might be able to return home, Dire could only conclude that someone else had gotten involved. Someone else was now going to be a part of the closing act of the story.

The intrigue both excited and concerned the bald man in black.

Mr. Dire knew that Jim was coming in the same way that he knew many other things that he couldn't have explained if you'd asked him - knowledge that became available to him as a member of The Scion. He'd been playing on that particular team now for ninety-three years - as a result, he was starting to get the hang of things.

The fact that Mr. Dire could still feel James Miller --nearby and also approaching-- was most certainly the result of there still being the tiniest amount of saurian venom in Jim Miller's body, in his tissues. Even though Jim was dead, and that death --along with the resulting natural processes of rot and decay-- were going to eventually put an end to whatever venom he might 'possess', it seemed that the essence was still there. That lingering trace put Jim on Dire's radar as a weak blip, and the advent wasn't going to take long, as far as the old man could tell.

And, wonder of wonders, that he'd 'return' on the eighty-sixth anniversary of their traipsing little trip into the back field of the property, the excursion that had cost the sister her life. The trip that had cost Mr. Dire a complete saurian crop that fall. That certainly couldn't be a coincidence, could it?

The Scion needed every saurian that they could raise. The saurians --and their venom-- were a very important part of the group's plans. Those two meddling kids had unwittingly upended a plan with a global scale, all those years ago. Admittedly, it hadn't taken Mr. Dire very long to get things back on track -- after all, it had been less than a dozen of the creatures, all together.

The real problem, the real reason why Mr. Dire was still sore about the whole thing all these years later was that Mr. Dire had a real difficulty with holding grudges.

Of course, he felt all of this, inside of him, swirling around in a spiritual stew of sorts, a mix of emotions and intuitions and premonitions. And, as much as you would think that a 153-year-old man would be better at sorting out all of his internal strife, if for no other reason than the extra experience that comes with extra years, Dire was still pretty mediocre, emotionally speaking.

The most important feeling for him to focus on, at the moment, seemed to be this feeling of developing energy, of a potential moment. It was gaining an intensity, gaining a dangerous capacity, for him and for The Scion. For all of his confusion, he was pretty sure that something was going to be happening this evening. He was going to have a little bit of work to do to see that the whole silly business with that field was brought to a final balance. Dire was becoming more and more convinced that it might be time to put paid to the history of Miller's Field, once and for all.

He would see to it.

* * *

"That was the best burger I think I've ever had. In my whole life. Ever."

Dean leaned back in his chair at the Hilltop diner, hands interlaced behind his head, exposing his distended belly. Of course, the distended belly of an athletic police detective in his mid-thirties doesn't end up adding up to a whole lot.

Kathryn looked at her brother and chuckled at his enthusiasm.

“And, I’ve got to say, my first ever country fried steak was quite the experience. Who knew we were going to travel all this way and the added bonus would be such an amazing dinner?” she replied.

Dean unlaced his hands to look at his watch, still leaning back on the diner chair on its back two legs.

“So, it’s 6:40,” he said, looking out the diner’s windows at the outside world, “and it’s already starting to get a bit darker out there, which means that dusk is coming. Do you have the address for this property we’re heading out to?”

“Sure do. Paul Brachman texted it to me during the meal. Here. I’ll send it to you.”

Kathryn tapped on her phone a couple of times, and swiped a couple of times, and then Dean’s phone chirped. He picked it up off of the table and looked at it. After a couple more swipes and taps on his end, he looked back across the table to his sister.

“Seems like the place is only a few minutes from here. Shall I settle the check and we can make our way out there?” Dean asked, offering his phone at arm’s length to his sister, to show her the map to the destination.

“Sounds like a plan, man.”

Dean caught the attention of their waitress --Juliette, according to her name tag-- and beckoned her over to the table to ask her for the check.

* * *

They arrived, the 'three' of them, at Miller's Field just as the sun was really starting to get serious about saying its goodbyes for the day. The light was golden in that special way that any photographer will tell you is specific to the time just around dusk. Long shadows issued from all manner of different pieces of this and that, sticking up out of the ground. Light was losing its war with darkness for the first time in many hours, and the skirmishes were happening all around - each shadow, oozing from each piece of detritus with any vertical profile to speak of, lying scattered all across the battlefield.

Dean and Kathryn pulled onto the path --that was supposed to have become Clint and Tami Shumer's driveway-- in their rental car, coming to a stop in front of the partially constructed house. The house that would never become a home.

Jim Miller's urn sat between Kathryn's feet on the floor in front of her.

The progress that Pioneer Construction made on the Shumer project --up to the point in time when they withdrew from the contract-- was enough for there to be, standing on the property, a skeletal edifice approximating a finished home in the same way that a set of bare bones approximates a human being - lacking in the 'finished product' department, but still quite a structure nonetheless. Most of the sides of the building were closed in with the flat sheet lumber that is commonly used in two-by-four construction for creating exterior walls, but many other openings still existed -- openings where windows and doors may have eventually been placed, had there not been a series of grizzly deaths occurring on the scene.

And, of course, there was the glowing.

Dean and Kathryn noticed it from Old Smith Road, even having been as far as a mile away from Miller's Field, for the red glow lit the sky in such a way that was hard *not* to notice. On the property itself, the glowing of the ground all around was as bizarre as anything either of them had ever seen. But, it wasn't so conspicuous as to outdo the glowing that was coming from inside of the Shumer home. Moreover, that particular glowing had a random pulse to it --not unlike firelight-- that the red glowing of the ground did not.

Dean and Kathryn got out of the car and each of them inexplicably felt compelled to head into the house, as if it were the most logical thing in the world to do.

It was then, as if on cue, that the two of them --Kathryn and Dean-- noticed a skittering sound coming from the house.

* * *

As Dean and Kathryn approached what was probably supposed to have one day become the front door of the house, the skittering that had grabbed their attention was getting louder as they drew closer and closer --a sure sign that the source of the sound was inside.

The open concept floor plan of the home, which was all the rage in modern home design, allowed for Dean and Kathryn to immediately have a view on everything occurring inside upon breaching the front doorway. While the home was not finished, probably not even in a state where it would have passed any initial inspections, Kathryn could --with some imagination-- envision what would have one day been a very lovely entryway onto a very lovely main floor.

However, her enchantment with what could have been was quickly overcome by the horror of what was.

A man, old enough to be their father and yet not so old as to be nearing the end of his life, presumably, sat cross-legged on the floor in the middle of the unfinished space. In front of him, a fire was burning, interesting in and of itself, since the concept of an indoor open flame in a space such as this was alarming. But, Kathryn noticed, the fire didn't seem to be burning anything at all -- she couldn't spot the fuel, be it wood logs, or sticks, or anything else flammable, at the center of the flames -- rather, the flame was floating about six inches above the wooden subfloor, an entity unto itself. Kathryn fought the urge to drop to the floor, on her stomach, to see if she could actually see underneath the flames, as they floated above the decking. Then, as she looked from the fire, to the old man on the floor near the fire, it occurred to her that it might not be that he was enjoying the fire, but rather that he was creating the fire through a level of focus from his mind.

If things like that were possible.

Like glowing red farm-fields or glowing red gravesites.

And while she had some questions about that fire, it wasn't even the most interesting --or alarming-- event going on in the space. It was at this point, seemingly for the first time, that the two of them simultaneously noticed the source of the skittering sound.

Thousands upon thousands of lizards were clamoring all over the floor. From wall to wall, from one end of the space to the other, they were writhing and pressing all over the floor boarding and all over each other, forming a reptilian carpet of chaotic movement. The individual members of the whole looked small, no wider than a couple of fingers, and much longer than they were thick. On top of each other, and underneath each other, side by side and also face to face, groups of them joined forces to create flows of them, coinciding with some groups while contravening others.

Kathryn noticed, upon looking, that there seemed to be several clumps of them in certain spaces, all over the room, as if they'd formed up onto something that had been on the floor as an obstacle. While Dean was wondering how it was that the old man didn't seem at all concerned with the concept of sitting on the floor in the midst of all of this beastly chaos --for it was enough to make him want to climb the walls just to try to get away from it all-- Kathryn was continuing to wonder what it was that was underneath those lizard formations.

The siblings stood, in the doorway, for moments that seemed like millennia. Watching the lizards. Watching the man. Looking and listening and just trying to process all of the sensory information that they were being presented with. Dean wondered mostly about the old man -- who he was, what he was doing here, what he had to do with them, all of them coincidentally being on the property at the same time. Dean's mind, in short, was doing cop things, detective things. Meanwhile, Kathryn was still unable to figure out what the lizards were molding up onto in different spots on the floor.

The old man, noticing Kathryn as she was noticing the lizard piles, broke his own silence.

"Lizards are mostly carnivorous, and there just so happens to be about twenty thousand of them in this room right now. That's a lot of take-out pepperoni pizza, and I'm not a man of unlimited means. And so, they are able to dine on what I am able to find."

Kathryn examined the lizard pile closest to their location, as they were still standing at the front-door opening of the building, and she was then able to see it. Breaks in the fabric of the lizards on top of the form revealed it to be a medium-sized carcass, probably belonging to some woodland mammal, pieces of its exterior flesh ripped away to reveal gaping holes leading into body cavities and such. Kathryn felt her stomach retch at the thought of the dead animal being consumed and deconstructed right in front of her. It didn't do her mind any good to realize that it was happening at a dozen different locations all over the main room.

“That’s him, isn’t it? There in your arm?”

The old man, who was quite bald and --at the same time-- in possession of one of the most perfectly triangular beards that Kathryn had ever seen, was pointing at the urn that she was carrying, snuggled in her arm. She’d tucked it like a running back hoping to make it to the end zone without coughing up a fumble.

“I don’t understand.” Kathryn replied, obviously at a disadvantage for not having understood everything that was occurring in this place and time.

“Perhaps I ought to allow you some leeway. Your minds must be reeling with all that they’ve been forced to choke down in the past couple minutes. I, on the other hand, have been looking forward to this moment for more than eight decades.”

The bald man stood with an agility that suggested that he was physically fit despite the appearance that he was heading toward the twilight of his life, just as the day was itself heading toward twilight. He stepped around the floating flame, making his way toward the two of them. The space that he left on the floor behind him was almost immediately filled in by thrashing lizards that seemed to almost be in a frenzy of some kind. Each of the steps that the man was taking, making his way toward the three of them --including Jim-- was clear of lizards only just before his feet touched the floor. Obviously, the lizards were aware of the man, his movements and actions, in a way that seemed unreal, beyond what average reptiles were normally capable of.

"The man whose remains are in the urn you're carrying was a very special man. For reasons that go beyond your level of devotion to him. You came all this way, under orders from him no doubt, and that noble dedication indicates something about him, or perhaps about you, but I am here to tell you that he was quite unique among living people on the planet. You might say, one-of-a-kind."

The two siblings looked at each other, each clueless as to what the bald man was getting at. And so, they waited for him to continue.

"Jim Miller was an eleven-year-old boy during the fall of 1932, and he lived on this property, with his mother and father, and his sister Patsy. I had a special business arrangement with Tom Miller --Jim's father-- that fall, an arrangement that Jim and his sister violated with their meddling into my affairs. As he may have already told you, his sister died for her obtrusion. Jim, however, paid a different price."

It was at this point that the bald man was standing right in front of Dean and Kathryn, close enough for them to carry on a conversation without having to shout over the noise that the lizards were making, what with their slithering and scurrying. He reached out both of his hands to Kathryn, wordlessly requesting to hold the burden in her arm. She couldn't imagine any reason for refusing him -- what would he do if she did refuse, she wondered. As such, she handed the urn over to him.

The bald man, dressed in a black dress shirt and black slacks, wearing a blood red tie, looked at the urn in his hands as if it were a priceless relic, the object of a life's pursuit. He even seemed interested in the urn itself, looking at its simple embellishments through the rimless glasses perched on the very tip of his nose. Kathryn noticed a copper medal, hanging at the bottom of a chain around the bald man's neck. The medal consisted of an outer copper ring, inside of which hung a suspended emblem, an insignia of some kind. Since most of the area inside of the medal was hollow, she could see the red color of the tie backlighting the medal.

"Oh, Jimmy-boy. Such a tortured life. Such a price to pay for interfering where you shouldn't have. So tragic."

The bald man handed the urn back to Kathryn, and she took it from him, freeing him of the burden.

"Did I mention that I was there, at the end? Yesterday morning. I was there when Jim died."

Kathryn's confusion prompted her question.

"What do you mean by 'there'? I was the only person in the room when Jim died. It happened right in front of me. In Santa Fe. Were you in Santa Fe yesterday morning?"

"No, I wasn't. Matter of fact, I was here. In this very room."

"So," Kathryn's retort was a little sassy, "can you explain yourself, then?"

The bald man locked her eyes with his and it felt to Kathryn as if he was trying to bore into her essence with just the power of his leer.

However, she was not the kind of person who was quick to break under pressure.

"To be blunt, I'm under no obligation to explain myself to the likes of you, young lady. It suffices to say that, while he was dying in front of you, he was also dying in front of me. His death, after almost a century, was at the same time overdue and also somewhat preventable. He may have been the victim of the slowest poisoning in history."

Dire stepped away from them, then, judiciously moving toward the nearest 'feast' that was going on. The man reached down and, after wiping away a couple of the creatures to give himself a clean purchase, lifted the carcass off the floor and into the air. Dozens of lizards fell off of the meat, screeching as they fell to the floor.

"These lizards," the bald man looked down as they crossed over the toes of his boots in an agitated turmoil, "are called saurians. They are a very rare breed, indeed. The only ones that exist on the planet are all in this room right now. And, speaking of rare, the two of you are now in a very exclusive group --because you've seen them-- for very few people have ever seen the saurians and lived to tell anyone else about them."

He dropped the dead whatever-it-was --hard to tell for as much as it had been picked apart-- that he'd been holding and crossed back over toward them. As he did this, he chuckled in a way that wasn't obviously malevolent, while Kathryn and Dean wondered how something could be considered rare while at the same time seeming to be in such obvious supply.

"Like I said, the only saurians that exist in the world are all in this room right now. Their existence has escaped the eyes of scientists and explorers for centuries. I possess --or rather, my organization possesses-- all saurians on the planet because we are particularly interested in their species and what it can do."

"So," Kathryn responded, attempting to punctuate the monologue that was developing, "what's so special about these "saurians"?"

The man in black slowly raised his two hands to chest height, palms facing each other, flexing in exertion all the while. In front of him, between the palms, a book appeared, floating in mid-air.

"Dean, take the book." the bald man said.

Dean felt compelled to comply with the instructions of a man who had power enough to know his name without him having offered it, and power enough to conjure a book out of thin air. He took the book from in-between the bald man's upraised hands. When he did it, Dean felt a bit of a surge, a charge of sorts, as his hands gripped the tome. As he drew it closer to himself, Dean noticed two marks on the book, bound in a dark hide that didn't seem to be a familiar leather to him. A large 'S' was gilded into the front cover of the book in a golden script, just above an emblem that matched the one that the old man was wearing around his neck.

"'S' is for saurian." the bald man spoke to the two of them, looking at the book.

Dean opened the book, and was immediately reminded of the encyclopedias that he and his sister had used, as children growing up in the last decade of the last century. He started to flip through the pages, making his way past the 'SAL's and the 'SAP's, heading to the entry on saurians. The two siblings, both very interested to know what they might be able to find out, started reading the entry, which took up almost all of the left-side page and the entire right-side page, at least.

As they were just getting started, the bald man loudly clapped his hands in front of the two of them, and the book poofed out of existence. Each of them spent an extra second or two, staring down into the space between Dean's upturned hands, where the book had just previously been, trying to process the fact that it was gone. Astonished by the disappearance, they both then looked up to the bald man, to see what he might do next.

"Let me spare you the reading -- I'll give you the synopsis. Saurians are dangerous little creatures because they are both poisonous and venomous. There aren't many beasts on the planet that can claim to be both. And, among all of the animals that are both poisonous and venomous, these saurians are the rarest. That man," he said, nosing toward the urn in Kathryn's arm, "is the only person on earth to have ever survived a saurian bite. It happened eighty-six years ago, on this very night."

Kathryn looked down at the urn in her arm, and wasn't surprised to notice, out of the corner of her eye, that her brother was looking at Jim's urn as well.

"Venomous creatures," the bald man continued, "bite or sting and their venom is injected in those acts. Poisonous animals, on the other hand, store poison in their tissues, and the poison sickens whatever other animal might eat them. Quite interesting when you think about it. Being venomous is a predatory adaptation, while being poisonous is defensive. In being venomous, a saurian is able to kill as a hunter. In being poisonous, a saurian is able to kill as prey. Of course, anything stupid enough to eat a saurian will suffer a fate of no consequence to the saurian, for obvious reasons. But --in nature-- it's pretty rare to find an animal that is suited to being lethal as both the chasseur and the quarry."

Neither Dean nor Kathryn had much to say to interrupt the old man's monologuing, so he continued.

"The fact of the matter is this -- when the Miller family children destroyed the saurians that they did, eighty-six years ago on this night, they released into the soil of this property a poison more powerful than the venom in any single bite from any of the saurians alone. The creatures themselves, as deadly as their venom might be..." The old man lifted his eyes from the two of them and looked off, past them and out into the yard. Kathryn turned to see what he was looking at, and she recognized the object of his gaze, for there was a patch of ground glowing more brightly than the rest, out past their parking spot. She wondered about Patsy's grave, but she spun back around when the old man continued. "...they are far more deadly as a poisonous prey."

Kathryn broke her stare at the lizards - saurians- all over the floor, to look at the man dressed in black with a question on her mind.

"If Jim was bitten, all those years ago, how did he survive the experience? How was he able to live all of those years after being bitten?"

"Well, there were a few factors working in his favor, the first of which was the prematurity of those saurians on that night. You see, they'd hatched before their time, in order to protect themselves, and they weren't fully 'ripe'."

"Ripe?" Dean replied. "You're speaking of them like they were garden vegetables. They look like lizards to me, and lizards don't 'ripen'."

"So," the old man replied, "what might look to you to be a lizard, of sorts, is actually something quite different. You've been taught to think of living things as belonging to one sub-group or another. That a vegetable isn't a bird and that a bird isn't a fish."

"Right." Kathryn responded.

"What if I told you that there are plenty of lifeforms on this planet that don't fit into the conventional scientific molds that you've been indoctrinated to think about? What if I told you that saurians aren't reptiles or plants, but rather that they are reptiles *and* plants."

Dean could tell by the look on his sister's face that he wasn't the only confused New Mexican in the half-finished building. But then, Dean watched as understanding dawned on Kathryn's face.

“Do you mean like a platypus?” she interjected. She wore a look of satisfaction on her face, believing herself to have come to understand the old man.

“Kind of. But not quite. How about this -- what if I told you that the book you were just reading from a moment ago was a single book from a series of volumes discussing all kinds of knowledge --that your scientists don’t have-- about plants and animals, from all over the world. That knowledge, about these life forms, is being guarded by the organization that I work for --The Scion-- because it’s knowledge that would change your entire understanding of existence.”

“But,” Kathryn replied, impatiently, “none of that explains why Patsy had to die that night. Why this man” -Kathryn shook the urn just slightly- “had to spend his life without his sister and at odds with his father.”

“THEY RUINED MY PLANS!” Dire screamed.

The bald man’s reaction, his immediate jump from slightly excited school science teacher to enraged lunatic, shocked Dean and Kathryn into each taking a step back from him, more out of reflex than any conscious decision. Dean’s foot came down clean, but Kathryn stepped on something that both smooshed and splintered under her foot.

The sound of it couldn’t have been audible, not in the midst of all of the reptilian tumult in the room, but she felt the sound through the sole of her shoe. The sound seemed to travel to her ear from inside of her, through the interconnectivity of the bones between her skull and her heel. The crunch and the sploosh were foreign to her, a young woman who'd not ever previously stepped on a sizable living thing. But, she also knew exactly what she'd done. In her mind. Unmistakably.

Every saurian in the room stopped instantly and turned, some twenty thousand of them, to face the three humans. This was stunning mostly because of the sudden volume change in the room -- previously, it had been hard to hear anything at all besides the saurians. But, as they all simultaneously ceased their movements, it became so silent as to be disconcerting. As all of this suddenly changed, Dean made a decision in his mind about his next move.

Approximately eighty thousand beady black eyes were now trained on the only people in the room. Whereas --previously-- the saurians had been ceaselessly moving, now not a single one of them even wavered. Motionless statuary, each of them seemed to be, all trained on three possible targets.

"Well now," the bald man began in a hushed tone, almost a whisper, "look what we've done, the three of us. I guess I should've mentioned that the saurians are awfully sensitive. I certainly didn't mean to startle you with my outburst. I've just been harboring quite a bitter resentment these eighty-some years. Probably not very healthy. Now, we are in a place, the three of us, that isn't easy to get out of. You see, as Shakespeare once wrote, 'blood will have blood'. The saurians are now quite intent at this moment to see what they ought to do next. Each of them is watching us to see what we'll do, as it will determine what they'll decide to do in response. They have a hive mind that is completely unique to all of reptilian life on this planet, and they are conducting a meeting amongst themselves at this very moment. Deciding what to do."

"In all likelihood," the old man said to the two of them, "not one of us will be alive five minutes from now."

It was then, before she'd even had a chance to think about what he was doing, before she'd even had a chance to object, that her brother pulled out the handgun that he always had on his person and shot the bald man right between the eyes. His movements were fluid and smooth, the sign of an individual trained in the use of firearms by profession. The back side of the man's head bloomed in a red cloud, a disparate mix of blood, and bits of brain, and pieces of skull. He slumped to the floor in a lifeless heap, the dark hole at the bridge of his nose --which hadn't been there a second ago-- trickling a single bead of dark red blood down the dead man's cheek and onto the plywood subfloor beneath. The sound of the single gunshot was so loud that it pierced Kathryn's perception of reality before she'd even come to understand what had happened, before she'd even been able to process all of the information from the previous four seconds.

She turned to look at Dean, even while all of the saurians were looking at the two of them.

"I made an executive decision."

"No kidding. But it doesn't really get us out of this situation." Kathryn motioned at the lizards.

"For that, I suggest running."

* * *

Patsy Miller and Jim Miller had run from the saurians, eighty-six years prior, and had almost been able to escape, the both of them. Of course, on that evening, the two of them --an eleven year old and a fourteen year old-- had been fleeing fewer than a dozen saurians, rather than twenty thousand of them.

Kathryn and Dean, however --full on adults and lacking in that magically nuclear kind of power that seems to propel only the youngest of humans-- were probably at a disadvantage, because of their relative age and because of the number of lizards from which they were compelled to flee.

Or, it's more accurate to say that they *would* have been at a disadvantage, if any of the saurians had decided to give chase. Dean and Kathryn completed the most pointless of fear-driven dashes, arriving at their rental car, Dean running around the front to the driver's door and Kathryn bringing up the rear but actually getting to her car door first, only to discover that not a single one of the lizard creatures were behind them.

"What the?"

Kathryn looked over at her brother, over the roof of the rental car.

"I know, right?! I would have sworn they were nipping at the heels of my shoes."

Dean squinted his eyes, to try to see better something that still wasn't going to be there, no matter how hard he looked.

"If they weren't interested in us...." Kathryn began.

"It doesn't even matter." Dean replied, fingering the remote fob of the car, unlocking the doors to allow the two of them in.

"Wait." his sister objected. "We can't leave yet."

"Why not? I'm not going to hang out to come to discover that the saurians are warming up on the bald guy in there and reserving us as the main course."

"You think those lizard things are in there, eating the corpse of the man that you just shot? That's quite a disturbing possibility."

"Well, since neither of us is going to head back in there to find out, having just set land-speed records to get out here, I guess we'll never know."

"Will you at least wait for two minutes?"

Before he even had a chance to answer, Kathryn was making her way around the front of the car. She knew he was going to wait. And she also knew what she needed to do.

"Be right back."

Kathryn continued walking, urn tucked under her arm.

* * *

The piece of property that the old man had nodded toward a few minutes earlier couldn't have been glowing so brightly when they'd arrived -- otherwise, Kathryn would have noticed it. It was out a ways, from the house and from the driveway, glowing so much brighter than the surrounding land, that it begged for attention. As she made her way toward it, Kathryn heard footsteps close behind her, and she only knew of one other human on the property at the moment.

"What do you think that is?"

"Based on what I read in those letters, it could only be one thing." Kathryn replied, taking Jim's urn into her two hands

Kathryn thought back to her last major conversation with Jim, of all of the questions she'd asked him --questions he'd freely answered-- and she became quite sure that the glowing spot on the ground, the spot glowing brighter than the surrounding glow, was Patsy.

Asking for their consideration.

And so, they meandered to the graveside.

* * *

She would have sworn, had she ever been asked about it by anyone after the fact, that the urn had been pulsing, throbbing as they stood there, which of course isn't possible. But, considering all of the other oddities that had already occurred that evening, things that were beyond her or her brother's ability to explain logically or reasonably, the fact that an urn -- containing the remains of a man who'd spent almost his entire life mourning a sibling's death-- might quiver at that sibling's graveside, didn't even end up registering on the top five crazy things to happen that night.

Dean kept looking back at the house, every thirty seconds or so, expecting to eventually see the wave of saurians coming to wash them away.

Remembering Jim's tale, and the details that she'd been able to glean from the letters, as they stood there in solemn memorial, Kathryn tried to picture what the original farmstead might have looked like. With Patsy laid to rest in the front yard, Kathryn looked off a little to the east to imagine a modest house, with a barn north from there.

Then, Kathryn imagined where the "tomato patch" had been, that proscribed piece of the property on which Tom Miller had taken the family's fate into his own hands, at such a detrimental collateral cost. She imagined all of the pieces that she needed to envision, in order to be able to play out a version of the narrative in her mind's eye. With her sibling by her side, Kathryn took a moment to picture those two siblings, nearly a century ago, invading the far-off parcel of land, releasing onto themselves the wrath of the little lizards.

* * *

Mr. Dire got up from the floor of the unfinished living room and dusted himself off. He wiped the three or four saurians that had clung to him as he'd risen, off his jacket. He removed the rivulet of blood from the bridge of his nose and his cheekbone with a kerchief from his pants pocket. He straightened his tie and reseated his spectacles on the end of his nose. As meticulously as he was doing these things, Mr. Dire also seemed to be rebooting -- re-engaging his mind, reorienting himself to his location, the circumstances of his surroundings, and the most recent turn of events.

From his position near the front door opening of the building, he exited the unfinished domicile. Into the night.

And the saurians followed after him.

They flowed out behind him, all twenty thousand of them, like the train of a formal dress he wasn't actually wearing.

He made his way out onto a lawn that was only partially lit, for the moon was between phases. His eyes adjusted to a dark landscape devoid of any signs of life or activity. The glow of the property was dying down now, for dawn was probably only a few hours away. The night was becoming emaciated, a mere shadow of its former self.

The part of the lawn that had been glowing all night, to a higher degree of brilliance than the rest, was still doing so. Mr. Dire sniffed the air in a fashion not unlike those approaches used by animals to detect the faintest of particle traces on the breeze, and it was toward this part of the property --toward the grave of Patsy Miller-- that Mr. Dire continued his walk.

And the saurians followed after him.

As he neared, the faint trace became an overwhelming stench. Mr. Dire knew still some twenty yards off what had taken place while he had been waylaid. The saurians picked up on the scent --tongues pulling particles from the air-- and waited behind Mr. Dire no longer, deciding instead to swarm the ground of the grave.

Mr. Dire stopped, allowing the saurians the space that they needed --all twenty thousand of them-- to form up on the grave, on the ground where the ashes of Jim Miller had been spread. As they did so, and as the ground beneath them continued to glow its angry red, the crimson light fought its way out from underneath the reptilian pile, under-lighting the saurians in a manner that Mr. Dire thought was pretty damn picturesque.

He stood back and watched. He knew that the saurians were eating the ash, consuming it --despite the fact that the ash would've been bereft of any nutritional value-- because they detected in it their own essence. The poison that Jim Miller had carried around in his tissues, for almost his entire life, was being returned to its owners, and Mr. Dire thought that there was something cosmically correct about the restoration of ownership rights.

As they gobbled whatever remaining ashes they could find, Mr. Dire thought about his wins and his losses. The night had not gone according to his plan, but it hadn't gone as poorly as maybe it could have. For that, he was appreciative. Kathryn and Dean Santos, of Santa Fe, New Mexico, were not likely to turn up in this neck of the woods again any time soon. As such, Mr. Dire didn't really consider them a part of the overall equation.

Aside from the ire that comes when a man vacates the contents of your skull with a bullet from his gun, Mr. Dire wasn't harboring any ill will toward the two of them.

They had, after all, returned Jim Miller to his proper resting place.

Mr. Dire chuckled at the thought as he watched the saurians finishing the clean-up.

* * *

Easterly Way, the road into which Old Smith Road terminally intersects at its southern end, makes its way out to M-192 --if you take it far enough east-- which is the highway that runs north and south through Knox County. So, from Miller's Field, it's slightly faster to take Easterly Way east to the highway and then take the highway south --toward Indiana-- if you want to get to the HIBS, as opposed to going into Bangor Springs and then having to navigate the lower speed limits in town and such.

Earlier in the evening, Dean Santos had connected his cell phone to the radio in the rental car, to be able to receive hands-free calls, among other things. This served the two of them well, leaving Miller's Field, since it allowed Dean to make an important phone call.

"Hello. This is 9-1-1. What's your emergency?"

"Yes, I'm calling to report gunfire."

"Okay. What's your location, sir?"

"I am northeast of Bangor Springs, out on Old Smith Road."

"Well, sir, that's not a residential area, per se." the female dispatcher answered. "Gunfire out in that neck of the woods isn't necessarily illegal. Are you sure that you didn't hear it coming from a private residence?"

Dean --on the fly-- steered the conversation away from where it was heading.

"Well, it seemed suspicious since it was coming from…"

He'd forgotten the name of the property. He turned to Kathryn, who mouthed 'Miller's Field' to him.

"...Miller's Field." Dean finished his thought to the dispatcher.

"Are you on the property yourself?" the dispatcher asked.

"Nope," Dean replied. He saw the rest of the conversation playing out the way that he wanted it to go, and the increase in his confidence level made his tone sound less dubious. "We were just passing by, heading south into Bangor Springs, when we heard the shots. We also saw a strange red glow coming from the field, and it looked like someone had a fire lit inside the building on the property."

The dispatcher paused, and Kathryn and Dean both heard her typing into a computer keyboard during the delay. A moment later, she responded.

"We'll send someone out to investigate. I'll just need to collect some information from you for the casefile."

Dean disconnected the call, knowing that most Sunday nights are slow nights in the 911 call center; the fact that they were willing to dispatch someone indicated as much.

By the time he'd completed the call, he was only a couple of minutes from their hotel. A couple more minutes past that, and Dean would be working on making whatever cocktail he could concoct from the contents of the mini-fridge in their hotel room. He and his sister would find whatever garbage they could find on the hotel room TV, and they'd probably both fall asleep to the din of that TV.

If either of them ended up being able to fall asleep at all.

Later…

A couple of nights later, out of the blue, Paul got a phone call from his best friend's ex-wife's sister-in-law.

"Hello?"

"Hello, Mr. Brachman. It's Kathryn Santos, from Santa Fe?"

"Yes, Ms. Santos? It's nice to hear from you again. I trust your stay in town this past weekend was enjoyable."

"Well, no, not exactly."

"Really? That's a shame. We didn't fall short somewhere on hospitality here in Bangor Springs, did we?"

"Nope. Not at all."

"Well then, what can I do you for?"

"If you've got the time to listen, I'd like to tell you the final chapter of the story of James Miller -- and of Miller's Field."

"I most definitely have the time, Ms. Santos. In fact, nothing would please me more."

* * *

The next evening, Bruce Randolph called Paul from his bar. He often called Paul on Wednesday nights, since the action at a bar on any given Wednesday night is usually pretty tame -- it gave the two of them time to catch up with each other on a pretty regular basis.

"So, what's been going on lately with my favorite newspaper reporter?"

"Well, you'll never guess who our town hosted as guests this past weekend?"

"Arnold Schwarzenegger and Maria Shriver?"

"Nope. I don't even think they're together anymore."

"Sonny and Cher?"

"Nope. In fact, Sonny's dead, Bruce."

"Well, then, was it…"

Paul interrupted him.

"You know, when I say, 'You'll never guess', I don't really expect you to attempt any guessing, right?"

"Yeah, I know. It's just fun to irritate you."

Paul waited for Bruce to stop his smart aleck commentary.

"So, tell me, who did we entertain over the weekend?"

"Your first wife's new husband and his sister."

Bruce was silent on the line long enough for Paul to wonder whether or not Buck had been upset by the news.

"What'd you say, Paul?"

"It's a long story, my friend, but I'm not going to tell it to you over the phone. I'll be down there in a few minutes, so clear me out a spot at the bar, and pour me a cold one, would you?"

Paul hung up the phone, knowing full well that there would be plenty of spots at the bar on a Wednesday night for Bruce and him to have a conversation.

* * *

A couple of weeks later, it was all over. During that time, a whirlwind of activity and interest descended on the property previously owned by Tom Miller, previously owned by Bob Smithers, most recently owned by Clint and Tami Shumer. Old Smith Road, near its southern intersection with Easterly Way, was a flurry of passing cars and investigators coming from and going to the scene. The police investigation that Kathryn and her brother had prompted from their 911 call that night had been the first investigation to conclude. Apparently, when the police had arrived to investigate the scene, minutes after Dean placed the call to emergency services, they didn't find any of the things that Kathryn and Dean thought that they would find.

A dead body.

A throng of mysterious lizards.

A burning fire in the middle of a half-finished residential construction project.

None of those things had been there when the cops showed up.

Except for the glowing.

In the end, the glowing had ended up being enough, all on its own.

* * *

Following the initial police presence on the evening of October 21st, a series of dominoes fell that ended up being quite spectacular inasmuch as they brought people into the tiny burg of Bangor Springs who would have never been here otherwise.

And Paul Brachman got to survey the whole thing, as the local newspaper reporter, of course.

Most of the people in town never even noticed this temporary increase in the popularity of the town. The management at the HIBS noticed, as investigators who were in town --from out of town-- needed a place to stay. Juliette and her fellow waiters and waitresses at the Hilltop diner noticed, for wait staff are always aware when the people that they're waiting on are strangers or not. Maud Patton noticed, one morning, as he was asked to deal with a customer who'd presented one of his cashiers with a "Federal Requisition for Fuel - DOT FORM 736". Maud gave free gas to a half-dozen cars within a couple weeks' time at the end of that October. He ended up getting reimbursed for the gas from the federal government the following spring.

The neighbors in the area of the southern end of Old Smith Road noticed, most of them just hopeful that things weren't too serious. They were confused about the differences between the DHS and the DHHS --just like anyone without a working knowledge would be-- but most of them came to understand that FEMA and the CDC were different federal agencies belonging to different executive departments.

A few of them even came to understand that, if the CDC and FEMA were working together on a project, it was pretty damn serious.

* * *

As nearly as Paul could tell, by the time the dust settled northeast of town, the federal interest in the situation was an interest in what was making the ground glow an angry red during the evening hours at Miller's Field. As much as Paul could ascertain from attempted interviews with government investigators that weren't interested in being interviewed, the CDC was on-site trying to find out whether or not the glowing posed a risk to the health of the public and FEMA was just looking for an authorization to lock-down all of south-central Knox County like the end of the movie about the extra-terrestrial -- surely, you've seen it.

But, as time went by, and as it had been happening for eighty-five seasons prior to this particular one, the glowing got to be less and less, after the actual anniversary of Patsy's death. A week later, and the glow was barely even detectable.

Government agents interviewed some of the locals, but they were especially interested in the people living most closely to Miller's Field. Those half-dozen families, mostly to the south of Miller's Field on Old Smith Road, all seemed pretty normal. Not obviously contaminated by any pathogen of any kind.

In the end, it all kind of just fizzled out.

Paul wrote up the story, as best as he could, for the Bangor Springs Gazette once it was all over. He did his best to include what he could, but he didn't want to end up sounding ridiculous. In his attempt to describe things without making it sound like he'd lost his marbles, Paul was happy with the copy that he'd written.

He waited the couple weeks before writing up the story because things were still developing out at Miller's Field, and it's hard to fully *tell* a story that's still developing. But, as it turned out, Paul had needed some time between Jim's death and the formulation of his thoughts in writing. Much to his own surprise, Paul had ended up grieving James, in a way.

Or, maybe it was more accurate to say that Paul's measure of grief was for the end of the chase. It's hard when you seek after something for so long, and then you end up with it, not to be a little overwhelmed by the end of the hunt. We become accustomed to the quest, and then the receipt of the goal puts an end to the pursuit. The grief for Jim's end, and for the end of the mission, made it hard for Paul to write anything that ended up sounding any good to him.

The story, when it finally ran in the paper during the second week in November, ended up generating some interest from his readership, mostly from the same people who always emailed him. People wanting to know how he got the 'inside scoop', people skeptical about the story and whether he was telling everyone the truth. Paul was happy that Kathryn and Dean Santos had long since returned to their homes in New Mexico -- it made them "unavailable for comment".

The construction site at Miller's Field, after the end of the investigation by the CDC and FEMA, was mostly left alone. Snows fell in Bangor Springs, as they tend to do, in November and December, and Miller's Field slept its way through another winter under a blanket of white.

An anonymous benefactor, in the spring of 2019, after the thaw, saw to it that the former construction project that was to be Clint and Tami Shumer's home was demolished. The demolition of the place went about the reverse of construction, ending with someone from Krieger Excavating coming out to fill in the foundation. When it was all said and done, the changes to the property, inflicted over the course of the past calendar year, were mostly unrecognizable.

Clint and Tami Shumer ended up building in northwestern Indiana, as it turned out. Cheaper property taxes.

The Mystery of Miller's Field, Solved
November 9, 2018
By Paul Brachman

I've been reporting on the local news here in Bangor Springs for just about fifteen years, give or take a few months. In

all of that time, I've tried my best to put rumors to rest, to bring facts to light. In this article, I need to tell you all about Miller's Field, and what I've come to know.

In the late 1920s and early 1930s, a small young family lived on the property out on Old Smith Road -- Tom and Norma Miller were parents to two youngsters named James and Patsy. They farmed the land, as best as they could, until a tragedy struck that took the life of Patsy and forever changed the dynamics of the family. They dealt with their grief and the loss for many years thereafter.

That tragedy most certainly had its effects on the family, but interestingly enough, it also had some effects on the property that we've all come to know as Miller's Field. As many of you know, or have heard from others, there have been some strange events associated with that piece of land, over the years. And even, just recently.

What many of you may not know is that Miller's Field was recently purchased by a husband and wife living two thousand miles away. You see, we were all set to have some new neighbors living out in the two-thousand-block of Old Smith Road. Clint and Tami Shumer -- originally from central California -- were building a home out there earlier this year, but Miller's Field wasn't set to receive any new guests, as it turned out.

This article is written, in part, as a memorial to Jorge Gutierrez, Nick McCoy,

Luke Lang, Emily Carson, and Dexter Booker. May they each rest in peace.

Back in the late 1980s, the land was purchased by a farmer who'd wished, not long afterward, that he hadn't. Bob Smithers tried for a number of years to get crops to grow on that land. By most accounts, Miller's Field is incapable of sustaining life. And, may he rest in peace, Mr. Smithers died in the early spring of this year, having never successfully harvested anything from that piece of property. This allowed for the sale that hooked the Shumers.

There's a lot of death associated with Miller's Field, come to find out. And that's what I want to talk about. I wish to put all of you, reading this article, on notice.

I believe that we have an evil among us. I've encountered him on a number of previous occasions, and I believe he's been at the center of the goings-on at Miller's Field for decades. He goes by the name of 'Mr. Dire', in case you ever happen to make contact with him. If you ever do come across him, I'd like to know about it -- please feel free to contact me here at the offices of the Bangor Springs Gazette (pbrachman.bsg@gmail.com).

Without getting into the gory details of Mr. Dire's impact, I do have to tell all of you that he's a menace to our fair town, and he was indirectly responsible for the original calamity that beset the Millers all of those many years ago, the calamity that killed young Patsy. If he were ever to read this

article, he needs to know that we are all set to be more vigilant about his presence in our midst.

I mourn the recent passing of James Miller, returned to Bangor Springs to revisit scenes from his past out on Old Smith Road, a few weekends ago.

March 6, 2019

The closest, upright, green, living thing to Miller's Field, for many, many years, had always been a tall, majestic oak tree, standing easily eighty feet in the air, in its spot on the west side of Old Smith Road, opposite the farm that hadn't been a farm in more than three-quarters of a century. Pursuant to the events of the fall of 2018, that mighty oak tree across the street suddenly died, for no obvious reason that anyone could ever surmise. Come the following spring, when it would have been expected to bud and leaf as it always had, it just stood, dead and leafless.

Nevertheless, it continued to stand, as trees so often do after they've died, either without the decency to fall over and let the rest of us know of their death, or without the weakness that usually afflicts dead things.

As that tree continued to stand, in its death, for days and weeks and months after having died, so had James Miller stood, for many, many years after the night of Patsy's death in October of 1932, and after the night of his injection with a tiny bit of saurian venom. Jim put on airs and he hid what was wrong inside of him, hiding from almost everyone who'd ever gotten to know him, the true depth of his pain, physical and emotional.

That tree lasted through 2019, and even into 2020, when a freak spring windstorm blew it over, causing it to slump over from the roots, landing it in Old Smith Road and creating a headache for the Knox County Road Commission crew, assigned to clean up the mess.

The tree, as it stood --lifeless, yet upright-- did however get to bear witness to the wonder of Miller's Field in the weeks and months following Jim Miller's death. In the spring of 2019, more than eighty-six years after the horrible events that doomed Miller's Field to so many decades of infertility, when the Michigan winter snows all melted, and the temperatures began their rise toward higher averages, the small weeds and wild grasses that you would have normally seen on any other field also began to sprout and grow in the dirt of Miller's Field.

The curse, and the mystery, were through.

THE END

Made in the USA
Monee, IL
10 November 2022

17459631R10174